D0444275

Also by Maisey Yates

Secrets from a Happy Marriage

**Welcome to Gold Valley, Oregon,
where the cowboys are tough to tame,
until they meet the women who can
lasso their hearts.**

*Smooth-Talking Cowboy
Untamed Cowboy
Good Time Cowboy
A Tall, Dark Cowboy Christmas
Unbroken Cowboy
Cowboy to the Core
Lone Wolf Cowboy
Cowboy Christmas Redemption
The Bad Boy of Redemption Ranch*

**In Copper Ridge, Oregon, lasting love with
a cowboy is only a happily-ever-after away.**

*Part Time Cowboy
Brokedown Cowboy
Bad News Cowboy
The Cowboy Way
One Night Charmer
Tough Luck Hero
Last Chance Rebel
Slow Burn Cowboy
Down Home Cowboy
Wild Ride Cowboy
Christmastime Cowboy*

Look for Maisey Yates's next novel
THE LAST CHRISTMAS COWBOY
available soon from HQN.

For more books by Maisey Yates,
visit www.maiseyyates.com.

MAISEY YATES

The Hero of Hope Springs

HQN

Recycling programs for this product may not exist in your area.

ISBN-13: 978-1-335-01351-4

The Hero of Hope Springs

Copyright © 2020 by Maisey Yates

This edition published by arrangement with Harlequin Books S.A.

For questions and comments about the quality of this book, please contact us at CustomerService@Harlequin.com.

HQN
22 Adelaide St. West, 40th Floor
Toronto, Ontario M5H 4E3, Canada
www.Harlequin.com

Printed in U.S.A.

For the caregivers.
You might not be thanked for what you do
every day, and sometimes you might be
taken for granted, but what you do matters.
You matter.

The Hero of
Hope Springs

CHAPTER ONE

FOR AS LONG as Ryder Daniels had known Sammy Marshall she had been his sunshine.

She had come into his life golden and bright and warm at a time when everything had seemed dark and cold.

And like anyone who had been lost in the dark for a long while, he'd squinted against the light when he'd first seen it. Had felt like it was just too damned much.

At first he'd wrapped himself up in a blanket of his own anger and bitterness. But soon all her gentle warmth had broken through and he'd shed some layers. Some. Not all.

And only for her.

Much like the sun, he never got used to her brightness. Time didn't dull the shine.

Even now as she spun circles out in the middle of the dance floor at the Gold Valley Saloon, he could feel it. Down in his bones. Her blond hair swung around with every movement, tangled and curling, her arms wide and free, the bangles on her wrists glittering in the light with each turn. The white dress she wore was long and loose, but when it caught hold of her skin it was somehow more suggestive and revealing than any of the short, tight dresses out on the dance floor could have ever been.

Ryder looked, because he was only a man.

But Sammy was his sun.

His source of light. His source of warmth.

And much like the sun, he knew that getting close enough to touch it was impossible.

There were two men dancing with her, spinning her back and forth between them, and she was laughing, her cheeks red and glowing. Then with a light pat—one for each of their shoulders—she abandoned them and made her way back over to the table where Ryder was sitting with his siblings, most notably his sister Pansy, and her brand-new fiancé, West Caldwell.

They had called them all out tonight to make the announcement. But Ryder already knew.

West had come and spoken to him like he was Pansy's father.

And in many ways, he supposed that he was.

When their parents had died, it had been up to him to take care of his siblings.

When their parents had died, all the light in his world had gone out.

It had left him frozen.

Sammy had gotten him through.

And he knew that Sammy would say something entirely different. That he was her guardian, her protector. And that was true in a way. But she had saved him. Had saved him in ways that she would never fully understand.

Laughing, Sammy plopped down at the table, right beside him, her shoulder brushing up against his, the touch a sort of strange familiar torture to him.

It nearly went by unnoticed.

Nearly.

"Does anybody need another drink?" she said, pushing her mane of hair out of her face and treating him to a smile.

"Your friends might want one," he pointed out.

She cast a glance back at the dance floor. Then she made a dismissive noise. "They're not in the running to becoming my friends," she said.

He was relieved to hear it, even though he wouldn't ever say.

Sammy was everything wild and free. Everything that he never would be.

He had no desire—ever—to try and bottle up that freedom and use it for himself. To limit it. Whatever he thought about it sometimes.

"I'll get the drinks," Colt said, getting up from his seat.

One of the cousins that had grown up with them, Colt was only a couple years younger than Ryder. He'd been fifteen when their parents had been killed. His brother Jake had been seventeen.

Reining in the older kids had been one of the harder parts of the whole thing. Because how did you tell someone who was basically your age that they needed to quit staying out all night and maybe try a little bit harder at school?

Well, you just said it, but it didn't always go down well.

Ryder had been a teenager, not a parent. It wasn't like he'd been a model for anything good or decent. The only reason he had kept his grades up when he was in high school was because he wanted to stay on the football team. That had been his life.

And he had been untouchable. Golden.

Until he wasn't.

Until he had discovered that his family was more than touchable. They were breakable.

Until he had to give up college scholarships and other aspirations so that he could take care of everyone.

Not that he would have made it into the NFL after college. He just would have been able to use football to get through school.

It didn't matter. He had never wanted to be a rancher. He wanted to get out. He wanted to leave home and see the world and have something different. Different than his uncle, who had lived on one plot of land for his whole life.

Different than his father, who had been the police chief of the town he was born in. The town he'd never left.

And here he was. The same. Just the same. And only about ten years younger than his dad had been when he'd died, too.

That was a real parade of cheer.

It didn't take Colt long to return with drinks, and he passed around bottles of beer. Pansy took one and stood.

His younger sister was pocket-size. A petite anomaly in a family that was otherwise of above average height. Pansy had followed their father's footsteps. She was currently the youngest police chief Gold Valley had ever had. And the first female. He was damned proud of her. But he didn't believe for a moment that it was down to something he'd done right.

Pansy was just good all the way through. Determined and strong. She'd had to be.

She'd only been ten when their parents had died.

Poor Rose had been seven.

Yeah. It had been a certain kind of hard to deal with

the teenagers. But comforting children who were crying helplessly over mothers who would never hold them again…

That was a hell he didn't like to remember even now.

So instead he just looked at Pansy, a grown woman with a man by her side.

That had been the first time he had to deal with something like that, too.

West Caldwell had come and asked him for permission. And Ryder had a feeling that he should have rejected that. Told him he didn't need it.

But he felt like he did.

He felt like he needed it for each and every one of them. Because they were his.

Even Sammy.

Because while she might be the sun in his life, he was her protector.

It was his job to make sure nothing bad ever happened to them.

"West and I have an announcement," Pansy said, smiling. "We're getting married."

SAMMY MARSHALL WAS in a whole mood. And Pansy's marriage announcement somehow made her feel even more tender.

She'd come out to have a good time. To forget life and all its irritants. And for a moment, on the dance floor with those guys, it had almost worked.

They were into her. That always made her feel good. A little attention she could control. A little attention that didn't cost anything.

But then she'd looked over at the table and caught

Ryder's eye and something about *him* had brought her back down to reality.

Back to who she was.

Though it wasn't his fault the confrontation she'd had earlier with her estranged mother had lodged itself in her chest and wouldn't let go and it...enraged her.

She didn't want to care what her mother thought of her. Or their relationship. Or anything at all.

But when she'd shown up at Sammy's workshop—an out-of-use barn at Hope Springs Ranch that Ryder let her put all her metal working equipment in—with a tale of woe that was nothing more than a Trojan horse, all sad and wilted with a request for money hiding in the middle, Sammy had made the grave error of letting herself give a damn.

Of course when she'd told her mother she couldn't give her everything she was asking for, the resulting explosion had been...predictable.

You don't have any loyalty, Samantha. You never have. You left us.

I couldn't stay with you.

Because you don't understand love. How can you? You don't have kids. And you'd be a terrible mother if you did.

Sammy gritted her teeth and looked over at Ryder, choosing to push her own issues to the back and focus on his. She could tell by the strong, certain lines of Ryder's profile that he wasn't shocked. Whatever he thought about his sister getting married, she couldn't say. But the announcement wasn't a surprise to him.

Not that he would have reacted a whole lot more visibly even if it was.

The whole rest of the table had been fractured by noise

the minute that she had made her announcement. But the Daniels family, and extended members, had never been accused of being quiet. No, in fact, they were loud and they were boisterous, and that was one of the things that had drawn Sammy to them in the first place.

Her world had been silence, walking on eggshells punctuated by explosions of violence.

And then next door had been this...wonderful, ridiculous collection of people—children—who had been living without parents. It reminded her of Neverland. Like they were the lost boys. And she had wanted so desperately to fly out of her bedroom window and join them.

The chaos had appealed to her. The anarchy of children running their own lives. But above all else, the tall, strong figure of Ryder had been something of a fantasy in her life.

He was the leader. And she had recognized that immediately. From the mantle of authority that settled over his broad shoulders.

Even at eighteen, she had found him mesmerizing.

Ryder commanded respect with nothing more than a firm nod of his head. Her father, for all his red-faced yelling and bruising fists, hadn't been able to squeeze respect out of a rock, much less beat it into a rebellious teenage girl.

But Sammy had learned at an early age that there was no amount of perfect that would ever please David Marshall. And so she might as well settle for being as imperfect as she possibly could be.

She had moved out of the house and into an old camper on the property when she had been fourteen. It had helped her keep her distance. Her mother had liked it because she felt that without Sammy's fractious presence in the house, her father might be calmer.

Sammy suspected that might have been true. But regardless of the truth of it, the arrangement had been better for her.

And it had allowed her to sneak over to the Daniels's ranch with much greater ease.

It was when she had put her plan into place. Operation: Befriend Ryder Daniels.

The memory made her smile even now. Then she looked at Pansy, and something turned over in her chest.

Pansy had been a little girl when Sammy had first started spending time with the family. And now she was getting married. Starting a family of her own. Pansy was one of the few who had moved out right at eighteen.

The rodeo boys came and went with the season. There was no reason for them to not bunk up on the property when they traveled so much. Keeping a permanent residence didn't make any sense.

Logan lived in the original ranch house on the property. Rose, Iris and Ryder lived in the main house. Sammy herself had moved her camper onto the ranch when she'd been about seventeen.

Sitting there looking at Pansy, Sammy still felt about seventeen, but somehow Pansy was a grown woman, getting married and…

The way that West looked at her. West loved her.

Sammy had never been particularly drawn to romantic love. For obvious reasons. Her experience with it—with her parents' marriage—had put her off.

She liked to have a good time; that much was true.

She gravitated toward men who had a light, easy approach to life.

But it was all starting to feel a little bit...

She felt achy. She felt like she wanted more. The fight with her mother today had made it feel even more stark, and the vague longing had started to feel crystallized earlier.

You're not a mother. You don't understand.

You'd be a terrible mother anyway.

It was insane.

Except it kept coming up in her mind, again and again, and she kept dismissing it because it was crazy. Absolutely and completely crazy.

She came out of her deep thoughts just in time to key in to Ryder giving a toast to the newly engaged couple.

"To West and Pansy," he said.

"Thank you," West said, grinning.

"If you hurt my sister, I'll rearrange that pretty face of yours into something no one would ever recognize as human. Count on it." He said it with a smile.

"I believe you," West said.

"Good," Ryder responded. "You ought to."

Ryder was teasing. Well, kind of.

Ryder was protective. He always had been.

It was one of the things that had drawn her to him in the first place.

And seeing it now, seeing it play out with Pansy made her feel... He was so sure and solid. Everything here was sure and solid. For the longest time her only goal had been to have a family.

She had made something of a family with the Daniels. More than something. They were better than the one she had been born into, that was for sure. But… Pansy had broken off and now she was making a life for herself, and it reminded Sammy that she was no closer to doing that.

And you want something to change.

She did.

She was doing really well with her handmade jewelry business. Online marketplaces and an interest in craft fairs had done very well for Sammy. She had something of her own.

She wasn't dependent. Not anymore. But… Well, but.

It was her mother. The *sameness* of her mother combined with the accusations her mother had spit out.

Sammy's mother was the same as she always had been. Brittle and angry, her skin pulled too tightly over her bones. Committed to misery and bad decisions, when before the death of her father Sammy had been convinced she'd been committed to him.

But her father had died five years ago. A heart attack. Which felt right. A heart ill-used, turned hard and scarred. A heart that allowed the abuse of a child. That didn't burn at all when he'd turned his rage and fists on the little girl she'd been.

It seemed right a heart like that would give out early. Poisoned by the spite that surrounded it.

Though she knew death found many good people that same way, so it was probably just a random occurrence.

It comforted her to think otherwise.

When he'd died she'd believed that maybe she and her mom could…that maybe with the enemy gone they could find a way to having a relationship. But no.

Paula Marshall had proven that while she hadn't made the particular kind of misery she'd found with her husband, she hadn't wanted to find anything else in life, either.

And she was angry at Sammy for leaving. For walking out on the abuse.

I wouldn't do that to my child.

She hadn't said it to her mother earlier, but she *thought* it now in defiance.

She would be a better mother. She knew she would be.

And she could change at any time. She wasn't frozen the way her mom was. Her mom was still in that house. Like she was tied to it.

Sammy wasn't like her. She could…she could do whatever she wanted.

And that feeling in her chest, that insistence, expanded.

Without thinking, she turned to Ryder. "Can I talk to you?"

Ryder looked at her, one brow arched. "Sure." He stayed rooted to his seat, as if he didn't understand that she was clearly asking to speak to him alone.

"Outside," she said.

He was going to tell her she was crazy. She totally knew that. But she really wanted to talk to him about this. About her idea. About what she wanted to do to move her life to where she wanted it to be.

She was thirty-three years old. At some point there had to be more than just sponging off her best friend's family, using his kitchen and parking on his land. At some point she had to make something for herself. Something of herself.

She didn't want to be her mother.

Never changing.

Tied to something that had no real power to hold her anywhere anymore.

What if she wasn't destined to be like her mother at all?

That had been itching at her brain now for a while, a restlessness in her soul she hadn't been able to define.

Until today.

And even though she knew that Ryder would tell her she was crazy, she wanted him to know what she was thinking.

Because his opinion mattered, even if she didn't ultimately do what he suggested. It just mattered. He mattered. He always had.

"If you're asking me my opinion on any of the guys out on the dance floor, it's grim."

She laughed, reaching out and placing her hand on his shoulder, the connection instantly soothing her. "No. I already told you none of them were in the running for my particular brand of friendship."

"Good thing." She laughed at his stern mouth. Honestly, he could be such a…brick wall.

"I'm not asking you to help me pick out my date for the evening. I am not asking for your opinion on my choice of bra."

He shook his head. "Thank God."

She'd only done that once. She'd been seventeen. And she wasn't sure what had possessed her to do it. A need for attention, most likely. She had narrowed down quite a lot of her behavior to that one root cause. When she had been young, she had been almost entirely driven by that need. She had settled into something a lot more comfortable over the past years. More comfortable with herself, which had translated into her being more comfortable with everyone around her, and a whole lot less… random and volatile.

"I've been thinking about something for a while," she said as they walked out the front door of the saloon and onto the main street.

The streets were crowded, and it was dark. The air was warm, the sky clear, the golden glow from the streetlamps doing nothing to dim the light from the stars, which were like crushed silver against black velvet.

She loved a country sky.

As long as she could see those stars wherever she was, it could feel like home. And she had done a bit of roaming over the past few years in her camper van, selling her jewelry. But she always came back here.

Always came back to her touchstone.

And she was starting to wonder if that was keeping her stagnant, rather than simply holding her steady.

"Yeah, I've been thinking," she said.

"Okay."

"I'm so proud of Pansy. Of how she's grown up. And that makes me sound about a thousand years old but…"

"Hell, you practically raised them," he said.

"No, you raised them. Iris did. But I was there. And watching her and Rose particularly become the women that they are is really inspiring. But Pansy… She's in love. She's making her own family. An offshoot of what you have. And that's an amazing thing. It's so brave."

"Sounds exhausting to me," Ryder said.

"Yes, I know your opinions on marriage and the institution thereof. Also your stance on children. And I don't blame you. I really don't. You know why I first started giving you sugar cubes?"

"Yes. And I told you a thousand times. The sugar was not required."

She smiled. It had started with sugar cubes. There had been a spot where she'd gone, in the mountains, and she'd looked down on the ranch imagining she was part of them. Until she had ached with it. Been full with her longing for it. She had begun sneaking into the barn, and she had given the horses at the ranch sugar cubes. And then she had started leaving them behind. Leaving them for Ryder. It was how he had first known someone was sneaking into the barn at all. She had begun doing it to get away from her father's rages. Had gone hiding out at Hope Springs, because the name had appealed.

She'd needed some hope.

Ryder had suspected someone was in the barn, but he never found her. Until one day she left an intentional trail of sugar cubes that led right to her.

She could remember it like it was yesterday. Looking up into those stern, brown eyes.

Who are you?

Would you believe I'm the sugar fairy?

And she held up a sugar cube. Reflexively, he held out his hand, and she had dropped it into his palm. You took my treat, she said. Now you can't be mad at me.

And somehow after that, she had found a way to make sure she was never away from there—away from him— for very long.

At first he had been grumpy about it. And very un-friendly. But he had let her follow him around while he was doing ranch chores. And after a while, she just couldn't remember what it was like to go a day without walking around Hope Springs Ranch in Ryder Daniels's boot steps.

The idea of changing that, of ending it… It made her whole chest ache.

But Sammy wanted more for herself.

And she only had two real thoughts on how to do that.

"I think I'm going to leave," she said, determinedly looking down the street.

There was a truck stopped at the four-way that headed out of town, two girls hanging out the windows, catcalling the cowboys walking down the street. One of them stopped to do spontaneous push-ups and the girls started howling.

"Okay," Ryder said, his tone neutral.

"No, not like I do sometimes. Like…really leave."

"What?" The question was sharp. She could feel him looking at her, but she didn't look back.

"Not like…forever. But…for longer than I do sometimes. I think I need to strike out on my own a little bit more."

"What brought this on?" She could hear the frown in his voice. Laced through with stern disapproval.

She shrugged, as if it wasn't a big deal and not something that had been nagging at her for ages now. "Pansy. Pansy making her own way. Her own place. Her own family."

Ryder looked like he wanted to say about ten different things at once, which was strange, considering he never looked like he had more than one thing to say at a time, if that. He said nothing.

"I think it's the right thing to do," she said. "Because... I'm happy. But I'm not whole. I have been doing a lot of thinking about what I need to do to have the kind of life I want. I'm not a kid anymore. And it's all hitting me really suddenly. I've always thought of Hope Springs as Neverland, Ryder, but I have to grow up."

"Is anyone stopping you from growing up?"

"I'm stagnant."

"You're not," he said, his eyes far too sharp and focused. Far too insightful.

"It's my mom," she said finally. "She came to the workshop today and...she's just...stuck, Ryder. She's committed to her bad choices. I thought my dad held her back but it was her. So what if I'm the only thing holding me back, too?"

"Holding you back from what? Sammy, you're building a successful jewelry business. You're a one-woman manufacturing machine."

"But I'm... I don't know how to explain it. I'm the same. I'm...alone."

"You have us."

Yes. She did. The family she'd crashed.

"I know. I don't mean that but I... I look at my mom and I see someone so bitter about everything. So stuck in these choices she made, and I don't want to become that. I don't want to realize someday that I missed out on something I really wanted."

You'd be a terrible mother.

Rage kicked in her chest. Rage and a desire to prove her mother wrong.

"I want to be more than I am. More than she thinks I can be. Just… Ryder…" She turned to face him finally, and the look in his brown eyes nearly took her breath away. But she continued on anyway because her mind was made up, and it was too late to turn back now. "I think I want to have a baby."

CHAPTER TWO

A LOT OF strange things had come out of Sammy's mouth in the past seventeen years, and Ryder had been audience to many of them. But he had to admit that this one was up there as far as crazy went.

"You...want to have a baby."

"Yes," she said. "I want... I want a family. You know that. You know what my home life was like. You're the only one who does. And you know that I..."

"It's not a labradoodle, Sammy," he said. "You don't just decide to go get one."

"Why not?" She was worked up, that Sammy energy crackling around her like a glitter fire that he could feel somehow rather than see. "My mom told me I don't understand her because I don't have a kid. Can you believe that? Of all the insulting... I don't need to have a child to know that she didn't protect me. To know that I'd do better. And I want to. It's my chance, Ryder. To know what it really means to have a mother-child relationship, because God knows I'm not going to get it with mine."

"But there are other things you might want to get first."

"You think I need white picket fences and a soul mate? Why should I sit around waiting to go through some magic chain of steps to have the life that I want?

It doesn't make any sense. That's how you end up brittle and alone."

He couldn't make sense of *that*. Because as far as he was concerned life could only function by the chain of command that it ran in. And when things went out of order on that chain, life got particularly unpleasant.

Yes, children expected to bury their parents. But not when they were eighteen. Not both parents at the same time. An aunt and uncle, a woman who might as well have been an aunt to him. There was no order to that. To all those little kids that were left behind without parents.

Parents were supposed to sacrifice for their children. And when they didn't you ended up with a situation like Sammy had.

The order of things was a damned goddess as far as Ryder was concerned.

"You live in a camper," he pointed out, because if he knew one thing about Sammy it was that what seemed logical to him didn't always track with her line of thinking.

"So?" she asked. "Have you seen how much space babies take up?"

"Sammy," he said. "You don't…"

"I'm not going to go and buy one tomorrow," she said. "I'm thinking about *having* one."

"Are you *with* someone?" With Sammy standing there in white, her blond hair lit up by the streetlamps, he was forced to imagine her in a wedding gown. With a man standing beside her. And suddenly, he could easily see a baby in her arms. Cradled close to her breasts. For some reason, the image made his stomach turn sour.

"No," she said.

The image still refused to vanish, in spite of her assurance that there was no man.

Sammy was a free spirit. The idea of her being tied down to some kind of domestic… Well, he knew what it was like. There was a reason he had no interest at all in getting married. And having a family of his own. He'd raised children. He loved them, with everything he was, and he had stood at the front lines of life protecting them for years. He didn't want to do it again. He knew what a grim parade of responsibility it could be, and Sammy had no real idea. The relentlessness of it.

How sometimes you just wanted to go to sleep but you had two little girls having nightmares. Teenage boys sneaking out.

One time Colt had up and disappeared for two days. The fight they'd had after that had been extreme. Ryder was only three years his senior, but he was in charge. And all he could think of was…

The responsibility had been left to him. Whether or not their parents had intended that, it didn't matter. His aunt and uncle were gone, and it had been up to him to keep Colt safe. And at fifteen Colt had most definitely felt like they were essentially the same age. But Ryder felt a burden of responsibility that his cousin would never have understood.

Because Ryder was in charge.

Because he was the one who was supposed to protect everybody. And it didn't stop. Twenty-four hours a day, it didn't stop.

Hell, it didn't stop now that they were adults. And it was ridiculous because he wasn't a father.

He had just been a kid who'd had to become a man very, very quickly.

And Sammy had no idea what she was signing herself up for.

"As someone who had the benefit of parenthood without all that baby fever stuff, let me tell you, it's not fun."

"I don't need it to be fun," she said. "It's not like I'm wanting a baby as an accessory. I just want… I want to make a home and a family. I don't think that's weird. I want a baby. That's… Biologically we're kind of geared toward wanting that. At least I am. I understand that you had your fill of it. And I don't blame you. I don't blame you for not wanting to do it again. But I've never done it. You've taken care of me most of my life, and before that I was by myself. No one took care of me. I want to take care of someone else. I want to… I know it doesn't make sense necessarily, but there's something I need to heal. Something that was broken by my parents. I can't have a mother-child relationship with my mother. You know that. But I can have one with my own child."

"Sammy, you need a plan. You need a house. A real job…"

"I make money with my jewelry."

"Health insurance."

"I'll figure it out," she said.

"Sammy, life is expensive. And when you think you got everything under control, one of the dumbass kids that you take care of goes hiking, slips off the trail and has to get airlifted out. And where do you suppose that bill goes? How much do you suppose health insurance covers of air transportation? A lot, but twenty percent of thousands of dollars is still thousands of dollars. You're one accident away from being absolutely buried."

"That's thinking a little bit further ahead than I need to."

"You have to think further ahead," Ryder said. "You have to. That's having children."

"Ryder, whether or not I go out and get pregnant tomorrow, I need to make some changes in my life. And you demanding that I submit to a life plan is not going to change what I want."

He had half a mind to accuse her of wanting to do this out of sheer stubbornness. Or try and call her bluff, because with Sammy, it was very difficult to tell the difference sometimes between a harebrained scheme and a provocative statement.

She lived to be unknowable, and usually, from his perspective, that made her easy enough to decode. But with this he honestly couldn't say.

"All this and you want to leave, too?"

That got him. The idea that she might not be there. That for the first time in seventeen years Sammy might not be steps away from his front door.

"Yes," she said. "You have... You have Hope Springs. It's yours. You work the land, and you make something wonderful out of it. I admire that. I have my...my thing. But I need to be..."

"So what is this about? Your mom or Pansy?"

"Both. I mean, one fed off the other."

He shook his head and huffed. "Women get so weird about weddings. Is it just because you're feeling competitive because she's younger than you and she's getting married?"

Right then he knew that it was the wrong thing to say. Sammy was a beacon of light. Sammy was all sunny smiles and glitter. Until she wasn't. And very few people knew what it looked like to watch those summer-blue eyes shift and sharpen into shards of ice. But he did. He knew it well.

And that was just what they did then. Sharpen until he was sure he was about to get stabbed clean through.

"Is that what you think? That I'm in some kind of marriage competition with your little sister? I don't need a man to realize my life plans. And that includes you. I don't need your input. I don't need your advice. I'm not a child, Ryder, and this is the problem. I haven't given you a reason to think that I'm not. But you… I'm two years younger than you. I understand that you were put in a very weird position where you were basically raising people your age. But I was never one of them."

"No," he said, agreeing to that easily. Because he had never felt like he was raising Sammy. He had felt like the barbarian standing at the gate. Keeping the monsters at bay. Ready to die for her. Ready to kill for her. His sunshine.

Currently, his iceberg.

"Since when have I ever given the impression that I was desperate to have what other people consider a normal life? I'm not."

"Sammy, you know that I didn't mean that."

"It's not about your sister. It's about my whole day. This whole town. My whole life. I really believed someday my mom and I could be fixed. But we can't be. I'm not sitting around waiting for my family to heal. I took a good long look at it today and saw how broken it was.

I… I can be a good mom, Ryder. I can. I can give a kid what my mom didn't give to me."

She said it with such deep, emotional determination that he felt a sliver of guilt lodge itself in his chest. "Of course you'd be a good mom, Sammy." The words scraped his throat raw. "And I didn't mean to offend you. I'm just trying to understand you."

"I didn't ask for your understanding."

"But you did want to talk to me. You wanted to tell me. Did you think that you were going to tell me you want to have a baby and you weren't going to get any kind of advice back? What in our past history has given you the impression that I was not going to weigh in?"

And that was when he realized. That was what she wanted. She wanted a fight. She had wanted something to get all righteous and het up about. A dragon to slay, because Sammy knew how to be an underdog. And he played right into that. But she was better at games, played either with herself or other people, at building cases and setting stages. He just sort of…knew how to endure. Two very different skill sets.

"I tell you what," he said. "Let's go home and sleep tonight off. If you still want to talk about it tomorrow, we'll talk about it."

He could sense that his measured tone was only tightening the screws on her irritation. But he didn't much care. Because he knew Sammy well enough to know that even if this bothered her, she wasn't going to outright show it. Because that would mean letting on that she knew that he was on to her, and she wasn't going to do that.

"Fine," she said. "We can talk tomorrow. But nothing is going to change."

"All right," he said.

He could feel her bristling with indignation, because she didn't like to be dismissed, but dismissing her was the best thing for both of them right now.

They turned and started to walk back toward the saloon, but Sammy paused, treating him to one last look that still held a glint of the ice she had treated him to moments ago.

"You know, instead of thinking about it I could bring one of those guys inside home."

He stopped, everything in him resisting it.

He didn't mind watching Sammy flirt. There was an ease to it that he had always admired.

But he had never watched her take a man home, and he wasn't about to start doing it now.

"You do that," he said, "and I will follow you and I will drag him right back out of your bed."

Her lips twitched. "You can't save me from everything, Ryder. Least of all myself."

"But there's no point to me if I don't try."

And in that moment they were at a stalemate, because she knew it was true. Because she knew as well as he did that she had told him all this to give him a chance to weigh in. That she was goading him and taunting him to see what he would do. And that if he did nothing she would be damned disappointed.

It was Sammy all up. It was part of how they were. Her father had hurt her with his fists. Her mother had hurt her by not protecting her.

Ryder in turn protected her. Kept her safe. Treated her like she was glass sometimes.

And there were times Sammy pushed for that, especially when she felt wounded.

This was coming from her fight with her mom. It was coming from her feeling injured and wanting a shield.

He could indulge that. It wouldn't hurt him.

"I suppose that's true," she said, clearly pleased she'd gotten a reaction from it.

"No suppose about it," he said, holding the saloon door open for her. She scrunched her face at him.

"Sometimes it's a damn menace that you know me so well."

"Well, you can still surprise me. Let that keep you warm tonight."

Because God knew if another man kept her warm tonight he wouldn't be able to sleep.

Mostly because he was worried she would go ahead and follow through with the pregnancy thing.

And not for any other reason.

As they took their seat back at the family table, joining everyone, who thought nothing of the fact that the two of them had slipped off for a few minutes of alone time, he cemented that fact in himself.

This was just a weird, crazy night. And that was all.

Nothing was going to change.

Nothing major. Sammy liked a shock, but that was it.

In the end, she would listen to reason. She always did, if only because he was there to act as the reason.

She might say that he didn't need to protect her, but he knew the truth.

And that was what he would do.

CHAPTER THREE

SAMMY AND RYDER had a long-standing gentleman's bacon agreement that she was seriously considering ignoring today. Still, she had woken up before dawn, which was when she had to wake up if she wanted to do breakfast with Ryder, and her body had automatically sensed that it was Saturday morning, and that there should be a bacon situation.

On Saturday mornings she cooked it for him. On Sundays, he did it for her. Unspoken, unwritten, but very real nonetheless.

He didn't deserve bacon. Not at all.

Not after the way he had spoken to her last night. But…the problem was… The problem was it was hard to stay mad.

Well, maybe it was just hard to resist bacon. But she had slept on it. And actually, as she rattled around in her camper and pulled out a skirt, bangles, a thin T-shirt and a pair of sandals for the day, she felt even more resolute. She began to make a mental list. A mental list of all the things she had going for her.

She'd felt an indefinable sense of being incomplete for about six months now. Just the sense that she was on the edge of some new evolution or metamorphosis and she didn't know what shape it would take.

Then her mom had said all that to her yesterday. Issued a challenge, essentially, and Sammy was a stubborn creature all the way to her soul. So the challenge had hooked itself in there and hung right on.

Then there was Pansy.

Pansy demonstrating what it was to grow. To move on. To make a life.

It was enough to bring everything into a crystal-clear vision in her head.

And Ryder didn't trust her.

Fine. She would prove to him she wasn't being spontaneous, crazy Sammy.

Well. Not *just* spontaneous, crazy Sammy.

He was worried about the camper, but she was going to ignore that for now. Because to her mind the camper was all that she needed. It would fit a bassinet nicely, and she intended to be a single mother, so there was no reason to dress it all up any differently.

As for health insurance, he did present a good point, and she was going to figure that out. It was on her list. Then she was going to have to figure out the whole father-of-the-baby situation. And that went on her mental list, too. So there, that was some planning. He wouldn't be able to fault her for that.

She was being responsible.

Just like he had demanded.

With a bounce in her step and intent in her heart she made the trek across the field, to the edge of the gravel up to the front porch of the farmhouse. She loved this place. She had spent the first fourteen years of her life in her parents' house, before moving into the camper. And for as long as she could remember it had felt like being in the den of some frightening and foreign creature.

It hadn't felt like home. It hadn't felt like a refuge. It had felt mean and like the whole house was made of the most brittle glass. And one breath could shatter it all.

She had learned to walk carefully. But she had never quite been able to master not breathing. And so the shattering had been inevitable.

But that wasn't the main point right now. What mattered now was breakfast and forcing Ryder to admit that she wasn't as silly as he seemed to think. He was such an obnoxious, self-righteous…

When she opened the door and walked into the kitchen, her line of thinking was stopped completely by the sight of him standing in front of the coffeepot. He was wearing a pair of low-slung jeans, and that was all.

His broad, muscular back was just…there.

As if the universe wanted her to take a good, hard look at the shoulders she had been resting on for the past seventeen years. He was like he had always been—like something unreal to her. Like a rock carving come to life. Strength and angles and an otherworldly perfection that had always made her think of him as some kind of…

Something more than a man. Infallible in some ways.

When she had become his friend she had begun to feel a deep sense of pride over his looks. Because he was her friend. And in some ways, she felt like he belonged to her. She felt that same sense of swelling pride now as he turned to face her, his body a triumph of hours of hard labor rather than hours in the gym. Lean and toned and well-defined. He was bigger than the men she typically gravitated toward. Taller, broader. More muscles.

"I didn't expect to see you here," he said, lifting his coffee cup to his mouth.

"Where else would I be? It's bacon day."

"You were mad at me," he pointed out.

"Not really." Except she was. "We stuck a pin in it." As if that was enough to staunch the flow of her rage. "Remember. You set it aside and decided to deal with it later. You told me to sleep on it, in fact."

"That I did."

"So *I did*."

"And do you have clarity?"

"I am the queen of clarity," she responded, making her way to the fridge and pawing around after the bacon. She pulled out a carton of eggs, as well.

"All right, reigning queen of clarity. Do you have thoughts?"

"I haven't had coffee. I have few thoughts."

"That's a lie. We both know there have been thoughts buzzing around in your blond head since the moment you rolled out of bed this morning."

She squinted. He knew her much better than she would like sometimes.

"Maybe."

"Say what needs saying. Do it quick, because I gotta get out of here and get working so I can be back in time to watch the game."

Ryder was married to football. Any football. College. Professional. Any team. Didn't matter. She sometimes wondered how much of his enjoyment of the game was wistful, given he'd given up a football scholarship to care for his siblings. But he never acted like it was.

"Speak your mind," he pressed.

"I don't need an invitation to do that."

Except there was a time when she did.

The slow unfolding of herself after she had escaped home had been a whole process.

And that had hurt. For a while she...

She had quiet rebellions from the time she was far too young. Mostly with boys at school. And she had confused being touched with being cared for and had found a way to make some of the ache of loneliness go away.

Then she had moved to Hope Springs and she had found a kind of safety. And as she felt safer and safer, she'd been like a butterfly who'd come out of a chrysalis. Her wings had been wrinkled and wet, and it had taken time for her to be able to spread them completely. But gradually she had begun to do it. And for a little bit of time afterward she had been...manic.

Giddy with freedom and unsure of what to do with that half the time. Some of it had been self-destructive, though she hadn't meant for it to be.

Time had mellowed her. Though Ryder might disagree with that. Especially at the moment.

"I made a list of everything I need to get in order before I go having a baby," she said, taking the bacon out of the fridge and moving over to the stove.

"Okay," he said, his tone grim.

Obviously, this was not a subject he wanted to be in the middle of. Too bad for him.

"Health insurance is the one I'm not sure what to do

with at the moment." She got a pan out and turned the burner on, letting the bacon settle in the pan.

"And you think that you have to leave to take care of the baby?"

"I don't know," she said. "It all feels like it goes hand in hand with growing up."

"You are grown-up," he said. "You can trust me on that one."

"I'm not independent."

"Take it from me," he said. "Independence is over-rated. As somebody who had my security pulled out from under me at a very young age, I can tell you there is no shame in banding together. Or did you forget that? Did you forget that it's how we got through all of this?"

"I didn't forget," she said. "It's just that I want... change."

"Change is terrible," he said, getting out his own pan and putting it on the burner next to hers. He cracked a couple of eggs into it and grabbed the spatula.

"Not always," she said. "A certain amount of change is a normal part of life." She picked up the tongs out of a canister next to the stove and flipped the bacon. "And I've been stagnant for too long."

"What part of this thing is nonnegotiable for you? Leaving or the baby?"

She had no real idea what leaving would give her apart from change, in the broadest sense. There wasn't a particular place she wanted to go. It was more that she was reacting to fear. The fear of being her mother. The baby was something else. A desire for love. For a sense of family. Completion.

"The baby, I guess."

"Think about it," he said. "If you stay here when you have the baby then you'll have us to help out."

"I don't want to do that to you," she said. "You already raised kids."

"I did," he said. "And to be clear I am not offering to raise your kid. But, Iris will be here. Iris loves babies."

"I don't know that your sister would appreciate you deciding that she can babysit."

"I don't care," he said. "She'll live."

"Very sensitive of you."

"I never said I was sensitive." They both turned to face their respective frying pans, and their shoulders brushed together.

"I just… The whole point of this is… I don't want to be like her. She's…she's just still here and she hasn't changed and it made me worried maybe I haven't done enough to move on from everything we went through, either."

"If it's just to change things, then you can do that in a much less permanent way than having a baby, you know? Get a tattoo, Sammy."

"Tattoos are permanent, Ryder. Or did you not know that was the point of them?"

"All right, but you don't have to feed a tattoo. Or change its diaper."

"It's more than that," she said. "You have all this family that loves you. I don't. I never did. I'm an only child from a couple of miserable people and you know that. You're the only one who really knows. I want to fill my life with something…sweeter. Better. I want to make a family that I love that loves me back."

"We're your family," he said, his voice rough.

"I know," she said, shaking the pan slightly and letting the bacon pop and sizzle.

"But it's not enough for you?"

She didn't know how to answer that. Ryder and Hope Springs Ranch had been enough for her, more than enough for so many years. They had been the fulfillment of dreams that she hadn't even been brave enough to have when she was a little girl. Dreams that had been nothing but whispers and echoes inside her as she had listened to the violence that tore through her house on a nightly basis.

But it wasn't about enough. It was about shifting and changing and growing.

It was about…this restless empty ache inside her that never seemed quite filled or solved no matter how much she wished that it were.

It was about the desire to prove she could be better than her mother. That her anger wasn't misplaced. That it wasn't actually so hard to simply love your own child.

"Why a baby?" he asked.

It was what they'd been talking about this whole time. But the way he asked now, with his voice husky and serious, his shoulders set rigid even as he flipped the eggs in the pan. She couldn't deny him an answer. And that meant looking deeper inside herself than she would like. But she owed him that much. And for Ryder she would suffer a little bit.

"I know you feel like you already did it. And I know you think I don't understand the responsibility. I do. Because I saw what it cost you. The way that you took care of everyone. The way you took care of me. I just… I ache, Ryder. For a connection. For that kind of deep love that people talk about. That magic that exists between a mother and a child. I don't know what that is. Because my mother wouldn't have laid down her life to protect me. She had ample opportunity to, and she didn't. There was no sacrificial anything on her part. I want… I want to know what it is. I want to feel it and hold it in my arms. I want a child to grow inside my body. And I'm thirty-three. I know that's not… I know it's not too old, but if I don't do it now, when am I going to do it? I keep asking myself what I'm waiting for when I know this is what I want. I guess I was waiting for signs from the universe that it was time. By which I mean a guy that I wanted to share the kid with, but I really don't want that. I mean… I don't ever want to get married."

It was the truth from the deepest part of herself. He was the only one who ever got to know those things.

He was the only one who'd earned them. By being there. Protecting her. Being her constant.

"You don't?" he asked.

They had never really talked about this. But then, they had never talked much about the kinds of changes that either of them might want. Mostly, they had just existed alongside each other. And it had been nice.

"No. I can't imagine giving that kind of control of my life to another person. The very idea makes my skin crawl. I don't want to share my baby with a man. But I do need a man to make one."

"Were you thinking… You know…"

His discomfort, stoic and monotone though it was, amused her. "Turkey baster?" she asked, her lips twitching.

"Yeah," he said, his face contorting slightly.

"Does that disgust you?"

"Now that you mention it I find the entire conversation somewhat disconcerting."

"Oh, grow up," she said. "It's all basic biological functions."

"Look, you seem to think that your biggest issue is figuring out health insurance. But it sounds to me like you're going to have to find…a bank of some kind, or…"

"A *sperm* bank?" she asked, grinning when he blanched.

"Yeah," he said. "That."

"I'm sure they have one down in Tolowa." She frowned. "That wasn't really what I was thinking, though. I kind of want… I know this might sound weird to you, but I would just kind of like it to be…done the old-fashioned way."

He went stiff like a salt pillar beside her. "I'm sorry. Why?"

"It seems… I don't know. I don't like the idea of going and doing it in a doctor's office."

"Well, the alternative is actually dealing with a guy, rather than disembodied… That."

"Sure," she said. "Both have drawbacks, I suppose."

He continued to look at her skeptically, and she took a breath and carried on. "Look, I'm not saying I wouldn't use a doctor if I needed to, but in most cases nature has given us a built-in way to accomplish this and I feel like… why wouldn't I try it that way first? It's more connected and organic and…and I want that. The idea of going to the doctor to do it seems impersonal to me."

"I don't understand how sleeping with someone random is less of a big deal."

"*Sex* isn't that big of a deal," she said.

He treated her to an arched brow. "Okay."

His skepticism was noted. But in her experience sex was…well, it was nice. It made her feel good about herself. She liked that there was a way to feel close to someone without having to dig deep and spill all her darkest secrets.

And frankly, she enjoyed that she had the power to make men a little bit weak. To make them react to her. She'd never actually…well, she didn't let go during sex. But it was enough that they did. That she could have her control while they lost theirs.

Anyway, there was something… Going to a doctor felt very intentional. Not that she wasn't being intentional. But there was something slightly more…

You want to be able to blame it on fate. Meant to be or not.

Yeah, well. Maybe.

"All right," Ryder said, flipping the eggs out of the pan and putting them onto a plate. "I'll make you a deal, Sammy. You agree to stay here, and I will help you find a man to father your baby."

OF ALL THE THINGS that he had ever offered to do for Sammy in the name of friendship this had to be the strangest one. But things had solidified for him when she had shown up at his house this morning on the same schedule that she always did. It was bacon day. And that meant that Sammy would be here early in the morning to cook for him. And tomorrow he would cook for her. It was a tradition that went back seventeen years. And it mattered to them. It mattered to her, and he could tell because she was here. Even though she was angry at him, she was here.

And it had hit him then that what he wanted more than anything was for things to stay the same. He had done the hard yards. He had sacrificed, dammit. And his life was finally in a place where he could call himself happy. Where he could say that he was content. Finally, he felt like things were coming together rather than falling apart.

But Sammy leaving… That was unacceptable. If she wanted to have a baby, she could damn well have a baby, but she could stay here.

He shoved the thought of her round and glowing and pregnant to one side. That didn't matter. That wasn't the mission. He would find her a guy and get her exactly what she wanted so that she would stay with him. He could do that. That was what he did. He fixed things. He could fix this.

"You're going to help me find a baby daddy?"

"I am. Look, I know everybody in town. If you want to find somebody that you know a little bit more about, you want things to be personal."

"So you're going to act as my pimp?"

"Don't say that," he said.

"Well, I'm just saying, it's a little bit weird."

"You're the one that has an aversion to donors."

"Fair," she said.

"Why do you, exactly?"

"I told you," she said. "It's clinical. And honestly… I want to know that the guy is a good guy. I don't want to just guess. Anybody can put stats into paperwork and lie about who they are. And granted, I don't really trust anyone enough to settle down with them and build a life with them, but knowing somebody... Their reputation, getting to talk to the people that know them..."

"Are we going to conduct interviews?"

"Would you?"

"I will do whatever the hell you want Sammy Marshall. Because that's what I do."

She stared at him with wide, doeish blue eyes. "I suppose you do. And...thank you. I guess."

"Okay," he said, taking the pan out from in front of her and dumping the bacon onto the plate beside the eggs. "What is your top criteria?"

"Don't take all the bacon." She grabbed another plate and divided the food up evenly. The two of them walked over to the long, empty dining table that still had some plates on it from the night before, and they shoved them down to the side.

"Criteria," he said.

"Kind," she said. "Probably... You know, kind of smart."

Leave it to Sammy to try and make this somehow soft and sweet.

"Looks?" he pressed.

She laughed. "Looks don't matter."

He arched a brow.

"They don't," she said. "I mean, there are plenty of people who are awful and very good-looking."

"Sure," he said. "You're going to sign up to sleep with a guy that isn't good-looking, and also is going to be passing on half of that poor genetic material to your child."

She sniffed. "I'm not comfortable evaluating somebody that way."

"This is literally the best time to evaluate someone that way," he said. "You're basically shopping for baby ingredients."

"That is the most distasteful thing you have ever said." But she dug into her eggs nonetheless so he couldn't be that distasteful.

"You don't want to put flawed ingredients into your baby cake, Sammy. That's all I'm saying."

The conversation was bordering on absurd, but there was actually no way to have a conversation like this without straying into the absurd.

"Fine," she said. "I would like him to be tall. I'm not very tall. I would like to make sure that the gene pool is…you know, boosted."

"All right," he said. "There's quite a few tall guys around."

"True," she said.

"Tall, smart, decent. Laz, from the bar."

Immediately, he imagined Sammy in the arms of the other man, and suddenly his stomach turned sour and he didn't much want his bacon. But he did his best to remain stoic and not to demonstrate any of the feelings that were swirling around inside him.

"He would be good," she said. "Good-looking, kind. Makes a good cocktail, which would help me not at all during my pregnancy, but maybe he'd give me free drinks after. I mean, I guess I would have to ask him if he would be comfortable having a baby that he doesn't have a lot of involvement with." She frowned. "You know, it would be okay if the guy saw the baby sometimes. Like a favorite uncle."

"Sure," Ryder said.

"Or, you know we can have your cousins ask around amongst the rodeo guys. Maybe they wouldn't mind."

"Right," Ryder said, gritting his teeth.

He'd agreed to do this. He'd offered. He had no call getting annoyed now.

But he couldn't even imagine just how an offer like that might go. Offer a guy the chance to have unprotected sex with a gorgeous blonde who didn't want you to hang around and deal with the consequences.

The problem was most guys that were super on board with that probably weren't actually all that decent.

But he suspected that what Sammy really meant when she said she wanted a good guy was one who wasn't violent.

Sammy's father had lived as long as he had only because there had been no way that Ryder would take the chance on getting sent to jail. He'd had too many responsibilities. And if he hadn't…

The night that he had discovered Sammy wounded like he had… Well, her father had been arrested, but he had barely served any jail time because her mother had failed to press charges.

It was a sad story, and it was all too common. And unforgivable when it came to his friend.

That was when she had come to Hope Springs on a permanent basis.

He had made vows in his heart about the way he would take care of her.

This was no different, not really.

Sammy was hell-bent on this, and when Sammy was hell-bent on something there was no stopping her.

There was only standing there to catch her if she fell.

Or in this case, making sure that the fall wouldn't hurt badly.

"This is killing you," Sammy said.

"Look, I don't love it," he said. "Would you like to help me find a woman to knock up?"

She laughed. The little minx laughed.

"I would definitely ask you if you had taken to the bottle, Ryder, because you and I both know that you would never do that. It's not in you. Honestly, I think the only reason this really bothers you is that it's so un-conventional." She wiggled her eyebrows and took a bite of bacon.

He thought there had to be something wrong with him. The way that he watched her straight white teeth close over the crispy meat, the way that his focus was completely captured by how she chewed.

But everything about her was ethereal.

Even her bacon-eating.

And years in her presence hadn't done a thing to ac-climate him to that.

"Well, you seem to take a particular kind of joy in being unconventional."

"What did convention get me? Look at my parents. Conventional as could be. High school sweethearts. You know, I don't know… If he turned into a monster after they got married or if he always was one. If she… If she knew when she married him, or if he changed on her. I wish I did. I wish I did, because it definitely changes the way that I think about trusting people. Whether or not I think other people are less trustworthy, or that your own self is."

"Either conclusion isn't much good," he said.

"But it's important," she said.

"You're not your mother," he said.

"I know," she said. "I've pretty much gone out of my way not to be. Hence the lack of convention. I refuse to care one bit what somebody else thinks about what I should want or what I should do. My life is my own, Ryder. And I fought very hard for that."

"I know you did," he said.

That girl had carried more weight on those slim shoulders than anybody should have to. And she stood strong and brilliant in spite of everything that she had endured.

"So you're going to help me find the guy. And..."

"Nothing."

"Well, you want me to stay. What do you want me to do?"

He looked at her, and his breath caught. The words caught right along with it. "Nothing," he said. "I just want you here."

They didn't speak after that. And Ryder found that suited him down to the ground.

He didn't have anything else to say.

CHAPTER FOUR

SAMMY WAS FEELING much better about life in general by the time dinner rolled around and she was in the kitchen with Iris slathering butter onto French bread.

The house had often been chaotic over the years, and she couldn't say that she was the best housekeeper. Iris was a lot better at the cleaning and organizing than Sammy was, but ultimately none of them were going to win awards.

But cooking… That was something that they had sunk into.

There was something about it that had felt like creating all the lost hugs that they were missing from parents who were gone. Or in Sammy's case, parents who should have loved her more.

They had made holidays feel like something merry because they spent hours on cookies, cakes and pies. Roasting turkey, making stuffing.

Neither of them had learned it from their parents. But Iris had an old recipe card box that had belonged to her grandmother, and with that the two of them had made mealtime at Hope Springs one place where no one felt like they were missing out on anything.

"The bread is a little bit pale," Iris said critically, looking at the slices that Sammy was buttering.

"It's fine," Sammy said, making sure to layer it on thick because if there was one thing she knew, it was that life was short and butter was delicious.

But Sammy hadn't made the French bread today so she felt appreciative of it and not critical in the least. She knew that it was much harder to take a neutral view on bread when you were the one responsible for trying to get the rise, bake and color that you wanted.

"It's delicious," Sammy said, taking a pinch off the loaf.

"You're a bread slut," Iris said.

"Yep," Sammy agreed. "But luckily for you so is everyone else in this family, so no one is going to care. Not one way or the other. No one is going to have any opinions beyond the fact that it's delicious."

Iris smiled and turned her focus back to the oven, where the meatballs were currently browning.

Iris was pretty in a very unassuming way. She never wore makeup or anything like that, but she had clear, pretty skin, amber-colored eyes and an easy smile. Her hair was dark and straight, and she often kept it clipped up high, out of her way, out of her face.

Sammy sometimes wondered if Iris did anything that wasn't strictly necessary. She was deeply practical, and the only place where flourishes seemed to exist in her life was with her baking.

She knew that her relationship with Ryder, her relationship in the family in general, was sometimes strange to Iris. But the two of them had grown close, in spite of the fact that being close to the same age meant that Sammy had somewhat usurped her position as older sister, and had done it in a way that Iris didn't always approve of.

Sometimes Sammy thought Iris seemed a good ten years older than she was, rather than two years younger.

And the idea of telling Iris that she was going to leave did not appeal. So on that score she was very glad that she had decided to take Ryder's deal.

Her stomach clenched.

She had agreed to stay, which would mean doing this whole baby thing here.

But when she thought about it… Of course she should stay. Of course she should raise her baby here.

Oh, eventually she wouldn't be in Hope Springs. But… she loved it here. And these people had been her family. Her child would have better than a mother and a father. He would have the entire clan here. And that was something that most people didn't get.

It wasn't a traditional family, but it was a wonderful one.

"You're quiet," Iris said.

Sammy couldn't decide if that was a simple observation, and inquiry, or an expression of gratitude.

"Thinking," she said.

"About?"

"Does it…" She hesitated before she finished the sentence, but she had started. There was no going back now. "Does it bother you that Pansy is getting married?"

"Bother me?" Iris laughed. "No. Why would it bother me?"

"I just mean from the perspective that…"

"Oh, that my younger sister is marrying some super-hot cowboy guy more age appropriate to me but I'm here essentially a dried-out spinster that might die alone?"

"Well," Sammy said. "Not alone. I mean, Ryder will probably live here forever eating the food that you and I make him."

"The food that I make him," she said. "You're not going to stay here forever."

"Actually… I'm going to be here for a while. Okay. I'm going to tell you something, and I need you to not make it weird."

"Oh," Iris said, giving Sammy a sidelong glance.

"It's just that Ryder already did. And I don't need additional…commentary."

"Oh, dear," Iris said, opening up the oven and flicking a couple meatballs to the side, checking their doneness. She closed the oven and turned to face Sammy. "What exactly is going on?"

"I've decided I'm going to have a baby."

Iris blinked. Multiple times. "You're going to…"

"Have a baby." She cleared her throat. "Ryder is going to help me find the father."

"Okay," Iris said. "I think I officially need to not know about this."

That was when Logan walked in, tall and broad-shouldered and better looking than any man had a right to be. Like her, Logan was not blood related to the rest of the family. But he was part of them all the same.

"Know about what?"

"I'm planning on having a baby."

"Seriously?" Ryder came into the kitchen sometime after. "You're just going to tell everybody."

"That's kind of my thing," Sammy said. "I'm not really known for my discretion."

Ryder looked like he might end up suffering a fatal surge of blood pressure. A moment later Rose walked in. "Sammy is going to have a baby," Logan said.

Rose's eyes went round. "What?"

"I'm not pregnant," Sammy said. "I'm just planning to be."

"This place is a damn circus," Ryder growled. "A *damn circus.*"

"I don't care," Rose said. "As long as there's garlic bread and no clowns."

"There are clowns," Ryder muttered, going to the fridge and digging around for a beer.

The rest of the ingredients came together shortly after that, and the crew helped set the table. A green salad, spaghetti and meatballs, and of course garlic bread.

Sammy wasn't afraid of awkward silences. And often, her grandiose statements seemed to force them. But she kind of enjoyed that in its way. Maybe it wasn't fair. To someone like Ryder who had such a strong sense of the natural order of things. But she had been nothing more than a cog in a machine in her parents' house. Her father had been the gears, so easily capable of grinding her into pieces.

She'd had no control there. None at all. So there was something gratifying about being able to take control of situations by being shocking. She didn't really care what that said about her. It made life interesting.

"Who's the lucky guy?" Logan asked.

"I haven't decided yet," Sammy said cheerfully. "Are you offering?"

"No," Logan said, giving her a wink.

She didn't know what she would have done if he'd have taken her up on it. A couple of months ago Iris and Rose had been teasing her about the possibility that Logan might have a crush on her.

The idea had unsettled her greatly.

She didn't want anything to come between her and this family. This family that had become her own.

Plus, she just didn't think of him that way. He was family.

Of course, as genetic material went, he would be a decent enough specimen.

But he wasn't offering.

"Can we not talk about this at dinner?" Ryder said.

"Why not?" Rose asked. "It's the most interesting thing that we've had to discuss in… I don't know how long. You're just going to find a guy to get you pregnant?"

"Don't get any ideas," Ryder said.

Rose made a face. "Oh, please," she said. "Do I look like I'm someone on the cusp of doing something like that?" Rose was dusty from a day out on the ranch, wearing jeans and an old, ratty T-shirt. She had on a weathered baseball cap, which covered stringy, braided brown hair. "I can barely take care of myself. Anyway, I babysit Logan out there all day. I don't need a kid."

The look that Logan gave Rose was inscrutable. And Sammy realized she was happy for it to remain inscrutable. She sort of didn't want to know what was behind it. There were just things she was better off not being in the middle of.

"You better not," Ryder said.

"Oh, but you're going to support Sammy?"

"Yes," he said. "I am."

"You're a hypocrite," Rose said. Mostly just to say it, Sammy knew, because as Rose said…she did not want to have a baby.

"I'm not a hypocrite," Ryder said. "It's just that you're my sister." His eyes met hers, and Sammy felt intensity. Heat. Radiating from across the table. Was he that angry at her? So angry that it poured off him in waves? "Sammy isn't."

Something about those last two words took the heat inside her and twisted it. And that sparked something that sizzled in her stomach. She cleared her throat. "Well, I hate to dominate the conversation with my potential pregnancy. There really isn't much to say right now. Except that when something is happening, I'll let you know."

They spent the rest of the meal talking about other things, but Sammy felt…regretful. Which she wasn't used to. More than that, she felt weirdly protective of Ryder. Somehow the whole conversation had been turned around to have something to do with him, and that didn't seem fair. Not after the way that he was supporting her. Well, grudgingly, but still.

She didn't often regret the things that came out of her mouth. Whatever she accomplished with them she was generally happy to accept the consequences. Most people kept everything bottled up inside them. Not her.

But she did regret it when it bothered someone she cared about. In this case, Ryder.

She was going to suggest that they talk after dinner, but judging by the look that he gave her over the table he already knew that. And he would demand it even if she hadn't.

Just as she put her last bite of pasta into her mouth, he pushed himself away from the table. "Outside," he said.

He was often a commanding bastard, but this was a little bit ridiculous even for him. He wore his irritation like a second skin. And when he rolled his shoulders back, the muscles there shifting, she gave thanks that she knew down to her bones exactly what manner of man Ryder Daniels was. Because when her father was at this level of intensity then a fist to the face couldn't be too far behind.

Ryder would never.

She didn't doubt that, even for a moment.

She had a feeling he might want to punch a wall right now, though.

He ushered her outdoors, onto the porch, and she turned to face him. "I'm sorry," she said.

"For what?" He crossed his arms over his broad chest, and she took a moment to admire the strength there.

Men like him normally made her uncomfortable, because of her past experiences. Men with intensity. Men with muscles.

The men that she dated tended to have slimmer builds, rather narrow of shoulder. Quick with a smile, slow to anger.

Ryder was none of those things. Broad and big and brooding as anything. But it was different. She wasn't dating Ryder. He was her... Hers.

"You're mad at me," she said. "Even if I don't fully understand why."

"Because you telling everyone makes it a hell of a lot more official," he said.

She touched his arm. "It is official. For me anyway."

"*Why* are you sorry, then?"

"Because you're upset. I'm not sorry I told them. I'm sorry that it bothered you because I care about you, idiot."

He sighed heavily. "Why do you always do that? Why do you… Why do you have to take everything public?"

She shrugged. "I don't see the point in keeping things to myself. It's not like it's a secret."

"You don't have a plan. You don't have anything in place. And… Honest to God, Sammy, I think you're a little bit too selfish to have a baby."

His words felt like a sword straight through her heart. They deflated her completely. "You… What?"

"You want to have a baby because you want something to love you. And that is the saddest damn thing that I've ever heard. And I've heard some sad things."

"I… I…"

He ran over her stammered half attempt at a protest. "But it's also about you. It's about you and what you want and how you feel, and not at all about the kid. Trust me when I say…you know kids don't belong to you. They're their own people. And if you're not there, they have to make their way without you. They don't exist for you."

"You don't think I know that?" She could feel her pulse beating in her temples, behind her eyes. Could feel blood rushing into her cheeks. She didn't get mad very often. She had seen the drastic effects that anger could have on a life. On people. And she had never wanted to be like that. Sure, she was a petite woman and not a man with big, bruising fists, but you didn't need to hit in order to cause pain. So she did her best to keep her temper locked down. But not now. Right now she was going to let it fly. "My father treated me like his own personal punching bag. And my mother treated me like a human shield. That isn't…"

"I know you know it," Ryder said. "But are you thinking clearly right now? Because you want this thing, and I know you, Sammy. You're impulsive. And you like to shock people. So do I think that some of this is you wanting to make a little bit of noise? Yeah. And do I even think that maybe it's because Pansy has something and you don't? Yes."

"I as much as said that. But you're twisting it to make it sound like I'm doing something to take the focus off her, and I'm not. It's just that what she did… Where she's at in her life, it makes me conscious of what I'm not doing. Do people want babies for selfless reasons? Or do they want babies because they want them. I mean, eventually I'll know the kid, and I'll know exactly what I want for them. But until then… I guess it starts with me wanting them, right?"

"Yeah, but because you want to give, not because you want to take."

"That you think I… That I would just take from my own child is about the lowest thing that anyone could ever have said to me. And I thought you knew me better than that."

It was what her mother thought. That she couldn't do this. That she would be a bad mom.

She had never expected for Ryder to say something like that to her.

"I thought I knew you, too, and then you looked up at me and said you wanted to have a baby. And everything in my life turned a little bit sideways. I guess I don't know you all that well, Sammy."

"This is…" She stomped down the porch steps. And then she stomped right back up. "This is bullshit," she said. "I deserve more credit than this. I have been here… I have been here all this time. And you have taken care of me. And I appreciate that. But I've taken care of you. Who cooked you dinner tonight? I did. And yes, Ryder, when I came over here it was because I wanted people to care about me. Because I looked in your yard and I saw happiness and chaos and freedom that I didn't have in mine. It wasn't about greener grass. It was about finding a life. So yes, when I came over here it was for me. But the love that I feel for all of you… What followed was my desire to give to you. And that's what has made this family for me. It's what's made this real. I know that's what's going to happen with the baby. I know it is. So don't lecture me." She took a deep, jagged breath. "Don't think so little of me."

"It's not thinking little of you," he said. "But it's uncharted territory. And I know you. I know you, Sammy, and you're great at a lot of things. You are capable of things that I can't even fathom. But this is what I know. Responsibility. What it means to have to set everything aside to care for other people. You were escaping something when you came here, Sammy, and that doesn't mean you don't love us. I was just handed a whole hell of a lot of responsibility. I didn't choose it. I didn't have something worse that I was leaving behind. I had something great."

"And you think that I have something great? What is that? My camper? Our friendship? Those are great things. But I'm not going to leave any of it behind. And… I am choosing this. I'm choosing this just like I chose being with this family. I'm choosing to expand my family. To make myself one. That's why I want… That's why I want to actually know the guy that's going to be the father of the baby. Because I want…connections. I want roots." Saying that, she realized for the first time that it was true. "In my experience roots have often been poison. But I want to grow down deep into my own soil and make something that belongs to me. Isn't that okay?"

"Just don't… Don't go building up fantasies that you're going to somehow find yourself a husband and everything this way."

It was like he had reached into her chest and grabbed hold of her heart. Twisted it. Everything in her recoiled from the idea, but there was fear that immediately jumped into the back of her mind. Fear that he might be right. That there was another layer to the fantasy that she wasn't allowing herself to acknowledge.

"I don't want that," she said. "I want… I want to raise my child here. I mean, not here the whole time necessarily. But this place… I'm glad that you asked me to stay. Because I can't think of anything better than giving my child this whole family. Maybe you think I'm selfish. Maybe I am. But I do want to share you with my baby. I want to give my child the happiest parts of my own life."

His dark gaze caught hers and held, and she found it difficult to breathe. She didn't know why. Maybe it was the way that he saw her. He didn't just look at her, he stared. Down deep. And she was afraid that he saw things there that not even she knew existed.

"If that's what you want, then I'm going to help you."

"You don't approve," she said.

"I know."

"Why are you helping me?"

"Because I'm your friend," he said. "It doesn't matter if I disapprove. I'm going to help you get what you want."

There was something heavy and unspoken at the end of that sentence, but she couldn't quite figure it out.

"Thank you," she said.

"Now, do you want to come back inside and have dessert?"

"Of course I do," she said.

And she felt a little bit like things were better. Like they might be close to being fixed. Because they had fractured slightly around that table, and it had hurt her.

He would support her, and whatever she did. She could have a new thing, and the old thing all at once.

And she found that enormously cheering.

CHAPTER FIVE

THE NEXT DAY Ryder was in a foul mood. He had taken that foul mood out on Sammy last night, and even though she had been the cause of it, he felt guilty about it even now. It made him even angrier. Which was why he was chopping wood with enough force to split a concrete pylon.

"Settle down there," Logan said, wandering up slowly, his laconic movements only serving to amp up Ryder's irritation. His friend was so damned laid-back. The kind of guy that people called for a good time, and an easy time.

Something Ryder would never be.

Except that he was a cowboy and about the furthest thing from a hippie as possible, Logan probably had more in common with Sammy than Ryder had with either of them.

"We don't all have the luxury of wandering around life waiting for things to be handed to us. Some of us have to put in a little elbow grease."

"Oh, yeah," Logan said. "I'm from a real charmed background. In fact, I think it might be the same one you're from."

"Still," Ryder growled.

"Yeah. I mean, when my mom died she did leave me a ranch, though, so..."

"Can I help you?"

"I just wanted to talk to you about what happened last night."

"Why did I have a feeling that you would?"

"Does she know you're in love with her?"

Ryder stopped; the muscles in his shoulders suddenly went tense. And he noticed he was grinding his teeth. He stopped. "What?"

"Sammy. Does she know that you're in love with her?"

"I am not in love with her," Ryder said.

"Sure."

His friend looked at him, far too deep. Far too sharp. It made him remember that Logan was the only one who'd ever seen him break.

Six months after his parents' death he'd lost it. Gotten drunk out in the barn and broken down. With Logan there as the only witness. A drunk one, but a witness all the same.

"I'm not supposed to be here," he'd said. "I was supposed to be a thousand miles from here. In college. Playing football. I wasn't supposed to be everyone's dad."

The responsibility, all that he'd given up, it had hit him like a ton of bricks then. His grief had finally cleared enough for him to see right where he was, and it had been…well it had been hell.

Logan had gotten him through that moment. Logan had seen the weakest part of him.

It wasn't long after that Sammy had shown up. And if not for her…

Well he'd have been sure to break down again.

That didn't mean Logan was right about this, though.

"I'm not. I don't want anything to do with that. Marriage and kids and all of that. It's not for me."

His feelings for Sammy weren't…marriage and kids feelings. It was nothing like his mom and dad.

It was all twisted up in the trauma he'd gone through back then. The place he'd been when she'd come into his life.

In the violence he'd saved her from.

His connection with her was feral, raw and too intense. He'd channeled it into protecting her, because that was the safest for them both.

What he felt for Sammy was all-encompassing. It was part of every breath he took.

But it damn sure wasn't love.

"Right. That's why you're still here. In this house. Doing the same thing that you've always done. Because the domestic life just isn't for you."

"Running a ranch on my own terms is not the same as being answerable to a wife or kids. It's not the same as having to take care of a pack of wild brats when you're trying to graduate from high school."

"Look," Logan said. "I'm not pretending to have any idea of what you went through when all that happened."

"The same basic thing you did."

Logan shook his head. "No. You know that's not true. You know it's not. We all lost the same, but you took care of us. And I get that's a thing. But… I also can see that Sammy means a lot to you."

"She does," he said, firming his jaw. "Basically everything. But that doesn't change the reality of who I am and what I want."

"What you want? Or what you're not scared of?"

"I ain't scared of shit." He swung the ax down on the wood again, and the sound of it split the air.

Logan chuckled. "So you're going to help her find a guy to have a baby with?"

"It was either that or she was going to leave."

Logan shook his head. "Well, maybe she needs to leave."

Ryder stopped, giving his friend an icy glare. "None of this is your business."

Logan shrugged a shoulder. "I don't care."

"Don't you have work to do?"

"You know you can let other people help you sometimes."

"Have you offered any help? I'm standing here cutting wood by myself."

"I'm pointing something out to you that you should maybe pay attention to."

"That you think I'm in love with Sammy." In love. That wasn't the right word for what he felt for her. He didn't like what he felt for her; he never really had. Because it was too big to breathe around, and he resented it. Because after his parents had died he'd been stripped of something essential, and in some ways it felt like Sammy had given it back to him. But it was on loan, and he was very, very aware of that. And if she removed herself, she would remove that, too.

And he would be right back where he started.

Hollowed out.

"Yeah," Logan said.

Ryder shook his head. "I'm not. I… I care about her."

"You want her."

That was the most disturbing of the things that he'd

said. That was the truth of it. Because of course he loved her. He just didn't consider that the same thing as being *in love*. But he cared for his entire family. Saying that there was no love involved would be stupid. He didn't stay here and work this land, didn't stay near everybody, because he felt neutral about them.

Wanting Sammy felt… Hell. He thought she was beautiful. Looking at her sometimes hurt. But him putting his hands on her… No. That was like cursing in a church. Treading on sacred ground in muddy boots.

He couldn't touch her.

So you'll let someone else do it?

He gritted his teeth and positioned another piece of wood for splitting.

"Hey," Logan said. "Maybe I'm wrong."

"You're wrong," Ryder said.

Because being in love with somebody was domestic and sweet. Because it was a bright and shiny memory from his childhood. The way his parents had been with each other. The way they had complemented each other.

It certainly wasn't the sharp, strange thing that he felt for Sammy. An overwhelming sense of needing to protect her. Of needing to…hang on to her.

He was everything that she avoided, and he knew it.

It was a relief in some ways that she tended to gravitate toward men that were so different than he was. Because it made his feelings for her clear early on.

Yeah, he supposed he could see where his feelings could have gone off in the direction that Logan was talking about. Yeah, if things were different. If life was different, if he was different, he could have easily fallen in love with all that bright, free-spirited beauty.

If he had been a different person with a different life. A man whose insides hadn't been crushed, compressed until they'd gone hard like granite. Tested by loss and by the deep burden of responsibility that had been placed on him at the age of eighteen.

And the first time he had ever seen her, curled up in his barn, he thought she was beautiful. Luminous and bright and a beacon of something. Hope. A light on a hill.

And yeah, he'd thought about kissing her.

But then he had started to realize that something wasn't right about the place she lived. That something in her life was broken. Some nights she would climb through his bedroom window and without a word, get into bed with him. And at first... At first he'd felt... tempted. To press a kiss to her head, to see where else it might go. But then he'd started to realize that she was afraid.

That when she curled up against his body she was trembling like a leaf.

And he'd known then that he could never...

That she would get in bed with him like that showed her trust in him. And he would never, ever do anything to break that trust. To violate it.

She was vulnerable, and she believed that he would protect her. He didn't know why. He didn't know why she had decided to come there. Why she had decided to come to him. But she had.

And then that night when he had been expecting her and she hadn't come... And he'd just known something was wrong. Felt sick in his gut about it. And he'd found her father, pounding on her with his fists in her little trailer that she slept in on the edge of her parents' property.

And Ryder…

Ryder had seen red.

And everything had made sense. That fear in her. That vulnerability. A man, a man she was supposed to trust had treated her with violence.

She trusted Ryder to protect her. And that day he had. Physically.

After that, she had moved the camper to Hope Springs.

Sometimes she'd still gotten in bed with him.

And it had been easy enough to take that thing inside him that wanted her, that felt sort of ravenous for her, and harden it. Turn it into a cold, dark obsidian. Sharp and unyielding. To put it between her and all the rest of the world.

Because he had experience enough with hardening the soft and weak things inside him. Because he had to do it the day that his parents had died. Because denying the things that he wanted had become second nature, and so he had simply done it with Sammy.

The idea of taking that and changing it now was unthinkable.

"It's not like that," Ryder said. "It's not."

"All right. I mean, aren't you worried that she's going to…do something stupid?"

"Yeah," Ryder said. "I worry about that with all of you. All the time. Except for Iris. I don't really have to worry about her."

"You don't have to worry about me, either," Logan said. "You know, since I'm thirty-three years old."

"Yeah, yeah," Ryder said. "Old habits."

"We're the same age now," Logan said. "So to speak.

And I know that it's hard for you to take that on board. But we are."

"That isn't how it works," Ryder said. "It just isn't."

"It can be, if you want it to be."

"Seriously, Logan, did you want something?"

"Unclench," he said.

"Really?"

"Yes. I mean, things are settled now. Pansy's getting married and you don't hate the guy, which seems ideal, really."

"I don't know that I would have chosen him." Still, the idea that his sister was old enough to get married was... Well, since the entire thing seemed unappealing to him, it was difficult to wrap his head around it all. Pansy was the most like him. Out of everyone in the family.

She was a straight arrow. Somewhat serious. Committed to doing the right thing.

And there was nothing wrong with her getting married to West Caldwell. It was just... It made him feel slightly abandoned and that was just stupid.

So maybe he had an issue with change.

It wasn't like the way that he was treating the whole thing with Sammy could disprove that. Quite the opposite.

But there had been so many years of struggle. Just so many. And was it so bad to want some settled years where things just felt...good?

"I'll tell you what," Ryder said. "You do your job. I'll do mine."

"Which is?"

"Raising hamburger," Ryder said. "Neither of us needs to give the other life advice."

"All right," Logan said. "Fair enough."

"What about you?" Ryder asked. "Are you ever going to get married?"

Logan chuckled. "I can't see it in the future."

"All right, so why are you here harassing me about it?"

"Because you're the best of us," he said. "Not me. It's not even close. I…" He shook his head. "Look, if anybody deserves normal, it's you."

"That ship sailed a long time ago. We were never going to get normal. Not after all that."

"That seems a damn shame."

"We have this place. Seems like that's good enough."

He looked around, took in the cloudless blue sky that was so clear it created hazy sunspots in front of his eyes. At the jagged green mountains capped with pine trees and the rolling expanse of fields all around him.

Hope Springs Ranch.

There had been a moment in his life when it had felt like all hope was dead. It had felt like this place and its name was an albatross around his neck. But gradually he had gotten used to the weight. And he had begun to find the hope buried here.

The salvation.

It had sustained him. His siblings, his cousins, his friend Logan.

And Sammy.

It would continue to do so.

He would be certain of that.

"So ARE WE going to go daddy hunting tonight or what?"

Sammy popped into the barn late in the afternoon, and could tell immediately by the rigid line that Ryder's shoulders created that she had led with the wrong sentence.

But really, he was the one who had said he would help her. And the fact that he intermittently acted irritated about it wasn't really her problem.

"Can you not call it that?" he said, turning around.

She sucked in a breath, momentarily frozen by the picture he created standing there at the center of the barn, backlit by the open double doors behind him. He had a black cowboy hat pulled low over his face, and there was dirt all over those high cheekbones of his. Ending just above his whiskers. He was thirty-five, but he looked weathered in the best way possible. Years had only made him more distinct.

She had known him since that face was smooth.

And as the years wore on, as he got all the kids in the house taken care of, as he expanded the ranch and steadily dealt with financial issues and all other manner of things that came with running a cattle ranch, he had added lines. By his eyes, his mouth, at the center of his forehead, between his eyebrows.

Like hash marks for each year they had known each other. A marker of the time, the hardships and the triumphs.

She had known him since he couldn't grow a beard. And now he needed to shave badly by the end of every day.

Ryder was part of her soul.

The fabric of who she was.

And she really hoped that he couldn't catalog the wrinkles and years on her face quite the same way as she could his.

She moisturized. So she liked to think that she hadn't crossed the border into rugged. It worked for a cowboy. Not so much for her.

"Sorry," she said. "Is there something a little bit more stately we can call it?"

"I don't know. Is there a way to make this…stately in any way?"

"Please take me out?" She gave him her best wide smile.

"Fine," he said. "I have to shower, though."

"Do you?"

In her opinion, dirt looked good on him.

"Hang out for a minute."

Trailing irritation and dust in his wake, he walked past her and she followed him into the house. Then into his bedroom.

"Excuse me?"

"Nothing. I just figured I would wait in here." She sat on the edge of his bed.

He had moved into the master bedroom of the house out of some necessity. She knew it had made him feel weird, but the other rooms were full, and there was no reason for him not to take this one. She felt comfortable in his room.

Back when she'd been a teenager and her dad had been in a fury, she had snuck out sometimes. The first time she'd done it…she'd been sure that Ryder would send her away. She had climbed through his bedroom window and got beneath the covers with him. And he had known exactly what she wanted. To be held. To be protected. To have some strength around her that made her feel safe, rather than battered and bruised and afraid for her life.

"Fine," he said, stripping his shirt off and taking his hat along with it, leaving both on the floor.

The wall suddenly felt slightly closer, and she didn't know why. There was something about the way he'd been looking at her the past couple of days that made her feel… unsettled, and no doubt it was responsible for the whole thing with the walls.

He went into the bathroom and slammed the door shut behind him, and she got off the bed slowly. She could hear the water turn on. She bent down and picked his hat up off the floor. The band of it was damp from his sweat. And when she picked the T-shirt up, she could feel that it was damp, too.

She held on to both for a moment, contemplating that.

And then she went quickly to the peg by the door and hung his hat up, before dropping the T-shirt into the hamper.

Touching his sweat should disgust her.

It didn't. She wasn't sure why. But maybe it was that whole thing about him being part of her. Now, why she had wanted to—for one moment—put her face in the T-shirt and smell it, she didn't know.

Maybe she was hormonal. Maybe that was why the whole thing with the baby suddenly felt urgent and…

She thought about what he'd said to her. About it being selfish to want a baby the way that she did. Maybe she was selfish. She wasn't sure she cared. Life hadn't given her much of anything. Except for Ryder. Life had given her Ryder. Hope Springs Ranch.

Through this place and her relationships with the people here she had a basis of support. The town had… The town had been there for her. She had gotten a job at one of the local jewelry stores where people had brought in artisan work, and she had developed an interest in metal-smithing and gemstones. Eventually, she'd been able to buy leftover material from her old boss and get into doing some of it on her own.

Now instead of selling other people's creations, her own designs were in the store.

So it wasn't that she hadn't accomplished things. She had. But there was something in her that still didn't feel satisfied.

She was just aching and empty all the time. And she was tired of it.

The bathroom door cracked open, and Ryder came out with a towel wrapped low around his waist. And she just stood there, frozen. Staring.

She had seen the man in a state of half-undress more times than she could count. She'd shared a bed with him when they were younger. They were platonic with a capital *P*. That didn't mean she didn't know that he was a good-looking man. She wasn't blind. And yes, she had been slightly... Well, she had been noticing those things about him a little bit more lately. But it was all to do with the fact that the energy around him had changed. The way he had looked at her at dinner last night.

But she was human. A human woman. And he was a man with a perfect, spectacular body wandering around with nothing on and water droplets rolling down his chest. Over his muscles. So many muscles.

Really, he had the best body she had ever seen. But she avoided bodies like his when it came to sexual situations because... Because they were scary. Intimidating. Because it was something that she would never feel comfortable with.

But Lordy, she was enjoying looking at it now.

"I didn't have clean clothes with me," he said, grasping the towel tighter and digging through his dresser.

"Don't mind me," she said.

"I don't," he said.

She didn't bother to look away. Because when she felt uncomfortable she tended to dig into the moment. So she supposed she would go ahead and own the fact that she was currently on a visual tour of every exposed part of him.

"Are you going to leave so I can get dressed?"

"I suppose," she said, treating him to her naughtiest smile. But for some reason her face got hot. And her heart hammered hard against her breastbone.

"Out," he said.

"Spoilsport," she said, leaving the bedroom and closing the door behind her. And for the life of her she had no idea why her heart felt like it was going to escape from her chest, or why it felt like she had put her head into a bonfire.

But it couldn't be because of Ryder's body.

It just couldn't be.

Because she had a mission to complete tonight, and she had plans. None of those plans included ruining the best relationship that she had.

CHAPTER SIX

THE GOLD VALLEY SALOON was packed full of people. Ryder hadn't been back since the other night when Sammy had said that she wanted to have a baby. And now, here he was, ready to help join in with her harebrained scheme.

He had to wonder if it mattered if the conductor of the train was a little bit more sane than the passenger if it was headed straight to hell anyway.

Which was maybe a little bit dramatic. Hell was probably not the right word.

Probably.

"Okay," she said. "There are some good options in here."

"Are there?"

"Sure," she said. "Laz, for starters."

He looked over at the bar owner, whom he quite liked, but for some reason he felt a little bit less charitable toward him at the moment. Well, okay, he knew the reason.

He wished that Logan hadn't come to impart his wisdom on him earlier, and he really wished that Sammy hadn't followed him into his bedroom before his shower tonight. Because none of that helped with this. Not with any of it.

Fundamentally, it didn't matter that in spite of his best efforts, looking at Sammy made him…

He'd fixed it so it wasn't lust, not strictly. He'd had years to climb that particular mountain. But he wasn't at the summit so much as camped somewhere in between.

Because all his feelings about that were just too tied up in knots. It wasn't straightforward, it wasn't simple, and if—and that *if* was pretty big—he was ever going to touch Sammy, it would have to be as uncomplicated as it could possibly be.

And there was no having that. So he didn't go there. So he drew a line around it in the sand and called it sacred ground.

"Well, you could just go ask them," Ryder said.

"I know that you don't actually think I should do that," she responded. "You want me to fail."

"I do not want you to fail."

"You do. And OMG what would you do if I got up right now, went over there and said, 'Laz, I want to have your baby.'"

He didn't even want to imagine that.

"I want you to be happy," he bit out. "But I can't say that I understand why you seem to think this is the way that you're going to be happy. I'm not exactly understanding that at the moment. I'm not going to lie to you."

She looked up at him, and the expression of desperation on her face made him want to reach out and touch her. But he couldn't. Not now. Not when things were still a little bit altered from that moment in his bedroom when he had walked out of the bathroom in his towel. He had been trying to get a reaction out of her. Because he had fashioned himself into a brick wall to separate Sammy from the rest of the world, and still sometimes he got a little bit upset when she looked at him and saw a wall instead of a man.

Sometimes he got angry, resentful that she didn't see him as a man, even though he didn't want to see her as a woman. Even though he knew all of it was futile.

"I don't know," she said. "I don't know if it will make me happy. But... I don't know. It's something people do."

"Don't do it because you're bored," he said.

"I'm not," she said.

"I trust you," he said. "Whatever reservations I might have, I have to come back to that. We've known each other for a long time, Sammy, and I might not always understand exactly what you're thinking, and I may not agree... But I don't have to. It's your life."

"Okay," she said. "So buy me a drink and give me your opinion on every man in this room."

"Okay," he said.

His back was still up when he went to the counter to order a drink from Laz, and he knew it wasn't the other man's fault. And if he sensed that Ryder was irritated with him for no reason at all, he didn't say.

He got one beer each for him and Sammy, and then joined her at the table she had snagged on the outer edge of the room.

Prime viewing area.

"You know," Sammy said as he sat down at the table. "While we're doing this, we could always find you someone to sleep with."

He was thankful that he hadn't opened the beer yet, considering, because he would've snorted it up his nose. "Excuse me?"

"It doesn't seem fair. Looking for someone for me."

"Yeah, but the goal that you're looking for is slightly bigger than an orgasm."

Something strange happened after he said that. Sammy's cheeks went red. And the redness spread. All the way up to the roots of her pale blond hair. He had never known Sammy to be embarrassed. Not about anything. Least of all sex. She seemed to live to pick at his more conservative spots, try to make him uncomfortable. And over the years, he had just stopped letting her. At least, he had stopped letting her see it.

And occasionally, he would do something like he'd just done. Be the one to go ahead and bring up orgasms. It never sat right with him. But he figured turnabout was fair play.

"What?"

"I... Nothing."

"I don't hook up with locals," Ryder said. "You know that."

"Yeah," Sammy said. "But I find it weird."

"It's just... It never seemed like the right thing to do."

He preferred to find women outside of town. If he needed to scratch an itch then he would go to Copper Ridge or Tolowa, but never here.

He preferred to keep that part of himself separate. From everything here.

From Sammy.

She had never extended that courtesy to him, but then, why would she? And in a strange way he had never really resented it. Because again, her freedom.

That easy way she had with herself, with her body... He had never wanted to do anything to hurt her, to stop that, to affect it.

And he could never be that person. Ever. So he watched her be that person. Be the person she never could have been if she had stayed under her father's roof. Light and happy and filled with joy.

Still, that was one thing. It was quite another to be discussing who she was going to have a baby with.

"Well, it feels greedy," she said. "You know, taking all the sex for myself."

And now she was back to her more typical persona. And he had a feeling that she was back with a vengeance for a reason. Because of whatever had made her so uncomfortable only a moment before.

"I'm really okay with it," he said.

"Well. Okay."

"What was that about? I mean, you blushed. I can't remember the last time I saw you blush, Sammy."

"Seriously? I thought we were here to have a grown-up discussion about which man in this bar should get me pregnant. Not about what made me blush."

"I didn't know our friendship had boundaries. You know, given the fact that I am here in this bar hoping to help you find a man to get you pregnant. I would think that we can have this conversation, too."

"It's not… It's not a big deal," she said, waving a hand. "And, has nothing to do with our objective."

"Orgasms made you uncomfortable."

The pinkness returned to her cheeks. He took a sip of his beer, long and slow, because he was enjoying having the control of the situation. It was honestly so difficult to get Sammy to react to anything, that having the upper hand here was somewhat enjoyable. And he knew it had nothing to do with why they were here, but he couldn't help but stop and enjoy it.

"Not uncomfortable," she said. "It's just…it has nothing to do with this."

"You want to make the baby the old-fashioned way. You want a connection. I assume somewhere in there pleasure is important."

"It's nice to be close to someone," she said. "It doesn't matter… It doesn't matter."

"Seriously?"

She shifted. "No. It doesn't matter."

He couldn't quite wrap his head around what Sammy was saying. "Orgasms don't matter."

"No," she said. "They don't. And honestly the idea that they do is just… It just puts pressure on people. I don't need that kind of pressure."

"What do you mean *pressure*? It's not something that you should have to worry about. The guy that you're with should… He should take care of that. He should make you feel at ease. He should make you feel good."

He couldn't believe that he was having this conversation with her. Like some kind of unholy sex talk. The kind he'd been forced to give to his siblings, but worse, because it wasn't just about basic bodily function but about…everything else.

"It's just that that isn't a goal for me when I'm with a man."

Anger poured through him, unchecked and unexamined. There were just too many aspects of this that bothered him to be able to apply a label to any one piece of it.

"You know why I don't like that, Sammy? Because it's the goal of every man who has ever touched you. The goal of every man who goes into a sexual situation. They want to come. That is the point. Especially if they are in a relationship with you. And if you aren't their priority…"

"How has it become this conversation. How?"

"Because I've never seen you this worked up about something like this. Usually it's the kind of thing you torture me with."

"I don't torture you," she said.

"You do," he said. "And you like it. So the fact that you don't find this funny at all makes me think there's something at play here that I don't know."

"We don't talk orgasms very often."

"Granted. But your reaction intrigues me."

"I've never had one with a partner," she said, the words coming out on top of each other. "Okay? I don't care. So I don't talk about it. It doesn't bother me. I can have them on my own, thank you. An exploration of self. A little bit of me time. I can relax and unwind with me. I know exactly what I like. Not a big deal. But yet…with guys…not so much."

"What?"

He couldn't wrap his head around that. Could not wrap his head around what she was telling him. Because…that was just bullshit. He was not a relationship guy. There was no room in his life for one. He was a sporadic one-night-stand guy or a meet-up-every-few-months-outside-of-town kind of guy. But he would never…

"How?" he asked.

"I mean I fake it," she said. "It's not really their fault."

"Oh, come on," Ryder said. "You can tell."

"You can tell?"

"If you're paying attention you can tell," he said. "There is no excuse for that."

"I've never asked for it."

"Why not?"

"I don't need it. I just told you. Anyway. Now that we've covered that delightful topic, why don't we get back to the subject at hand, which is just finding a guy to get me pregnant. And now we've covered the fact that I don't need him to be filled with prowess and skill. Because it would be wasted on me."

"So what do you require? Soft, nonthreatening hands and in possession of a concave chest?"

"You're being an asshole," she said. "I like the guys I've dated. They're nice guys. And they make me feel good. It feels good that they find me attractive. That they... I like that they get off. Whatever happens with me... It's deeper than an orgasm. I'm fulfilled. By the connected experience."

"Why can't you have both? It sounds to me like it's one of those ridiculous compromises that women are asked to make constantly. And let me tell you, when it comes to that I'm not a man who compromises."

He leveled his gaze at her, and when she couldn't stand to meet his gaze for too long he didn't look away.

Because yeah, this was straying into deeply uncomfortable territory, and yes, he was beginning to feel a little bit hot under his shirt collar, but the fact remained that she needed to hear this. No matter how uncomfortable it was.

"Why can't you have everything? When I go to bed with a woman her pleasure is my top priority, and I don't take mine until she gets hers."

"What if she's faking?"

"I told you already. You can tell."

"How?"

She was staring him down, her blue eyes glittering, and he knew that he was being issued a challenge. She was trying to make him back down. She was trying to make him uncomfortable.

It was not going to work.

Because if there was one thing he had learned over all these years of mastering his cravings for her, mastering the various needs that his body had, it was how to face a problem head-on when he wanted to turn away from it. It was how to hold steady when he wanted to crack. And he knew how to fake it. Since he had become responsible for an entire household he knew how to fake a smile when he didn't feel like it. Yeah, he'd learned all that. Sammy wasn't going to pull one over on him.

"First of all, her breathing changes. Her pupils dilate. Her skin gets flushed. Not a blush. Flushed. Color that spreads up your neck and into your face. Goes all the way down over your breasts." His heart was starting to pound heavily, his blood running hot in his veins. Because it was far too easy for him to build a picture in his mind that put Sammy into the position of lover. And that was something that he didn't do. But he was breaking a host of rules right now. With her. And he didn't know how to turn back now.

"Her nipples are tight. She's wet between her legs."

"That's arousal," she said breathlessly, taking a drink of beer. "That's not an orgasm."

"You didn't let me finish. Because then that's when the magic happens. Some women are quiet. Some women are loud. But their muscles tighten and shake. And if I'm buried inside them, or my fingers are, I can feel all that pleasure squeezing them tight, deep and desperate. It's almost as good as coming yourself. If you're the kind of man who knows the value of pleasing his partner. And I sure as hell do."

"Great," she said, her voice thin. "Thank you for the sex-ed lesson."

"Not a problem."

She was shaken by that. And a damn good thing, too, because so was he. He took a long drink of beer.

But maybe she might be too consumed by her own issues to pay attention to how he was looking right now. It was only sheer force of will that prevented him from being physically affected by that moment.

But he had a lot of practice not getting hard with Sammy.

So this was not an unusual experience for him.

"What about Lincoln?" she asked, gesturing to a man standing in the corner with a beanie pushed back on his head and one of those small French artist-looking beards that seemed like a man lacked either the testosterone or commitment to go with the full beard. Neither of which spoke well of him, in Ryder's opinion.

"Cool. If you want your baby to be a hairless, craft-beer-drinking snob."

"I don't think *snobbery* or beer taste is genetic."

"But you don't know that."

She huffed. "You're actually the one that sounds like a snob right now."

"I'm just saying."

"You're just saying a whole lot of toxic, stereotypical things."

"You like it when I'm like that. Because I'm the secret part of your brain that you never let out, Sammy. And I think we both know that."

He was making assumptions now. That maybe he was the hard, dark edge to her sunny sweetness. Just as she was any amount of optimism that he was able to access.

"This isn't helpful. I don't know why it should surprise you that I want a man that exemplifies the kinds of things I care about."

"Corduroy and beekeeping?"

"He's my type," she insisted.

"Your type doesn't turn you on," he said.

Their eyes clashed, and it was like lightning cracking over the mountain that night. Sudden and sharp and echoing down into the valley below. The valley of his soul.

"Fine. I don't need to be turned on. Maybe I just need to be intellectually stimulated."

"Baby, if you were stimulated on any level you would have come."

"I don't…" Her face had gone red again. "I'm done with that part of the discussion."

"We are actively talking about which man in here you should sleep with."

"For the purposes of *creating life*."

"You may have to sleep with him many times. You don't just get pregnant the first time."

"I'll check my ovulation. There are predictors for that. You could just buy them at the store. They're like next to the pregnancy tests and condoms and maxi pads."

"Thank you for that little verbally guided tour of the grocery store. But I did know that."

"*How* do you know that?"

"I've bought condoms. And maxi pads."

She squinted and looked at him through her spiky, golden lashes. "You've bought maxi pads?"

"I basically raised three daughters, Sammy. I have bought maxi pads. Tampons. You name it. I'm sorry. Does the kind of man you hang out with usually get disgusted by that?"

"No." She sniffed. "They're actually very enlightened. It wouldn't bother them at all."

"Sure. Or is it that you didn't expect me, caveman that I am, to be completely okay with that?"

"I didn't think about it."

"Have you ever gone and bought that stuff for the girls?"

Sammy frowned. "No."

"Who do you think talked to them about all that. I mean, Iris helped. But she was young herself. And somebody had to talk to her…"

"You did that?"

"Someone had to. And I was okay with it being me."

"Okay just…" she sputtered. "Make a list, put Lincoln on it."

"Fine."

"And Laz. Oh maybe that dude that rides rodeo and hangs out with Colt and Jake… Bowen?"

"No," Ryder said. "He's not your type. He's just a…a cowboy."

"Like you," she said. "You're not writing anything down."

"Do you hear yourself? You're acting like your damn biological clock just exploded and you're desperately trying to get ahead of the backdraft. Why don't you chill out?"

"Chill out? You're the one being an ass. You offered to help and now you're finding fault in everyone I suggest and you're not making suggestions of your own. *And you're not writing anything down.*"

"Believe me, I'll remember everyone you've suggested."

That she was comparing him to one of the guys she'd suggested for her list hooked something down in his gut that he hated to think about.

"Why are you being so difficult?" she asked.

"None of them are good enough."

He did feel that way; he truly did. And he liked Laz, but it just didn't seem right.

Because he didn't want any of the men in here, any of the men in town, any of the men in the world, to touch her. They all had their chance. The men of the world had failed Sammy Marshall. Hadn't given her what she needed.

"Well, all right, Ryder, maybe you should do it, then."

Her words landed in the middle of the table and just sat there. He was afraid it might bend and break beneath the weight of them.

"So many opinions about what I need the father of my baby to be. So many opinions on how that baby is made, my thought processes and blah blah blah. Put your money where your mouth is. Or your...your...you know, I can't even finish it. I think you can figure it out."

Her cheeks were on fire now, but she wasn't backing down.

Him.

She'd asked him.

And hell, he was supposed to be her protector. He was supposed to...

He was supposed to be her *protector*. He was supposed to be the one.

And suddenly, everything crystallized; it all became clear. He stood up from his seat and began to cross the bar, making his way across the weathered floorboards.

He looked around the room, at all the men present. All under consideration as Sammy's baby creator.

Him.

She'd asked him.

"I'll do it, Sammy. I'll be the father of your baby."

CHAPTER SEVEN

SAMMY WANTED HER STAID, predictable friend back. He had been nothing but absolutely out of character from the moment they had stepped into the bar tonight. From pushing her on the subject of…orgasms of all things, to this. This. She couldn't even actually believe that he… There was no way that he… He was lying.

She'd asked him because she'd known he'd back down.

Because she'd been desperate to reclaim the natural order of things.

But he hadn't backed down. Football had been playing on the bar TV and he hadn't looked at it once. He'd only been looking at her.

Him.

"You don't want children," she said.

She looked up at him, all handsome lines and angles and basically every dangerous fantasy a girl had ever had wrapped around the heart and soul of a really good guy, and she could suddenly think of no better man to father her child.

Honestly, it wasn't like it was a revelation that Ryder would be the best one, it was just that…she hadn't considered it. She hadn't considered it because she knew that it was something he didn't want to be a part of. Because she knew that there was messy, and then there was the kind of messy that was so tangled up you would never be able to unknot it. She and Ryder sharing a child was… Well, that just wouldn't work. It was one thing to think about having some kind of casual arrangement with a man in town. One who gave occasional visits and even support. One who kind of added to the casual, expanded family that she had created at Hope Springs.

But she lived with Ryder. Practically.

And how could they do a distance thing in that sense? How could he not be involved?

She supposed it was possible that he could act as a favorite uncle.

As for the conception… She wasn't going to think about that.

She was not going to think about the fact that she had just seen him wander through his bedroom in a towel, either. Wasn't going to think about any of that. Because that had nothing to do with the actual reality of what he was proposing, and it wasn't going to happen either way.

"I'm not letting you fall on your sword for me."

"Who said I was falling on my sword?"

"Because I know you. You're trying to rescue me. You're desperately trying to rescue me, and you're offering yourself up in an entirely impractical way in order to do that."

"I didn't say that it wouldn't come without conditions."

"What kind? I mean, honestly, how would that even work? You don't want kids because you've already been there and done that. You don't want unconventional. And I am the very essence of unconventional. Which is fine for a friendship, but how could we ever share a child?"

"It wouldn't be unconventional," he said.

"How is it not going to be unconventional?"

"Because. I'll be the father of your baby. You'll be my wife. We'll be a family."

"Are you… Have you lost your mind?" she asked. "That is…nothing like what I was proposing for this whole situation."

"And it's the only way I can see to make it work. I mean, with me as the father."

"I didn't say that I wanted you to be the father. And anyway, why would it have to be that way if you were the father? Why couldn't we live together on the property, and you can take kind of a secondary role? A favorite uncle."

"You are out of your damned mind, lady. That is not how I would do it."

"But you don't want children."

"And I don't do halfway. I can't, and I won't. I'm all or nothing, and you know it. If we were to have a baby, it would be everything."

"You are… You know you are an old man," she said, doing her best to beat back the crazy little what-if that was rattling around inside her chest. "You raised your kids, they went out on their own, you work your land, you read the paper in the morning, and you watch *60 Minutes* at night before you go to sleep very early."

"So what? I'm stable."

"And you're done. And I'm not. I'm not an old man."

"I'm well aware. It's called opposites complementing each other, Sammy. I thought that you would know something about that."

"No. Just no."

"Why not?"

"Because I don't want to get married. Because I can't be married to you," she pushed.

"And why is that?"

His eyes were so steady, and she wanted to just say yes. She wanted to lean into him and…

No. She couldn't do that.

"Because it would ruin everything. I'm not going to become this crazy ball and chain that you shackled yourself to because you didn't approve of the way I was doing something. It's nuts. Even you have to acknowledge that."

"I don't have to acknowledge a damn thing."

"No. If you want to do this my way, then… I mean, of course I can't think of a better person. A better man. But we're not… I'm not trapping you into eighteen years of a life that you don't even want."

"You marry me and you'll get health insurance. I have it through the farm union."

"Oh, my gosh. Are you genuinely proposing that we have a marriage of convenience? And a baby and…"

Suddenly it didn't seem crazy. For a moment it didn't seem crazy at all. It seemed unbearably tempting.

But then reality came to the rescue. Sense came to the rescue. Because she knew she didn't want this. She didn't. Not even a little bit.

There was a reason that she gravitated toward men that were so different than Ryder. There was a reason that she was opposed to marriage at all. There was a reason that she wanted to keep control of her life and her child.

And it wasn't because she didn't trust Ryder; that wasn't it. It was just… To trap him in a relationship he didn't want anyway…

He would never hurt her. She knew that. It wasn't

that she thought he might be violent like her father. She had lived under an oppressive cloud of two people who weren't in love living in the same house. She had seen firsthand what it did to people. She didn't want it. Couldn't stand it.

"I can't do that to you. To us. To me."

"You'd rather have a baby with someone you don't even know."

"Yes," she said. "That's the point." Except suddenly that didn't seem as appealing as having his baby except... "Why do you have to be so uncompromising? Why can't we figure out maybe a different way to do it? Why do we have to do it your way?"

"Because it's going to have to be my way if we do it. I can't be unconventional. You said it yourself."

"Yeah, but you can dig in and be miserable. You're good at that. I won't be the reason that you are."

She turned and walked away from him, anger bubbling up inside her. She knew that he wouldn't follow her, not when she was in such an irritated state with him. She went over to the bar, and she signaled for Laz. "Hi," she said.

"Hi," he responded, flashing her a grin.

He was a very good-looking man. In a genetic sense, he would make a fantastic father for her baby. And suddenly, her own thoughts seemed so ridiculously insane to her, and Ryder seemed less crazy, and she hated that. She pushed against it. Hard.

"Can I get another beer?"

"Sure," he responded.

He gave her a look that was far too canny. "Are you trying to make him mad?"

"Why do you ask?" She flipped her hair over her shoulder.

"Because I know when a woman is trying to make another man jealous. I'm not stupid."

She huffed. Then scoffed. Then huffed again. And realized that was one back-of-throat noise too many to be wholly believable. "He's just my friend," she said.

"Oh, I know that," Laz responded. "I know everybody's business. That's my job. But I'm just saying, it seems to me you're trying to make him jealous."

She wasn't doing that. Of course she wasn't. Ryder wouldn't care if a man was flirting with her, or if she was flirting with a man. And anyway, she was more trying to annoy him about the possibility that she was more willing to consider Laz as the father of her baby than she was him. Which was entirely weirder than what Laz was accusing her of, so she wasn't going to say that. Honestly, now she just felt absurd. And wrong. And it was Ryder's fault. It all felt possible before he had gone and said that to her.

"Well, if I were, what would you think about that?"

He arched a dark brow. "If you were flirting? Or if you were trying to make another man jealous? Because I have to tell you, I have a lot of experience with both. And my actions depend."

She leaned on the bar and worked her shoulders inward. "Well, what would you do with me?"

"Hey, I respect a lady's choice. If you're looking for a good time, you know I'm up for it. But I'd also like you to continue to buy beer from me."

The problem was she wasn't really looking for a good

time. And every awful conversation she'd had with Ryder was swirling around in her head.

"But," Laz said, "I do have an aversion to women thinking about other men when they're with me."

"I'm not," she said.

"Whatever's going on with you and your boy, you should probably figure that out."

She was going to tell him that he was not her boy, but she had a feeling at this point it was all futile.

"I'll take the beer and you can keep the life advice," she said.

"Sammy, if you ever want to come flirt with me when you don't have someone else on your mind, you know you're welcome to."

She took the beer and offered him a scowl before retreating.

"Did he tell you no?" Ryder asked.

"I didn't ask for a baby. I asked for a beer," she huffed. "I want to go home."

"You got a beer. You can't go out onto the street with it."

She narrowed her eyes at him, hoping it might help hone her irritation to a fine point he'd be able to feel. "You've made this weird."

"I made this weird? You're the one who asked me."

"Not seriously."

The look on his face made her feel like she'd swallowed a boulder.

He looked down for a second, then back up, his tone slightly hushed. "I made it weird that you're out here trying to find the right guy to get you pregnant?"

"Yes," she said, rounding on him, not caring that they

were in the middle of the bar, likely drawing attention to themselves. "First with your talk about orgasms, and then with all of your propositions. Proposals. Oh, my gosh, did you propose to me?" She let her hand holding the beer fall slack at her side.

"If you want to think of it that way."

"I don't want to think of it at all."

"I'll tell you what," he said. "I'm going to go home. Iris can come pick you up when you're done, if you don't find a man to take you home. But you think about what I said. And if you find anyone in here that you think would be better than me, fine. I'll let it go. But I don't think you will. Because I think you and I both know, you can protest all you want about me protecting you and taking care of you and making sacrifices for you, but you want it. I'm the one who's been there for you all this time. Don't tell me you don't want me to be here for you now."

And then Ryder turned on his heel and walked toward the exit. And the son of a bitch actually walked out the door and left her standing there. She couldn't believe it.

She looked around the bar, taking a swig of her beer and no, she didn't want any of the men here. Not even a little. Not even at all. She felt like she'd been hollowed out. Like Ryder had reached inside her and taken everything she contained and everything she knew, and just stolen it from her. She had no idea who she was now. No idea how the world kept spinning. When it was so clearly knocked off its axis. And so she did a very stupid thing.

She turned on her heel and ran out onto the street. "Ryder!" she shouted. "Don't leave me here."

"I thought you were finished with me for the night."

"Stop being an idiot. I don't want to call your sister

to come pick me up. And I don't want to go home with some random guy. Stop acting like you had a personality transplant."

"You're the one who changed things," he said.

"Just take me home," she said. "I want a do-over. Let's just pretend that this whole evening didn't happen."

He laughed. "Fine. Whatever you want, Sammy."

They walked beside each other in silence to his truck.

"What did you do with your beer?"

"I just left it on a table. I didn't really want it anyway. I just wanted to irritate you."

"Yeah, I knew that," he said.

"Then why did you let me do it?"

"Hell if I know, Sammy. Sometimes it's easier than others to ignore your shenanigans."

"*Shenanigans*? You know, that's the problem, Ryder. That's what you think this is. You think I'm full of shenanigans. And you think that I'm selfish. And you think that I'm immature. And for one moment you don't think that maybe I… Maybe I'm responding to the same kind of thing you are when you say that you don't want to get married. When you talk about how you're just done with the life that you lived before. With the pain. With the past. Maybe that's what's wrong with me. Maybe I'm just done. I'm done being the person that my dad beat me into being. I have been done with that. But a lot of my life since then has been built on the reaction to that. And I'm tired of that, too. I just want to find my own way, my own life. I don't think that's terribly difficult to understand. And I don't think that you have the right to look at me and decide that what I want, and what I feel, and what I need are shenanigans. That the things that I really want are things that you have to save me from."

She got into his truck and slammed the door behind her. "It hurts me," she said quietly as he started the truck and pulled away from the curb.

He didn't say anything for a long while. They got on the two-lane road that headed outside of town, away from Main Street, away from the bar.

Farther and farther away from the scene of all that had happened tonight and closer to the familiarity of Hope Springs Ranch. Where maybe sanity would prevail. But she didn't know if she even wanted that. Because she just felt so raw and scrubbed the wrong way.

She didn't know if she wanted to keep fighting, or if she wanted to wrap herself in the blanket of home and pretend that none of it had happened.

"Well, the thing is, Sammy," he said, his voice quiet, firm and steady. "You seem to think that the only reason I might have accepted was because I'm protecting you."

"Well, because you've made it very clear that you don't want to have kids."

"Maybe I don't like the idea of you having them with someone else. Maybe I do feel like that kid should be mine."

She had no idea what to say to that. She had no idea what he meant. And she still didn't think she was wrong, because all of it was that same old possessiveness stuff. Ryder was hers, and she had felt like that for a long time. But she knew pretty firmly that Ryder also felt like she belonged to him. And she had a feeling it was more about that than it was anything else.

"Don't," she said. "That's not fair. Don't put that on me. You don't mean it. You don't really want any of this."

"You just know that?"

"Yes, I do know it. Because I know what you've been through. I care about you and I want you involved in my life, and looping you in on my major decisions is part of that. You accepted because you're retired. A retired old man living in his golden years, in his thirties. And you don't want anything to change. You don't want to lose a comfortable relationship, a comfortable setup that you have. You're not worried about me having a baby. You're worried about things changing."

"I said as much," he said. "I said I didn't want things to change."

"Well, you can't have your way. Not in this. It's going to change. I'm going to do things the way that I want. The way they make sense to me."

He turned off the main highway and pulled beneath the sign that said Hope Springs Ranch. It was a beautiful sign, one that had been there since before his parents had died. Silhouettes of horses and cowboys all around the letters.

She waited for the comfort of home to wash over her when they turned onto the property. But it didn't come.

Because the man that should have helped provide that homey feeling was like a stranger to her right now.

Which was maybe a touch dramatic. But it didn't feel like it. Not right now.

When he pulled up to the house, she got out quickly and began to walk back toward her camper.

She could hear heavy footsteps on the gravel behind her. She knew that he was following her. She paused, letting out a long, slow breath. "Did you have something else to say? Because I think we should sleep on it."

"Go ahead and go to sleep," he said. "But you ask yourself what you need, and then you ask yourself who you think is going to be able to give it to you."

Ryder left her there, standing alone in the middle of the drive after that.

She walked back to her camper slowly, replaying his words over and over in her mind.

Think about what you need. And think about who is going to give it to you.

She knew what he meant. He meant: Who was going to help her provide stability? Who was going to be her counterpoint?

And truth be told...when she thought of raising a child, she saw him as a figure in that child's life. Being... Ryder. The influence on the kid that he had been on her.

He meant health insurance and he meant practicalities.

But for some reason she kept flashing back to the conversation they'd had in the bar. The one she had tried to avoid.

The one about orgasms.

The way he had reacted; the things he had said.

Ryder was beautiful, but she did her best to think of him in terms other than real, human man.

She found it comfortable to think of him as a statue. A man carved from granite. As a guardian. Some kind of supernatural protector. Not a man she could touch. A man whose hands could touch her.

Not a man who knew his way around a woman's body. A man who might be more proficient at it than any other she'd been with before.

But then the idea of that… Of him touching her… Of him taking control of her in some way, even if it was for pleasure, made her break out in a cold sweat.

She didn't like that. The thing she liked most about sex was the closeness; she hadn't been lying. And also, she liked feeling like she'd affected a man in a positive way.

She had been so afraid of men after the way she'd grown up, and then Ryder had taught her that some men could be trusted. The guys she had grown up around at Hope Springs had only reinforced that.

And when it came to sex…

Boys at school had been grateful to her for it. And after that, it hadn't really changed. Sixteen or twenty-six, men weren't all that different.

And that made her feel…valuable and powerful in a way that she could contain all inside herself.

One that made her partner not matter quite so much as she did.

Ryder was talking about uncharted territory. Not just for their relationship but for her.

He was… Was that what he was expecting, really? To request that he give her a baby, or was he thinking to give her an orgasm, and to…

She couldn't even wrap her head around it. So she decided not to.

A skill she had acquired growing up in a home that contained reality she found distasteful.

She was so good at deciding to be finished with thoughts.

And so she decided to be finished with that one, because she could not sort it out, and she didn't like that. Didn't like the uncertainty of certain lines of thinking.

She approached her camper, tiny but home, and jerked the door open, which caused the whole thing to rattle slightly.

This place still felt familiar. Smelled like her incense and candles. Things that Ryder really wished she wouldn't have in her camper, because he was concerned about it being a fire hazard, in spite of the fact that she told him she only ever lit any of that stuff when she was watching it.

He didn't trust her.

She frowned.

He didn't really trust anything.

She crossed the tiny space and sat on the edge of her bed, batted the netting that hung from the ceiling and cocooned it in a diaphanous veil out of the way.

Ryder not trusting her didn't have all that much to do with her, really.

He didn't trust life. He didn't take anything for granted. He never assumed that things were simply going to work out just because.

Of course he wanted to get his hands all up in her baby plan.

That was the wrong way to think about it. That made a flush creep out over her skin.

She was not going to think about her friend that way. Not anymore.

But for some reason, she couldn't just banish these thoughts. And they played over and over in her mind. Her best friend in a towel. Her best friend talking about orgasms. Her best friend offering to be the father of her baby.

And by the time she woke up the next morning her entire mind was a tangle of all these thoughts, and she wasn't any closer to sorting out anything.

There was only one person she could talk to about this.

She got up and angrily dragged herself toward the main house.

Thankfully, she knew that she had missed Ryder for the day.

But Iris would be there.

Iris would be in the kitchen at this point heating up something delicious for breakfast.

Sammy walked into the main house without bothering to knock and angrily stamped toward the location of her friend.

"Wow," Iris said when Sammy appeared in the doorway. "You look rough." She winced. "Did you…sleep rough?"

She had a feeling that was her friend's delicate way of asking if she'd hooked up.

"I did, but not the way you mean."

"What's going on?"

"I'm in a fight with your brother."

Iris cleared her throat. "Well, after all that the other night I can't say that I'm surprised."

"It's not his business," Sammy said.

"Sammy," Iris said, affecting a humorous, deep voice. "Everything the light touches is his kingdom. He absolutely is going to think that this has everything to do with him. You're part of his… His whole thing here."

Except, she didn't really think she was. She was a part

and different. And she didn't think that just because he had essentially proposed marriage to her. But because of the way he had talked to her about sex.

It wasn't the same.

And that wounded her in a strange way, too, because it made all this feel precarious.

And she didn't like it.

"I know," she said, feeling it was best to gloss over any of her internal rambling. "But I don't like it. And he..."

She didn't know how to tell Iris, actually. That was the problem. Standing there now, pondering it, she wasn't sure that she wanted to.

Because Ryder saying yes to the baby meant he was saying yes to the two of them having sex.

That thought, cold and blatant, stopped her cold. And she knew she wasn't supposed to think of any of this in those terms.

Because it was all supposed to be about conception, of creating life and babies. But he had brought up orgasms. So now there it was.

He had brought up marriage, so that was something else entirely.

And she was suddenly caught in a place where she didn't want to say what was on her mind. Where she didn't want to talk about everything that had happened the night before. Usually she would, and count on a little bit of shock and awe.

But she didn't want to. She wanted to wrap herself in this whole thing and sit in a corner with it. She wanted to stay quiet. She wanted to think.

And if she had thought that she couldn't be any more irritated with Ryder than she was, she had just proven herself wrong. Because as annoying as it was to be this confused, it was even more annoying to feel out of character.

To be confused by herself, and not just him.

"Why have you suddenly gone quiet?"

She looked over at Iris. "I just… I don't know. I need to think. Maybe I need to talk to Ryder."

"Well, normally that doesn't stop you from talking to everyone else first."

"I… Do you think I'm crazy, wanting to have a baby?"

Iris paused, staring at the back wall behind Sammy's head. "At first. Yes. My initial thought was that you were a little bit crazy. I'm not going to lie. But I don't know. Mostly I'm happy with my life here. And I'm here still because of choices that I've made. Nobody made them for me. But yes, sometimes I think about what it might be like to change things drastically. And I know if I did that Ryder would be the first person in line to tell me that I needed to go see a psychiatrist. But I don't think he gets a sense of quiet desperation being here. I think the quiet is something that he likes."

"Well, why don't you do something about it?" Sammy asked. "I mean, no one is stopping you."

"Because I don't want to do anything drastic. Drastic doesn't appeal to me. But you're you, Sammy, and I can see how you would be the first one of us to do something different for the sake of it. That's not a criticism. It just is."

"But you could do something drastic. If you wanted. I mean this is the thing. We all stay in our prescribed boxes, in our little houses, doing everything that's expected of us just because. And I can't help but think that even though there were deeper, more toxic things at play, to an extent my mother stayed with my father because she didn't know what else to do. We get entrenched in things and people and places, and we don't know what else we can be. Well, I don't want to be that. I want to be everything that I can be, and I don't want to wait around to have it."

"I have a feeling I'll just end up waiting around," Iris said, smiling sadly. "I just don't have it in me to do things the way you do."

"You could," Sammy insisted.

"Some of us are caged birds," Iris said. "Some of us aren't. I don't know if you can learn to be wild when you've been kept inside for so long. Afraid of everything out there."

"Is that the problem? You're afraid?"

Iris's smile turned sad. "I've been afraid of everything since I was fourteen years old."

Of course. That was when her parents had died. It was easy for Sammy to forget that she wasn't from the exact same background as the rest of them. Sometimes she felt like they were all the same merry band. In other times not. This was one of those times.

She had most definitely had her share of trauma. But it wasn't the same. She had never known what it was like to live in a safe house, not until she had come here. But this place was where they had lost their innocence. Where they'd had their childhood ripped away from them.

She had never looked at Iris and seen fear. She had always seen her friend as someone steady. Even-tempered in a way that Sammy herself could never be. Practical and industrious.

But now she could see clearly just how contained she was. How perhaps her practicality was more necessity than anything else. How it kept her rooted here.

Both Rose and Iris were very different from Pansy, who had gone out and made a life of her own. Who had so consciously patterned herself after their father by becoming the police chief of Gold Valley.

Rose, on the other hand, was irrepressible. She worked on the ranch, fizzing over with energy. She ran wild over the place, but she definitely had a territory and a range. She didn't venture out beyond the edges of Hope Springs, as it were.

And then there was Iris.

"You don't have to be what everyone expects you to be," Sammy said.

"Neither do you," Iris said.

"I'm not," Sammy protested. "I'm unconventional by design."

"Yeah. Well, don't be afraid to be conventional if you feel like it. You don't have to go around surprising everybody all the time. You could just be."

Sammy felt like the interaction had been flipped on its head and she didn't really like it. She was much more comfortable in the advisory role. Acting as the more experienced and worldly woman in the group. Honestly, if Iris had ever dated a man, Sammy didn't know. And Sammy usually managed to ferret out whatever information she wanted. And if she smelled a secret, she went right in for it.

And with Iris, she had never gotten the hint that there was one.

Rose wouldn't be able to keep it quiet if she'd found a guy. That meant there wasn't one. And never had been.

She looked up at her friend, who was staring at her with clear, amber eyes. And suddenly, Sammy realized she had been arrogant to think that she was the only one who observed anything about these people she lived with. Suddenly, she saw a world of opinions in Iris's eyes. Opinions about her.

She wanted to turn away from that. She was used to Ryder and his opinions, but she often brushed him off. She did that because she was sure that half of his issue was that he was stodgy and boring. That he was reacting to whatever she did, whatever she wanted from that standpoint.

It would be tempting to paint Iris with the same brush, but she wasn't like that.

And maybe the real issue was that Ryder had seen some things in her all along that she didn't want to acknowledge.

He might be closer to the right solution to all of this than she wanted to admit.

She closed down that part of her brain.

"Do you want anything?" she asked.

"What?"

It took her a moment to realize that she had changed subjects very abruptly and there was no way that Iris would have any idea what she was talking about.

"Jewelry," Sammy said. "I think I'm going to get going on some projects today. I have some sunstone from Eastern Oregon and some moonstone that I'm really happy to work with and figure out what kinds of combinations I can make. And of course, you know my current obsession is rose gold when it comes to settings."

"Oh," Iris said.

Okay, so it hadn't been the smoothest transition. And it was probably pretty obvious that the reason she did it was that she wanted to be done talking about deep things inside herself. It was one thing to kind of pry other people apart; it was quite another when they started doing it to her.

"So if you want anything…"

"You can surprise me," Iris said. "I mean, if you end up with something you don't want to sell."

"I'll let you know," Sammy said.

She left the kitchen and realized she hadn't even taken any food with her. But she didn't want to turn around and go back now. She also realized that given the inconclusive nature of that entire interaction it was probably clear to Iris that Sammy hadn't shared even half of what she had intended to.

She hoped Iris wasn't hurt by that. Iris was so difficult to read in that way. She was often serene in a way that made Sammy certain there was more going on beneath the surface than anyone knew.

Her ultimate conclusion was that while she hoped her caginess didn't hurt Iris, Iris hid enough of herself that she didn't have the right to be annoyed.

By the time Sammy was halfway back to her camper she was grouchy.

She felt completely topsy-turvy and turned upside down, and it was all Ryder's fault.

Her camper came into view, and she saw the silhouette of one tall, infuriating cowboy.

"Speak of the very devil," she muttered, kicking a stone to the side and trying to affect her best detached look.

"So it's ice today," Ryder said.

"What?"

"You're ice or fire, Sammy Marshall. And very few people ever see the ice. But I'm lucky enough to be on the receiving end of it every so often."

"Well, you deserve it. And you're the last person I want to see right now."

Mostly because when she closed her eyes now he was all she could see. Mostly because now when she thought about who should be the father of her baby he seemed to be the only answer.

No.

There were risks she could take in life, and had taken many of them gladly. But compromising her relationship with Ryder like that…

If he married you, he would have to keep you for basically ever.

She felt rent right down the middle with that thought. A jagged streak of terror on one side and a blinding, white-hot need on the other.

She was also starting to see herself the way that Ryder might.

And *lame* was about the only word for it.

She scowled. "Anyway, what do you want?"

"Just checking in."

"My answer is still no. I mean, we could do…some kind of agreement, I guess. But we can't do marriage."

"No," he said. "If you want to do this, then it has to be my way."

"Why?" It was so irritating and ridiculous that what

had started as a suggestion she'd made on a whim had turned into an outright obsession. She was angry at him, and angry at herself. Because the more she thought about it the more she realized that he would be the perfect father for her baby. Because Ryder was perfect. Because he knew how to take care of people. Because he knew how to take care of her.

And she refused to think about any of the other things, because they were complicated and messy and they made her chest hurt.

"You're asking me why I'm acting in character? What about you? Why would you ask that of me if you didn't want this response?"

She had thought that he couldn't possibly strip her closer to the bone, but then, there he went.

He made her feel seen.

He made her see herself.

She didn't like it.

"I didn't think you would take me seriously."

"Was it a joke?"

The seriousness in that gaze of his stole her breath.

"No," she said. "I just… I don't know why I said it. Because… Because you would be a good father. Because you're protective, and because you are an old retired guy. All those things that I said to you… I know that it was not very nice of me, but the thing is you complement me, and…"

"But I thought you didn't want a man to help raise your baby?"

"I don't," she said. "I mean…not really."

You do, though. Secretly. He's right. You harbored a fantasy of all of this working out as some big unconven-

tional family in your head, and if you didn't, then you would have just gone to a sperm bank like a normal person. But you're not handling this like a normal person.

She tried to ignore the needling voice in the back of her mind.

And then another one.

You expected him to take care of you. But you also expected that you could get your way.

That cut her in two.

Because she had to look at herself critically and ask if that was true.

Or maybe she didn't. Maybe she could just abandon everything right now. Everything could go on as it had before, and nothing needed to change.

"We should do something less complicated," she said, hushed. "I've been fighting with you a lot more than I want to. Which means... Fighting with you at all. I don't like it. I don't want to be in a fight."

"Tough to avoid when you started a fight, baby," he said.

"It became something it shouldn't have. I should not have asked for your help with this. I shouldn't have accepted it. It is weird, you're right. I didn't need to involve you in my sex life, and we crossed some lines." She used her best calm, rational voice. "But we won't cross them anymore. You're the most important person in the world to me, Ryder," she said softly. "I couldn't stand it if something affected that."

He didn't say anything; he only stared at her with dark, fathomless eyes.

"I have to go. I have a custom order and I need to get to work on it. I imagine you have some work to do."

He nodded once. "That I do."

"Okay. I'll talk to you later."

She slipped past him and into the camper, and it was only after she settled in with all of her fittings and gemstones in front of her that she realized he hadn't agreed to not let it affect them. And she feared that it already had.

CHAPTER EIGHT

RYDER WAS ALL bound up in the gut the next day, and on into the evening. He didn't know why he couldn't let the thing with Sammy go. She seemed to be ready to do just that, and that meant that he needed to do it, as well. But he found the whole thing difficult.

You're not her parent, though.

He was well aware of that. Nothing he felt for her was parental or brotherly or anything of the kind. It was something he'd never particularly liked. Something that he knew would be a violation of her trust in him. And so he'd done a really good job of keeping it pushed down all this time, but he was failing now more and more.

He gritted his teeth and returned to the task at hand— which was mucking stalls, an evening chore that he never minded.

It had been a long day moving the cows from one pasture to another, and in general dealing with cantankerous animals. It was nice to be back at the barn dealing only with the horses.

He pitched out the last of the foul shavings and took his wheelbarrow out of the stall, heading toward the back of the barn where he would find fresh bedding for the animals. And that was when he saw Sammy, lingering in the doorway, staring at him curiously.

In one of her typical Sammy outfits, she had on a long skirt that the backlight from the barn door lit up, letting him see the exact shape of her legs beneath the diaphanous fabric. Her blond hair was down around her shoulders, a pale cloud, and the golden glow cast around her hair could easily be confused for a halo if he didn't know her quite so well.

She was his sunshine, yes, but his angel, never.

Because she was something a lot more grounded than that. A wood nymph or an equally ridiculous creature that he would never normally think of, except Sammy put his mind in places that he would never choose for it to go. She made him think of things, want things that were crazy and impossible, and she seemed to put a whole new vocabulary inside his head on top of that.

"Hi," she said, clasping her hands in front of her and twisting them, the bangles on her wrists jingling slightly.

She looked…demure, and he didn't trust it, because that wasn't her. Not at all.

"What are you doing?"

"Getting ready to go out," she said.

And there was something in that that he didn't trust at all.

"You're getting ready to go out?"

"Yes."

"All right. And what aren't you telling me?"

"Nothing."

"Sammy…"

"I told you I wasn't going to involve you in this anymore, and I'm not."

She whirled around and he reached out and caught her arm, drawing her back toward him. Where he made contact with her skin felt like it was fire, and he couldn't tell if that was because he had finally touched the sun, or if it was because he was next to the door of hell.

"Be straight with me," he said.

"I think we decided that wasn't the best idea."

She was going to go out and find a man. She was going to do that. After everything. After she had asked him to be the father of her baby. After he had fired back with his ultimatum. After all that. He couldn't believe the gall of her. The nerve. And suddenly he didn't much care if it was wrong to grab hold of the sun. Because it felt like an invisible barrier had come down between them over the past few days. She had brought him into this.

Yes, he'd offered to help her find someone, and yes, it had been self-serving in some ways. But then she had asked him. She had asked him, and it had thrown his mind down a path he had done his very best to keep it away from for all these years. She had admitted to him that no man had ever given her an orgasm and that had put something else right underneath his skin. And she had taken those two things and she had…

He hadn't wanted it. He hadn't asked for it. But she'd done it all the same.

Sammy.

His reckless, brilliant Sammy, who was going out to give all that light to someone else. To get pregnant with their baby. To have sex that wouldn't even make her feel a damn thing.

What kind of protector would he be if he allowed that?

All the rules that he made for himself, all the rules he

made for her, starting when he was eighteen years old suddenly cracked, crumbled and fell. And left behind was a new world order that gave him a wide playing field and a reckless way to be.

He did something he'd told himself he would never do. He propelled her toward him, and she stumbled up against him, her delicate hands pressed against his chest. Her eyes were wide as she looked up at him, her mouth dropping open. She looked afraid, and he had told himself he would never make her afraid. But his heart was pounding too hard and his blood was pumping just a little bit too hot and fast, and he didn't know what he was.

He didn't know what he was.

He lifted her chin up, holding it tight between his thumb and forefinger, and he could see it in her eyes if only for a moment. A challenge. A dare.

And he was too far gone to not take it.

Somewhere in the back of his mind were the last vestiges of his sanity, and they were screaming at him. Screaming at him to get a grip, get it together, be the man that he had promised himself he always would be with her.

And he would've listened, if not for that challenge.

If not for the way she stood there, with an expression that basically said he didn't have the nerve.

Old. Retired.

Comfortable.

Steady.

That was everything he never wanted to be, so why hearing it all come out of her mouth had riled him like it did, he didn't know. But he was ready to disrupt that story she'd written about him.

Hard.

Before he could get another thought into his crowded brain, he leaned down and pressed his mouth to hers.

If sunshine had a flavor, it would be this. Because it was an explosion more than anything else. Heat and light like a full gut punch that immobilized him for a solid ten seconds.

He had spent so much time not thinking about what it would feel like to taste Sammy's mouth, that it was like seventeen years' worth of fantasies rolled out through his body in one brilliant flash. And when she parted her lips on an indrawn breath, a gasp that became a sigh when he slid his tongue against hers, it was like finding the answer to a question that had been dogging him for years.

And he made sure that kiss was nothing like she'd said he was.

Retired or old or steady.

She didn't wrap her arms around him. She didn't cling to him. Her hands were balled into fists against his chest, and she didn't pull away, but she didn't lean in, either. Didn't resist the explosion between them, but didn't return it, either.

And in the end, that was what stopped him.

He wanted to give, but there was a point where the way she was standing made it *taking*, and that wasn't what he wanted.

He took a step back and the look on her face made his stomach a hollowed-out pit.

"What was that?" she asked, her voice shaky.

"Something that had to be done," he responded,

amazed that he could even get the words out through his tightened throat. He could barely breathe, much less speak.

"You don't… You don't get to do that to me," she said. "You don't… That's not what you're for."

"You suggested we have a baby together, and you're very anti–turkey baster, Sammy, so how did you think we were going to accomplish that? Are you going to treat me like a prostitute? No kissing on the mouth. And were you going to lie there and think of England the whole time and make sure that you didn't enjoy it?"

"I didn't enjoy *that*," she said. Her breath was coming in short, harsh bursts. "And I didn't think it through. It was about *you*, who you are, not about us sleeping together. And now… It's not even about who you are."

"Oh, so now that I decided to make you face up to what it is you actually wanted to do you've decided you don't like me very much anymore?"

"What does that mean?"

"You know full well what it means. I made you face the reality of your plan. What it meant. You're the one that asked me if I'd be the father of your baby. And now you're acting like me introducing a kiss was a violation? What do you think would have happened? What do you think any of this entails? You're angry because you want your dream to stay frothy and cloudy and nothing that you have to figure out the logistics for. I'm sorry I brought it back down to earth, babe, but eventually it's going to land there, and you're not going to like it. And it isn't going to be my problem."

"It won't be," she said. "I'm going to make sure it isn't.

I'll go out and deal with it myself and you're absolved. Just go away."

"You're the one who'd have to go away, darlin'. I'll be right here where I've always been."

"Hanging out making Joan of Arc look like a self-preservationist with a selfish streak?"

Her words were sharp and they cut deep. "What?"

"You're a martyr, Ryder. Don't pretend you aren't. Don't you think I know what this is all about? It's not about me. It's about you. From your offers of marriage to that kiss. It's about you wanting—needing—to be the one to miserably sacrifice and fix me, and excuse me if I don't want it."

"That's not what this is."

"It's what your life is," she said, the words uncompromising.

Sammy was often shocking, but she wasn't usually uncompromising, and she was never mean.

But she was pretty mean right about now.

"Why are you still here? Why did you never leave? Because you were going to, you told me that. Before your parents died you were going to follow your football scholarship to college and get a degree. Major in engineering. Figure out how to make the things that hold the world together. You never did it. You settled right in here and you put on your hair shirt and kept it on even though you don't need to now. Even though you could change your life at any point. You don't. You keep yourself busy and you just keep on treating yourself like a beast of burden and why? So at the end of it all you can be the great hero, who never had to try and fail at living his own damn life." Blue eyes blazed into his, scorching his soul.

"Sammy..."

"You're not the only one who can see through a friend's bullshit."

Then she turned on her heel and walked away, leaving him standing there facing down the inevitable truth that he had jumped into this with both feet to keep things from changing, and now he was the one that had forced them to change irrevocably.

And she'd stabbed him clean through with those words, though they weren't as true as she believed because being with her—in her bed—oh no, that had nothing to do with him suffering at all.

But as he stood there with regret in his chest and the taste of Sammy on his tongue... He wasn't even sure he would change it.

Because one was stronger than the other.

A taste of sunshine was brighter than just about anything else.

CHAPTER NINE

SAMMY WAS INCANDESCENT by the time she walked into the Gold Valley Saloon. She was ready to approach the first man she found and ask him to put a baby in her.

Just to spite her best friend in the whole world for daring to put his mouth on hers. For daring to question her like he had been for days.

That was reasonable.

But he wasn't reasonable. He was calling out all of her secret fears and laying them bare in the light, and it wasn't fair. Not when she didn't push him. Not when she didn't make him feel bad about his life or himself or who he was.

And not because she didn't see him. Not because she didn't know that he was a man who'd turned away from the future he could have had if his parents had lived. He'd done it so deliberately that it was clearly a punishment and a shield all in one.

Her whole body was on fire, crackling like an inferno, and she wanted desperately to believe it was all rage, and not because the feeling of Ryder's rough, commanding lips on hers had been anything other than a gross overstep of their friendship.

And through all that she kept asking herself if he was right. If what he had said was true. If the reality was she

was just mad at him because he was asking her to face…
well, reality.

If the issue was that she had a nice idea of what it
meant to have a baby. It was true, she had a beautiful
vision of herself round with child standing in a field in
a flowing dress, and then later holding a beautiful new-
born, having it there in a bassinet while she made jewelry. Some kind of earth mother, bohemian existence that
was a completely unrealistic vision of how that would
actually be.

But she knew there was more to it than that. That vision was just a concrete picture of the longing inside her.

But underneath that longing was some fear. That she
still needed help. That she needed some real security.
Safety.

It was why she'd asked Ryder.

She had actually dated plenty of men who would be
fine with the kind of thing she was proposing. But Ryder
wouldn't be. He was right; she did know that.

And so he was right again to ask why she had thought
that she could ask him for that and get the outcome she
had imagined she would get from the made-up man in
her head. She wasn't thinking about Ryder anymore.
And she was ignoring the way her lips burned. Because
it wasn't fair, and she didn't like it.

Don't you?

She ignored *that*, too. She didn't like the way this quest
had thrust her into some weird situation where she had
to continually ask herself honest questions. That was
Ryder's fault, too.

The continual taker of her moral inventory. Her rock.

Her touchstone. For better or for worse. And in this case for maddening.

It wouldn't bother you if you didn't want to have his baby.

She gritted her teeth and made her way farther into the bar.

And she looked at the men there. Men that would be expected to touch her if she wanted to sleep with them. If she wanted to get pregnant. And she could only think of Ryder.

The problem was, she couldn't seem to banish thoughts of Ryder from her mind. No matter how hard she tried. No matter how many men she looked at.

His words kept echoing in her mind.

Your type doesn't turn you on.

That wasn't true. Of course her type turned her on. It was why they were her type. They were interesting to her in ways that went beyond the physical.

She could have orgasms. Just not with a partner. And she had decided a long time ago that worrying about that only stressed her out to a degree that made it all not very much fun, and therefore, she didn't want to do it. Therefore, she would just go ahead and focus on the sweet physical touch that she liked, and the conversations that she had with them before and after, and she would go off to her own space, her own bed and have orgasms when she wanted to.

None of that had to do with what she was doing here now. None of that had to do with any of this, and she was furious at Ryder for what he had done. For kissing her.

Kissing her.

Him.

It hadn't been like a kiss. Not the way she knew them. There had been no tentative question, no testing things at all.

He had pulled her up against his body—which had been hot like an inferno and hard as a brick wall—and he had claimed her mouth like he had every right to it. Like he knew what she would like. Like he knew full well how much tongue she wanted sliding against her own and how much pressure she wanted against her lips. Like he would know how fast or slow to touch her between her legs, how hard or soft, and when to ease up and when to go on.

She had never been with a man who had grabbed her quite so confidently, and he was the last man on earth who should have, since she hadn't indicated at all that she wanted to kiss him.

Maybe, just maybe, at the last moment she had dared him rather than retreated. Maybe she had seen in his eyes that she could have stopped him, and had chosen not to.

But that was only a maybe.

And the next thing she'd known he'd been kissing her.

And really, it wasn't like she should have reasonably been able to guess that was what he was about to do, even though he was holding her like that. Because they'd had seventeen years of not kissing, so the fact that they had suddenly started kissing was a whole weird thing.

She stood by the fact that he was the one who was wrong and not her. That he was the one who had changed things somewhat irrevocably and she could only feel annoyance about it.

She suddenly felt utterly and completely alone standing in the middle of the bar. She hated that feeling. It reminded her of being a child. Helpless. Standing in the corner while there was screaming going on around her.

Of when she would retreat deep inside herself and force that feeling because she hadn't wanted to be where she was.

She had even learned to do it when her father had turned his rage on her.

To just go to another place and detach.

This moment was oddly reminiscent of that and she didn't like it at all.

It wasn't long before the door to the bar swung open, and in walked Ryder.

She was getting really tired of this.

Really tired of him deciding that he was going to go ahead and be shocking when that was supposed to be her job.

He was supposed to be predictable and easy. He was supposed to be safe. But nothing that he was doing right now was safe at all. And she didn't know what to make of it. Not even a little bit, not even at all.

She started to back away from the door, but his eyes caught hers and managed to glue her in place to the floor.

And then the sensation inside her flipped, and it was like a whole other different kind of being alone. This was an isolation. It was as if the bar around her was falling away piece by piece. As if it were transforming into something else entirely. All of the insignificant bits were crumbling and dropping out of the sky like so many fallen stars, scattered around the floor at their feet. And it left her. It left Ryder. And this growing intensity between them that was thick and black like a night sky.

"You don't want them," he said.

And the unspoken words there were that she wanted him.

And she didn't know what to do with that. Didn't know what to make of it.

Didn't know what to make of this intense stranger who was in the place of the man she had called her best friend for so many years.

Except, was he a stranger? Or was this just the guardian unleashed? What happened to the man when he was pushed? And she'd pushed him. On purpose. Maybe this was her consequence. That he was here now. The warrior that she had always known existed beneath that protective exterior.

He had never even tried to rearrange the boundaries between them before. But he had always been capable of it, and she saw that now.

That everything he had ever done all these years had been him being controlling. Had been him protecting her. And suddenly, he wasn't protecting her from him.

Suddenly, he was everything that she had sensed he might be in all of its terrifying glory.

The kind of man that she had avoided all this time. She had favored those concave chests and smooth faces he had accused her of liking earlier.

Men who didn't just assume that she might want a certain kind of kiss, but who couldn't seem to figure out which one she did want even when she told them outright.

Almost as if Ryder knew something that she didn't.

None of this is about that.

She had to wonder if her body was doing some kind of weird female hormone thing.

And maybe that was true. Maybe it was more of a weird hormone thing. Suddenly, her body had identified that he would make a spectacular protector for a baby.

And why not? He had been the protector for her for all this time; of course he would make a great father.

Biologically.

But he was demanding all of these other things, and she didn't know how you were supposed to compromise with a brick wall.

They couldn't bend; you could only break them down.

And she had a feeling that she could grab hold of this one white-knuckled and still not come out the winner. Only come away with bleeding hands and destroyed fingernails, and he would remain as he had always been.

She waited. She waited for him to do something to make her comfortable. Waited for him to do something to defuse all of this between them. Because surely at some point he would crack a smile and revert back to being her friend.

Wind back the clock so that he was the man she had known for the past seventeen years, and not the stranger who had pulled her into his arms and scalded her with his heat. But he didn't. Instead, all of that intensity only seemed to grow as he moved closer. And she didn't have the heart to back away.

"Don't do it," he said, his voice rough. "I couldn't stand it."

She tried to breathe around the tightness in her chest. "You couldn't stand it?"

"No. Don't let another man touch you. Not after that."

"It was just a kiss."

He shook his head. "It wasn't."

Those words, simple and flat, terrified her under her soul.

"Ryder, I don't…"

"You know it's right. You know it is."

And she didn't know if he meant the kiss or him being the father of her baby or what. She didn't know at all.

And she wasn't sure she wanted to ask. Because she wasn't sure she could stand there and talk to him for a moment longer.

It was strange, because she couldn't hear the chatter of the people in the bar anymore. Couldn't hear the music.

She could hear the thunder beginning to roll outside, and she could hear the beating of her own heart. She could hear a warning sounding in her mind, pounding against her temples. She couldn't even see any of the other men in the bar; how would she leave with them?

And how would she kiss them with that brand of Ryder's still impossibly hot against her mouth. It was impossible. And she knew it. Pressure built behind her eyes, and she wanted to squeeze them shut, turn away. She wanted to be anywhere but here.

But she couldn't close this off, and she couldn't seem to make him or herself disappear. None of the tricks that she had used as a scared little girl seemed to be on hand to bail her out of this. She couldn't hide and make it go away, and she couldn't seem to brazen it out, either. And there was no rescue, no one coming. Not for her. Because the one who did all the rescuing was the one making her want to run and hide. But she only knew how to run into Ryder's arms, so that was making the moment decidedly more complicated than she would want it to be.

"Let's go," he said.

In the past when she had taken Ryder's hand, she had known exactly where he was going to lead her. She had trusted it.

Like Peter taking Wendy out the window into Never Never Land. Except, she would climb into his, and she would find safety there.

In that place full of lost children who had found each other.

But this time, he was leading her outside, and she didn't know where they were going to go.

Didn't know what was going to happen.

But somehow, she must still trust him, because she was going. She was going, even though it terrified her.

When they went outside, the air was hot and heavy, and the first raindrops from the summer storm were falling fat and heavy on the sidewalk, on her arms, her hair, and she knew that the blond mass was going to grow exponentially in the damp and humidity.

A silly thing to think about right now, but a safe thing. A certain thing.

And everything else seemed not quite so.

Thunder cracked through the sky, lightning splitting the air behind it and lighting up the street. And she could see his face, all hard and intense, and she hoped there wouldn't be more lightning, because she liked it better when she couldn't see him.

When she could imagine that it was still a familiar face, and not this one that seemed so different now.

He had kissed her first. And the grand tapestry of their friendship felt altered.

And she found that irritated her a bit, because why

hadn't she ever thought of it? She had teased him when they were younger. That time she'd shown him her bra. And he hadn't done anything. Hadn't made a move to touch her, hadn't even let his gaze flicker down to her breasts. He had been like stone, but tonight he wasn't stone. He was a man, and she realized that she had taken comfort in the fact that she thought him a mountain. And now he had revealed himself to be flesh and blood, and she didn't know what that meant.

But if only she had kissed him once. Just to taunt him. Just to tease him. Just to prove to herself what it could be, maybe she wouldn't be so surprised now.

It was why she went through life ripping Band-Aids off all potential wounds. So that she could never, ever be surprised. Ever. The rain was falling in earnest now, and her hair was sticking to her face, her tank top sticking to her body. He bundled her up into the truck, and didn't say another word. And she didn't dare speak.

The rain on the roof of the truck, on the windshield, the sound of the wipers moving back and forth. The motor. The occasional rumble of thunder. A familiar soundtrack, but one that seemed as different as Ryder's face looked. Like all the world around her was foreign and new and she had no idea what she might do with it.

No idea what would happen when he finished driving. Or where they were even going.

Just home, she realized. And she didn't know whether to be disappointed or relieved. A breath escaped and she couldn't tell if it was a sigh of relief or sadness.

Because something inside her had felt momentous; really, it had for a few days. It had led up to the whole pregnancy thing, and then somehow had brought her here.

And now maybe nothing was going to change, which should be a profound and great thing. Except…

He parked the truck in front of the house.

He didn't say anything.

She got out before he killed the engine, and she started to walk back toward the camper.

But he was behind her. She could hear his footsteps, and goose bumps raised up on her arms, the rain rolling down her skin. And he was there. Still.

Him.

And then his hand was on her, warm on her slick skin, as he stopped her from taking another step. She could pull away. She knew he would release her. But instead she turned to face him, because she wanted to know what this unpredictable version of her friend might do.

Because she was curious.

And she knew what they said about curiosity, but at the moment it was difficult for her to care.

But he didn't move. He just looked at her. The thunder rolled over the mountaintop, through her body and seemed to fill up her chest in a way that words couldn't right now. Propelling her heart on. Propelling them both further down some path she wasn't sure they were ever going to be able to find their way back from.

He took a step toward her. And she held fast.

Then he lifted his hand, putting it on her cheek. He had done that before. He had touched her before like this, but it was different. As he moved his thumb slowly over her rain-dampened skin, it all felt new.

The act of being touched. Ryder's hands.

The rain pounded down around them now, slid down her face, rolled off the brim of his cowboy hat, and as he tilted his head down, water poured from there. And she didn't care. She just didn't care, because she had to know.

She had to know.

And then he was pulling her close, bringing her under that brim and shielding her from the rain, angling his head and kissing her deeper than he had the first time.

She felt weightless. Breathless. And she *did* like it.

Those lips, firm and commanding and different than any man she had ever kissed. The stiff, scratchy feel of his whiskers against her face, the way he moved. Sure and certain.

And most of all, there was just something indefinably *him*. Something that went beyond anything as simple as the shape of his mouth or the strength of his frame, his beard or the squareness of his jaw. Something that went beyond physical and rested somewhere deeper.

Something like pixie dust.

Something that might make her fly.

There were other things you needed. She could vaguely remember how that line went.

Faith. Trust.

But then her mind was blank and she couldn't think anymore. Because his hands were big and rough and cupping her face, and there was something hollow and aching expanding inside her. Like loneliness but better because the creator of it might also be the completion for it, and he was right there, kissing her like it was better than breathing.

He moved his hands from her face, wrapping his arms around her, down her waist, her hips, to her thighs. Then he picked her up off the ground, wrapping her legs firmly around his waist. His stomach was firm, flat. And with every step he took toward her caravan she felt vibration between her thighs, and he was still devouring her mouth, making her feel things that no man ever had before.

How was this possible? It was never like this.

She didn't even want it to be. She didn't like it.

She liked for people to think she was out of control.

She even liked to pretend that she might be.

But she never really was.

The more outrageous she was the more she controlled the conversation. The more she controlled people around her. It made her feel safe.

She never wanted to actually be out of control.

She was close to it now, but it felt so good that even though her brain was screaming caution at her, she couldn't really resist it. Didn't even really want to, not totally. Because she was weak, and those hands holding her to his body were strong.

With shocking ease he pulled the door open to her camper, bringing them both inside, and slamming it behind them again.

As it always did, the rain pounded loudly on the roof, making it feel like the storm encompassed the tiny shelter. It was one of the things she loved about living out here. That she always felt enveloped by the rain, more than shielded from it.

It was comforting even now, though comfort wasn't the dominant emotion that she felt. Not even close. For so many years rain had been her lullaby, but tonight it was the insistent, pounding beat of her desire. Pulsing through her like a drum. It was crazy, she knew it. It was stupid, and she knew that, too, but Ryder was never crazy or stupid, and he was here. Touching her. Kissing her. So maybe it wasn't quite as stupid as she thought. It couldn't be.

Because he was doing it.

Him.

He set her down on the edge of her mattress, his hands tangling in her wet hair, and then he sank down in front of her, on his knees. He cupped her cheek, kissed her neck, dragged hot, openmouthed kisses to her collarbone, and around the neckline of her tank top. Then he jerked her shirt down, exposing her breasts. They were wet from the rain, and the air felt cold, her nipples going unbearably tight. Stinging.

Then he covered one with his mouth, and white heat exploded behind her eyelids.

She was stone-cold sober, hadn't gotten around to having any kind of drink in the bar, but she felt dizzy. Felt like she must be either drunk or hallucinating because her best friend's dark head was bent over her bare breast, and that simply couldn't be. It was an impossibility more than it was an improbability, and yet it was happening.

Because while she might be able to hallucinate the sight of it, she wouldn't be able to manufacture the feel of it. Because this was like nothing she had ever experienced before. And she wouldn't have been able to make it up. Not ever. He moved his mouth to her other breast, teasing the first one with his hands as he did.

His hands were so *rough.*

She'd never been touched like this, by hands like this. She hadn't known that she would like it. That she would want it. That she could crave it. That the scrape of a workingman's callus against her bare skin could be the most erotic thing that she could imagine.

Or maybe it wasn't a workingman's hand. Maybe it was that it was Ryder's, and he was her friend, her protector, and there was something dirty and wrong about doing these intimate, secret things with him in the darkened camper with the rain pounding outside.

Things they hadn't even done when they'd been teenagers and full of hormones and rebellion, which would have been the perfect time. Not when they were in their thirties and full of nothing but opposing ideals and a deep, ingrained desire to not lose anything that mattered to them.

It occurred to her then that it was a bigger risk now than it would have ever been when they were young.

But that thought was only a fleeting one, because after that he started pushing her skirt up her thighs, the damp fabric resisting, but before long she was exposed, and he was hooking his finger in the waistband of her panties and pulling them down her legs, wedging her thighs apart with his broad shoulders.

Then he dipped his head, and it was no longer her breasts that were receiving attention from that wicked mouth—a mouth she would've never characterized as wicked before this—it was somewhere much more intimate.

"I don't like that," she said, her voice a rushed whisper.

It always felt like too much pressure, too much attention, and she didn't allow more than a feeble gesture toward the act because she didn't like being set up for failure.

She was much more comfortable with things where the objective was her partner's orgasm and not her own, since clearly that wasn't the point or purpose of her getting naked with someone.

"Then no one's done it right," he growled, not put off by her protest.

She was about to protest again when his mouth made contact with her wet, aching flesh.

His tongue left a streak of fiery need behind as he traced a path through her folds to the center of her need for him.

And something unexpected happened. Something incredible.

A miracle, really.

He pressed his fingers down against her, parting her, spreading her wide as he explored her with his mouth, as he pushed her harder, farther, farther than she had ever imagined possible, not just with a partner, but to heights she hadn't even begun to achieve on her own.

She was panting, her breath coming in short, harsh gasps.

It was electrifying. Terrifying.

Because she had no control over this. She wasn't conducting the train, not now. And not ever, not with him.

She tried to flex her hips in time with the movement, follow the rhythm of the rain, make some sense of it, try and get ahead of it, try and bring it back under her control, but there was no doing that. Not at all.

Because he set the pace, and he set the intensity. Because he made it amazing and dangerous and wonderful. Because he was Ryder Daniels, her very best friend in the entire world, and the only man who had ever seemed to know what to do with her body.

Her friend, who she would have said was beautiful, but perhaps far too good to be wicked in quite this way.

But she'd underestimated him.

And as disturbing as everything about tonight was, that might have been the most disturbing thing of all.

But then he brought his hands in to work together with his mouth, and she could no longer have a care about how things should be, or what she found disturbing, because there was only pleasure as he pushed one finger deep inside her, followed by another, as he continued to focus his mouth on that sensitive bundle of nerves there, as he made her feel things, deep and rich and wonderful that she hadn't imagined she was capable of.

And then he looked up, those familiar brown eyes meeting hers, a completely unfamiliar light in them.

"Come for me, Sammy." She trembled, the muscles in her thighs shaking. And then he said on a low growl, "Samantha. Come for me."

And she broke. Utterly dissolved beneath his touch, beneath his mouth, quivering, shaking, near to shattering as the most powerful orgasm she'd ever experienced in her life tore through her like a twister over the plains. Uprooting everything inside her. Everything she knew. Everything she was. Possibly everything she had been on the path to becoming. Rearranging the landscape of what was possible in her. Around her.

She was raw and shaken when it was over, and then he rose up and kissed her on the mouth, the intense flavor of her pleasure evidence that couldn't be denied.

Her skin was damp. From rain and perspiration and desire.

"There," he said, his voice rough. "Now you've come with a partner."

Her body still felt like it might belong to someone else, and she was still grappling with that sensation when he began to move away from her. "I'll let you get some rest."

"I…"

But she didn't know quite what to say. And by the time she thought she might have something to say, he was gone. Leaving her behind in her caravan with nothing but the sound of the rain on the roof to ground her to the moment.

Her heart rate still hadn't returned to normal.

Because she just had an orgasm. With a man.

Not just with a man, but with Ryder. The only man that had ever really mattered.

The one she couldn't make do without. And suddenly, she was very glad he had left. Very glad that he had given her reprieve.

She peeled her wet clothes from her body and crawled beneath the covers, damp and shivering, still wearing her jewelry.

She didn't know what had just happened to her.

No. That wasn't the problem. The problem was she knew exactly what had happened to her. She just didn't know where she was supposed to go from here.

And the one person that she truly wanted to talk to, the one person that might be able to help her deal with the riot of emotions inside her, was the person who had caused them.

CHAPTER TEN

RYDER COULDN'T GET last night out of his mind. Couldn't get the taste of Sammy off his tongue, and frankly he didn't want to anyway. He had done a damned idiotic thing last night, and today he couldn't be bothered to care. He hadn't seen her all day, and by the time dinner rolled around, he was anticipating the sight of her like a blow to the face.

Perhaps not the most eloquent of similes, but the whole thing wasn't overly eloquent.

It had been desperate and dirty on his part, and she had fallen apart in his arms, and when it was over, he had known that one of two things was going to happen next.

He either had to leave immediately or he was going to strip them both naked and finish what he'd started.

As he held her, trembling, his face still scant inches away from the most intimate part of her, he had known that she wasn't ready for all that.

And frankly, he wasn't sure he was, either.

Things had gone further than he'd meant them to, and caution had been set the hell on fire.

He walked into the house and through the entryway, kicking boots to the side. Rose's and Logan's, already sitting there. "You're meddling." He heard his friend's voice coming from the dining room.

Rose and Logan were sitting at the table, each one with a beer. Rose was examining Logan with a bright kind of keenness that they all feared Rose turning on them.

The youngest of all the kids, Rose was irrepressible. And the meddler.

She meant well, but she tended to jump into things with both feet. Lead with her heart, followed up with her mouth, and as far as he could tell, her brain was typically somewhere well behind those other two things.

"I'm not meddling. I'm just...prying. And saying that I think if I'm right, you should go for it."

"If you're right about what?" Ryder asked.

Logan looked up from where he was sitting and gave Ryder a world-weary expression.

"She thinks that I have a thing for Sammy. And that I ought to ask her out."

The back of Ryder's neck lit on fire. "All right. Are you suggesting that he help her with her pregnancy scheme?"

"I'm just saying that if he likes her he needs to get in there, because he's going to have to stop her from doing that."

"When did I give you the impression that I liked her?" Logan asked.

"I just thought that you might. And, the two of you would be a great couple."

"What do you know about couples?" Ryder asked.

Given the conversation he'd had with Logan about Sammy only recently, he knew that Logan didn't have any kind of interest in her. His friend thought that Ryder was in love with her.

Difficult to think about now.

He walked into the kitchen and jerked the fridge open, pulling out his own bottle of beer.

"You're very serious," Rose said. "Sammy might lighten you up a little bit. Anyway, she's pretty, and you both live here…"

"I'm good, Rose, thank you," Logan said.

"I just thought that you might…"

"I don't," Logan said, looking up from the table and meeting Ryder's eyes again.

Rose turned around. "I think he's being ridiculous."

"Well, he clearly thinks *you* are being ridiculous."

"He usually does. I'm not really bothered by that."

"Well, why would you be?" Logan said. "Apparently, you only think I have good taste if it matches up with yours."

"Obviously," Rose said.

"I'm not sure that you'd make it as a matchmaker," Logan said.

"Why not? I think I have a pretty good sense for people."

"Have you ever even been on a date?" he pressed.

"What does that have to do with anything?"

All things considered, the conversation was a little bit overly ridiculous.

"You need to be with a woman who will lighten you up a little bit," Rose said. "Ryder needs a woman who will do things for him, so he doesn't have to be such a ridiculous martyr all the time."

He stiffened. Because it was the second time in twenty-four hours that someone had called him that. And he was beginning to wonder if it was true.

If Sammy was right.

If he'd gone straight for the thing that he said he didn't want because he was an eternal martyr climbing up on a wooden stake asking for life to go ahead and set them on fire.

But then Iris walked in, followed by Sammy, whose eyes met his, and then she jerked away like she'd been scalded.

And he knew that he wasn't as much of a martyr as his sister or Sammy seemed to think.

Because martyring himself would've been sitting back and watching her sleep with another man. Get pregnant with another man's baby.

Martyring himself would have been stepping back and letting her do what she wanted while he suffered.

And now that he had tasted her he knew that for sure. That what he wanted more than anything was her, whether or not he had tricked himself all these years into believing he was standing by holding sentry while engaging in some kind of courtly love.

There was nothing pure about what he felt.

Nothing like love about it, either.

Was he that basic that all this time he had never really been able to squash the lust that he felt for his best friend?

That in the end, it was stronger than wanting her to have the kind of happiness that she was after?

He feared that it was.

And if he were a martyr, he would have taken a step back right then. Let himself be consumed by his desire rather than seeking to satisfy it. But he didn't. Because everybody might think that he was like that, but he knew that he wasn't. Not in this. Not now.

So there. A victory, even if it was a hollow one. He would take what he can get.

Her blue eyes met his, and there was a strange glint in them that he couldn't read. Sammy was often enigmatic; it was part of her charm. And he knew it was somewhat intentional. He had to wonder if she was being intentional in it this evening.

"And how was your day?" she asked.

He felt like she was deliberately lobbing that question into the center of the room and not at him specifically. And the test was whether or not he would respond. But he wasn't sure if he was supposed to.

"Great," Rose said happily, taking the pressure off him in terms of who was meant to answer first.

"Just fine," he responded.

When her eyes connected with his there was a crack of electricity that hit hard and low in his stomach and then skittered outward. Downward.

If there hadn't been the faintest color in Sammy's cheeks he wouldn't have thought she was affected at all.

"Wonderful," she said. "I picked blackberries, so there will be a pie tonight."

She was all sweetness and light, sugary smiles and promises of dessert. He didn't trust it.

He knew that no one else thought it was weird at all, because they only ever saw this sunny side of her, so they didn't sense the false note there. But he saw the sharp side of her often enough that he could tell when it was lurking beneath the surface. He deserved it, quite frankly. But he wanted to know what manner of storm was coming. Because he knew there was one.

That distraction was enough to take his mind off the

intimacy that had passed between them. For a moment. Not for very long.

But hey, he was a man after all. So of course he was going to think about what it had been like last night. It had been a long time since he was with a woman. A long time since he had tasted one like that.

And you're going to pretend that's all this is? You fixating because you're a man and she's a woman and you did dirty things with her?

Not because it was your friend, and it was the culmination of years of suppressed fantasies.

All right. He couldn't pretend that. Of course it was about Sammy. Of course it would always be about who she was. It couldn't not be.

Sex for him was a pretty low-stakes game. He went out of town; he found women he had no obligation to. He made sure that nobody got hurt. He was safe; he was respectful. It wasn't intense. It didn't need to be. It was nice. A release.

But this had not been a release, and it wasn't just because he hadn't come. This wasn't a release because it had built up more uncertainty between them than it would ever let go.

Because it had caused him to violate some of the very basic tenets of his existence, and it was difficult to bring himself to even regret it.

Sammy took her position at the table next to him, her arm brushing against his. And she looked at him, out of the corner of her eye, and that was the only indication that he had that she even remembered what had happened between them last night. Because it was far too intentional. All of this was.

"How did you sleep?" he asked, looking at her with intent.

"Well," she responded, looking a little bit surprised that he had come at her like that.

A smile twitched at the corner of her mouth, and he had the sudden thought that she might actually just blurt it all out there at the table in front of all of his family. That she would just go ahead and say that he had given her an orgasm last night in her camper just to watch the world burn.

But no.

What was it she'd said to him the other night? That it hurt her, the way that he assumed that everything she did was simply down to shenanigans.

He was guilty of that.

As guilty as he was of the martyrdom she had accused him of.

That was his fault. Going around assuming that he had the correct read on her, but she didn't have one on him. But then, it wasn't arrogant so much as it was he didn't really think he had a lot of secrets from the world. Or himself.

He was a simple guy. He worked on his ranch; he took care of his family. They needed less from him now, but that was basically still the focus of his life.

He went out when he really wanted to. Found a woman when he needed to. He liked steak and he liked beer. He cared about his friends. Not that he had that many.

And she was the most important among them.

So it wasn't that he didn't think she was smart enough to see through him, so much as he didn't think there was anything to see.

She was making him question that slightly.

In making him question the way that he looked at her.

He did that with his siblings sometimes, didn't give them enough credit for the years and what they'd done to change them. For the progression of time and how it had matured them. He wondered if he did the same to Sammy.

And if so, then he had to backtrack and figure whatever she was doing now… It wasn't just to mess with him. Well, it was to mess with him for sure, but she must have another aim. One that served her broader purpose.

But it was difficult to think because she brushed against him again, and the electricity between them was the kind that made it hard to breathe or think. The kind that he'd only ever experienced with her.

When they were young.

He hated that. She was only two years younger than he was, but he'd felt ancient at eighteen, with the weight of the world on his shoulders, and a pretty sixteen-year-old that was at his same high school shouldn't have seemed so out of bounds.

All those times she'd climbed into his bed, right at first, it had been like torture. Until he'd learned how to push it down. And then he'd spent seventeen years since pushing it all down. Until last night.

Until now.

"Glad to hear it," he said.

"How is your baby thing going?" Rose asked.

Rose had ulterior motive embedded in her tone, and he was sure he'd have recognized it even if he hadn't already heard her talking to Logan about it.

Iris grimaced. "You can't ask someone how their baby…thing is going," she said.

"Sure I can," Rose said. "I mean the fact that we know it's happening means that I can ask. Anyway, Sammy would ask any one of us."

"Promising," Sammy said, a smile touching her lips.

"See?" Rose said. "She doesn't mind talking about it."

"I have no problem saying I don't want to talk about something if I don't want to talk about it," Sammy said. "I don't really have a problem coming out and saying anything."

"No," Ryder said. "It's whether or not you'll say what you really feel. That's the question."

Their eyes held. And he could read the unspoken communication there. Asking him if he really wanted to get into this kind of stuff in front of people. Because while he didn't think she was going to announce what had happened between them, he had a feeling she would push the line.

Well. Fine.

He shrugged.

"I mean," Sammy said, all cotton-candy voiced, "it's better than keeping everything shoved down deep and then dying someday of constipated emotions."

"Is there popcorn?" Rose asked, her eyes bright.

Logan gave Rose a long, hard look.

"What?" she asked. "This is the most entertaining thing that's happened here in a long time."

"You mean, ever since Pansy lost her mind and is marrying an ex-convict?" Logan asked.

Clearly, his friend was attempting to shift the focus of the conversation, because even if Logan had the wrong end of the stick, he knew that there were things happening between him and Sammy, which was something his younger sister would never pick up on.

"Sure," Rose said. "But if Sammy is going to call Ryder out, I want a front-row seat."

"You have one," Iris said. "With steak."

She got up from the table and went into the kitchen, coming back with the steak that had been resting. There was salad and green beans, too, and for a moment everybody was occupied dishing food and tearing chunks of bread off the loaf that Iris had made.

That meant that he and Sammy had a choice. They could call a cease-fire. Because with oral sex and an orgasm between them maybe it wasn't the best idea to be pushing all this out in the open.

But he wasn't in the mood.

"Better than trying to inflict your feelings on everyone else, I expect," he said. "Then other people might die of them."

"Oh right. Me and my harebrained schemes. Always inflicting myself on people. That's me. And yet…here you are. And here I am. So for all the trouble that I cause, you seem to need it. You seem to need me."

"Are we in the middle of a fight that we didn't see the beginning of?" Iris asked.

"Something like that," Sammy responded.

"I want to eat steak," Logan said. "You have a problem with that?"

"Can you not eat steak when there's tension around you, Logan?" Sammy asked. "I didn't realize that you needed to clear your chakras in order to enjoy your food. But I can burn some sage if you want."

Sammy had clearly correctly identified that Logan was on his side. And she was not happy about it.

"Oh, I'm fine," Logan said. And as if to prove his point he cut into the steak and took a bite.

Sammy was tapping the edge of her ceramic flowered plate. These plates had been gifts that Sammy had brought with her. Ferreted out of various charity stores and yard sales. She had compiled enough dishes for the expanded family, including her.

She had elbowed her way in. Made a place for herself.

And he had put everything she did down to shenanigans. He did treat her like she was a kid. Like she was running with her arms in a windmill doing things that had no point or purpose. But these nonmatching dishes had a purpose. Like all the other things that she did.

"It's fine," he said. "I'm sorry."

She blinked, her lips twitching. "What?"

"I'm sorry. I shouldn't have been poking at you."

"Somebody write this on a calendar," Rose said.

"I apologize, when I'm wrong."

"When you think you're wrong," Rose said. "Which is basically never."

"Well, I haven't had the luxury of running around thinking I might be wrong. Because usually I just have to make decisions and stick with them. But I was picking on Sammy, and that wasn't okay. So there. See? I can apologize."

"We'll have to continue the conversation later," Sammy said. And then she shifted, brushing up against him again, and he realized that was calculated, too.

They finished eating, and then Sammy got up to get her pie from the kitchen. "I'll help," he said.

"It's just a pie," she responded.

She said it so sweetly that he was sure she was making him push the fact that he wanted to be alone with her.

"There's ice cream. Anyway, it's chivalry."

The two of them went into the kitchen, and she leaned against the counter, crossing her arms. "Is there something you want to say?"

He thought about pulling her into his arms and kissing the smirk off her face, but his sisters were in the next room, and it wasn't the time.

"You okay?"

"Are you inquiring about my well-being postorgasmically?"

"Yes," he said, gritting his teeth.

"I think the time to do that would have been when you actually did it. Instead of leaving me."

"It was the right thing to do at the time."

"Was it? Because it seems to me that if it was the right thing to do, it would be the right thing to do now, not just at the time."

"Are you mad at me for leaving?"

She shifted her shoulders, making a strange little smirk with her mouth. "I wouldn't say that I'm mad. I just… I don't know. You're my friend. I expected you to stay and talk to me."

"It was better if I didn't," he said, his voice rough. "Trust me on that."

"Why?"

"Because," he said. "I would have taken things further. And it didn't seem like you were in the headspace to do that."

She huffed a laugh. "I was actually in a pretty great headspace to do that, all things considered."

"But it would have been taking advantage of that and it would have been too easy to make choices for you, choices for us, that would be better…discussed. And it didn't seem like the best idea."

"So you just left me there to sort it all out instead of having a little bit of self-control?"

He leaned in, grabbing hold of her chin with his thumb and forefinger. "I've had self-control for the past seventeen years. Last night wasn't just a lapse in it. It was an absolute destruction of it as a concept. And I didn't know what the hell I might do if I stayed there. So yeah, I figured that leaving was about the best thing."

Seventeen years. That was…that was too much for her to take on board. It made it hard to breathe. So she had to push it aside. "You wouldn't have done anything I didn't want you to," she said.

He lifted a shoulder. "You know that for sure?"

"Yes."

She turned away from him and took her pie off the counter.

"Get your ice cream," she said.

He opened up the freezer and grabbed the gallon, following her back into the dining room, and that was the end of their conversation.

But it wasn't really the end.

Because they would be talking about this more later. Of that he was sure.

One thing he knew, he had done something wrong, and Sammy was mad. Hell had no fury like a woman scorned. And hell's fury ran from Sammy Marshall when she was pissed. If he had half a brain he would do the same. Except he couldn't, because he had been the one to cross the line, so he would have to be the one to put it back, he supposed.

And let her go off with another man?

Hell, no. All right, maybe there was no moving the line back.

Ryder didn't like not having a plan. He liked to be in control. As best as he could. Mostly because life had proven to him that plans and control were a joke, so it made him want to cling to the idea of them even more. If he could build a facade of them, there would at least be that.

And right now he had no idea in hell where things went from here. And not knowing that made him feel like he didn't know much of anything at all.

CHAPTER ELEVEN

HE WANTED HER. And that changed everything.

Through all of this Sammy had imagined that he was acting out of some weird, misguided sense of chivalry. And he might very well be, in part, because it was Ryder, and that was how he was.

But he wanted her.

Last night his reaction to everything… Well, obviously he wanted her, but initially she had thought it was just a man responding to a woman's body. After all, that stuff was easy for them. It really was. It was why all the men that she'd ever had sex with had come, and she hadn't. Because they didn't need to want *her* in any kind of particular way, she just needed to be there.

Show up, bring boobs.

But she had the feeling now that Ryder wanted her. Her. And no man had ever made her feel like that during sex. And all right, they hadn't had full-on intercourse-type sex. And she hadn't seen him naked. And she wasn't really sure he had seen her so much as had his… Well, that was the most intimate thing she had ever done.

And it had felt wonderful. *Wonderful.* And nothing had ever felt like that for her. She had never been able to let go with a man like that. Moreover, she hadn't wanted to. And she had resisted at first. Resisted letting Ryder carry her off into that dark unknown with his arms around her and his tongue…there.

And all today she had been thinking… Why shouldn't she have that? She had some power here. He wasn't just coming after her because he wanted to save her from herself. No, he had offered because he wanted her. You couldn't do that to a woman and not want her; at least she didn't think so. Sex was one thing, tasting her like that was another. Certainly none of the men she'd been with had ever been… Well, some of them had tried, and she had immediately crawled off the bed. Nearly out of her skin.

The whole thing just had never appealed to her.

But Ryder had done it and…it was like her world had been burned to the ground. But not in a bad way. She had just been standing there watching everything go up in flames around her, and it had seemed beautiful and warm and wonderful.

She had gone up right along with it, and it had still seemed wonderful.

It made her feel different about the whole thing. About him. About his offer.

They were friends after all. Maybe they could manage to be friends with benefits. Maybe they could be friends who had that kind of sex and a baby between them. She had avoided him after dinner, which was maybe a little bit mean. But she was mounting a campaign. She had an idea. Then the very thought of what she was about to do made her feel sick inside, but it had to happen. Because she had to know. Before she made any kind of decisions about whether or not he would be the one. Before she decided how much she was willing to bend and break with his demands...she had to know.

She dotted the insides of her wrist with perfume and looked in the mirror. She didn't have any makeup on, but she often skipped makeup. Instead, she pinched her cheeks and wet her lips, fluffing her hair and looking at the woman in the mirror.

The woman who was about to take a step with her friend that she wouldn't be able to take back.

Last night was that step.

Or maybe it was several steps ago. When she had asked if he would be the father of her baby.

Or maybe before that when she had told him about her plan in the first place.

Maybe it had all changed sometime before she could even remember. Maybe there had just been the slow, inevitable walk toward something new. Something different. Maybe no matter how badly you wanted to stay in one place, the way things moved around you meant you couldn't.

She was filled with *maybes* and she didn't have a lot of answers. But that was the story of her life.

She was on a quest for something more concrete; if she wasn't then she wouldn't have embarked on the whole baby endeavor to begin with.

Ryder was the strongest, most solid man she knew. And so on that score she could see the value in agreeing to what he had asked her to agree to.

But beyond that... Beyond that was the way he'd made her feel, and when had anyone in her life touched her and made her feel that good? They hadn't. Not ever.

Didn't she deserve that?

Buried in all those thoughts was a concern about the way he had called her selfish. And if maybe this line of thinking was selfish, as well. But she wasn't sure she cared. She wasn't sure she could afford to care, not now.

Because now that the idea was in her head, that it should be him, now that he had touched her the way he had, kissed her...

And none of it was simple, because it was all bound up into many things. Because he was her friend, and because they had never done anything like this before. Because she had never felt anything like that before with anyone, because all of this was linked to the idea of having a baby together, and then because of him, the idea of maybe getting married...

Yeah, it was a little bit complicated and she wanted to reduce it right now.

To sensation.

To the way that he had made her feel, because it was new, and it was amazing, and it was different from anything she had ever felt before.

She opened the door to the caravan and walked outside, the warm summer evening washing over her skin. Her nipples pebbled beneath her thin top. She wasn't wearing a bra. She often didn't wear a bra; she didn't have breasts that were much of anything to write home about, so there wasn't a point when she wore tank tops. No use fussing around with strapless bras and things like that when she might as well just forgo.

But she happened to know tonight that the white tank top she was wearing was a little bit see-through. As was the skirt that she had put on.

She had put on underwear, but only because she had

a pair of very cute white lace panties that she thought he might like.

The idea sent an arrow of pleasure shooting straight through her core.

She didn't think she'd ever thought about sex and attraction in these terms before. The idea of wearing things for men... Well again, she just assumed that men kind of wanted whatever woman presented herself as available. So she had never gone out of her way to make herself particularly attractive to a particular sort of man.

She tended to attract the kind of man that she liked. She gave off a bohemian vibe, and she often worked at arts-and-craft fairs and farmers markets. She was primed to manifest the kind of man who frequented those places.

But that meant she didn't really try in a specific sense. But she didn't know what Ryder liked. Apart from the fact that she was now convinced that he liked her.

She had never known any of the women that he had slept with.

And if pressed, she would have said that he probably liked a neat, practical woman. One with contained hair. Possibly a brunette. Who favored T-shirts and jeans.

Except that he wanted *her*. She was sure. And she had only become more sure over dinner tonight.

And when he'd said...when he'd said he'd had seventeen years of self-control.

Seventeen years.

All this time.

It was mean of her to do it like this, she knew.

And maybe even a little bit cowardly. Because they could have talked about it. They talked about everything, though. And she was kind of tired of talking, because it hadn't gotten them anywhere interesting. No, last night had been the big advancement, and he hadn't been using his tongue to form words.

Heat spread through her body and she picked through the tall grass, heading toward the main house. But she didn't go to the front door. Instead, she crept behind the large oak tree that stood on the side of the house. She hiked her skirt up, another reason to wear underwear if she could ever think of one, and leveraged herself up onto the lowest branch. Then she began to climb. Higher and higher until she reached the second floor. Until she reached a very familiar window.

She hadn't done this since she was maybe…nineteen? Probably the last time she had ever done anything quite so silly as climb through this window and get into bed with him. But she was doing it now, and it wasn't for innocent reasons. Of course, he might have locked the window, which would ruin her plan.

And she had no other backup plan except maybe coming to the front door.

Which she was not above doing.

She made it to the top of the tree, and shinnied out on the branch toward the window. She reached out, testing it and finding that it gave easily. And then, with as much grace as she could muster, she slipped through the opening and into his bedroom.

She swallowed hard, looking down at his sleeping form.

She'd never thought about doing this. Not once. She had no idea how she hadn't thought of it. Especially when she had come in here so many times as a hormone-ridden teenager.

But Ryder had never been about hormones. He'd always been about safety.

And if she contorted she could pretend that there was an element of wanting safety and security here, too. But that wasn't the why of it. It was because she wanted— no, needed—to touch him.

Her breath caught in her throat. Now that she was there… Well, now that she was standing here she didn't know what to do next. Her certainty was gone, and he was so often her source of certainty that feeling this way about him was… It was terrifying. But the only way was through; she knew that.

So she had to make a choice.

She wrenched her shirt up over her head, and then pushed her skirt down her thighs, so that she was wearing only that pair of lace panties.

Then she heard him stir.

"Sammy?" His voice was rusty from sleep, and there was something in his tone that made it sound like he thought he might still be dreaming. And so she just did what she'd done so many times before. She crept over to his bed, lifted the covers and climbed beneath them with him.

His body was stiff beside her, and he was rigid, looking up at the ceiling, and not at her.

"If you think that you're going to climb into bed half-naked with me just so we can lie together…"

"That's not what I'm here for," she whispered.

She put her hand on his chest. His bare chest.

He had always worn clothes to bed before.

And then… Then she wondered.

"Do you always sleep naked?" She assumed he was

naked. Suddenly, it was like a torment to keep her palm still where it was on his chest when she wanted to let it drift down, explore more of his body.

"Yes," he said gruffly.

"So when I used to get in bed with you…"

"When you started coming to my room I made sure that I was always dressed. I slept that way until after you quit coming."

She blinked into the darkness. "For me?"

"I always wanted you to trust me, Sammy. But this… We can't share a bed like that. Not now. It's too late. It changed already and it can't go back."

"Well, I didn't take my clothes off for fun," she said. Then she laughed. "Actually, I did."

"What are you doing?"

"No one's ever made me feel like that before. And I want to feel it again."

"I'm not just going to give you an orgasm and let it be done."

"I didn't expect you to."

"Sammy…"

She scrabbled across the mattress and threw her thigh over his body, so that she was sitting on top of him. The hard length of him was settled between her legs, and she gasped.

She had a much better idea of his size in this position than she had last night. But then, she had barely touched him last night. And she could touch him now. All over.

She had never… She had never been with a man like this.

And moreover, she had never been with her friend. Both of those things combined to make this feel entirely new and different. Frightening and exciting and exhilarating.

She slowly let her fingertips drift across his chest. Across his chest hair. And she shuddered.

His hands came up, grabbing hold of her hips, holding her steady against him.

And his eyes blazed up into hers.

He was so handsome, her friend.

She had always felt a sense of pride about that.

That her protector was such a beautiful piece of art.

A man carved from stone. That perfect, square jaw and blade of a nose. His intense eyes and large hands. Broad shoulders.

He was wonderful. Wonderful in every way.

But she had never appreciated him physically in quite this way before.

And again she had to wonder at the inevitability of it.

She imagined most people would have thought that they'd done it a long time ago.

But it really hadn't been about this. Because then it couldn't have been.

And now it felt like it had to be.

So who was she to deny either of them?

She leaned down, ready to kiss his mouth, when he shifted his hands, bringing them behind her to cup her butt, squeezing her hard. She gasped. Then those big, rough hands started roaming over her bare body, her back between her shoulder blades and back down again. She gritted her teeth, trying to keep herself still. But her hips were rocking involuntarily, and it was difficult for her to keep herself steady.

"Let me," she whispered.

He growled, and suddenly she found herself flat on her back with him over her, his eyes looking into hers.

"No," he said. "Let's get one thing straight. I held myself back for a lot of years. And you bringing it here like this... Baby, I am not going to sit back and let you take control. You chose this. You're here. That was your power move."

"I knew you wanted me," she whispered, not quite sure what possessed her to say it out loud. Except that she wanted to find her own a little bit, and with him so hard and dark and powerful above her it was difficult to do that. It was difficult to breathe, much less feel power.

"Hell, yes," he said. "I want you. And I did my damnedest not to. Because you used to climb in my bed like this when you were sixteen years old."

"And you think I didn't know what happened between men and women back then? I wasn't a virgin."

What would she have thought if Ryder would have looked at her this way then? If he would have touched her then?

"I know that," he said. "But that wasn't the point. You came to me for protection. You trusted me. I would never have done anything to violate that. But now you're here." He planted his palm firmly between her breasts, let one finger drift over and touch her nipple. "You're here and you're like this. So you're the one that made it..."

"I want you, too," she said.

"You better the hell," he said. "Because I don't want you here just because you're trying to manipulate me, or say sorry to me, or whatever else this might be."

"No," she said. "That's not it. I would never take a risk with our friendship for those reasons."

"Nothing's going to risk our friendship," he said, his voice rough. "We've already been through all the hell a person can go through."

She found that comforting in a way. More than a way.

Because if they couldn't be broken outside this bed, through all the things they'd been through in life, then how could they possibly break in it? They were too strong, their friendship was too real. Ryder was and had been everything to her for seventeen years. There was no more defining relationship in her life. He was a man who had moved her from the darkness and into Neverland. But what she was discovering was that eventually everyone had to grow up. And why shouldn't he be the man to help with that, too? Why shouldn't he be the one to help her with that here?

It could just be part of who they were. And maybe part of who they were always meant to be.

She had to believe in fate. In the good of the world working to create a better end. That the hands of time had a point and a purpose, and that they were driving everything toward that inevitable place where love would conquer all.

Because wasn't that every story? Wasn't that the essence of faith?

A deep, real belief that seemed to grow from the center of the earth and up through the ground. The roots of humanity.

And there were villains; there always would be.

Men like her father who were selfish and wanted nothing to do with the good or beautiful things in life.

But it wasn't what the world was made of. It wasn't the deep essence or truth of what it meant to be a person.

And believing that like she did, she had to believe that her life was headed somewhere good.

That it had been from the moment Ryder had reached his hand out to her in that stall all those years ago.

It had to be.

He pulled the covers off them and switched on the bedside lamp.

"What are you doing?"

"I've waited seventeen years for it, Sammy. I want to see this happen."

"You really wanted this?"

"Yes," he said. "But I didn't let myself." That big, heavy hand rested on her breast, slid down her waist, to her hip bone. He moved his thumb up and down slowly, the callus scraping over her tender skin.

"You trusted me then," he said, his voice rough. "You trust me now. I'm going to take care of you."

Of course he was. That had always been true. Ryder had taken care of her from the moment she had passed into his sphere. From the moment she had become his responsibility, because it was who he was as a man. She loved that about him.

She squeezed her eyes shut tight, and then opened them again.

He was naked, but she couldn't see him, not in the position they were in. She could see the cords on his neck standing out, showing all of the self-control it was taking him to hold steady now. She could see the flex of the muscles in his shoulders, his chest. The intensity in his face. The deep grooves between his eyebrows, the firm set of his lips.

She couldn't see all of his body, but she could see him.

In a real and intimate way. In a way she had never seen him before.

And she could feel him.

The hard ridge of him pressed between her legs, against where she was throbbing for him.

It was such a foreign feeling, this deep, aching desire shared with another person.

She knew about arousal with a man in a bland way. It wasn't that she didn't get excited in this kind of situation. But not like this.

Not need that seemed to fill her to overflowing while hollowing her out all at the same time.

It was different, and so was he. Different as a lover, and different because he was him.

If she had been asked to imagine what it would be like to have sex with Ryder only a week ago, she would have said that it would be awkward.

That she might giggle and laugh because he was her friend, and what business did they have seeing each other naked?

But there was nothing funny about this moment. And sex for her often had a bit of lightness infused with it. But not this.

Not now.

It felt momentous and potentially altering, and normally she would have wanted to run from it. She didn't, though, not now. Because it felt essential to who she might become as a person.

Because it felt like a reclaiming of something she hadn't even known she needed.

To have a man look at her like this. Like he was starving for her. Like he was so hungry he might devour her completely. And maybe that was the real issue. She had never had a man look at her like this before because she had never been *ready* for a man like this.

She had never been ready for the commitment that was required to feel these things, to give back what needed to be given in order to create a connection like this.

Because it was so big, so intense, and there wasn't another man on the planet that she could've ever trusted to hold on to these feelings. Except she could trust him. Because he was Ryder, and he was wonderful. Because he had always taken care of her. And he would even now.

He hooked his finger into the waistband of her panties and started to pull them down her legs, revealing that last secret from him, even though he had tasted her intimately last night.

She knew he hadn't seen her. Not like this.

He let out a curse. Short and sharp, and somehow, it sounded more like a prayer.

Especially when he whispered her name at the end like a hallelujah chorus. Especially then.

He pushed himself up then, on his knees in front of her, looming above her where she lay. And she could see him.

Her mouth went dry.

She had never, ever thought of herself as the kind of woman who cared much about things like that. The size of a man, when after all, weren't there endless articles on the internet talking about how size didn't matter anyway? And that whatever women thought they might feel they were wrong, because the scientific fact was you couldn't tell, etc. etc.

But her whole body tensed with excitement looking at him. Hands down the biggest man she had ever seen.

Big all over. And on some level, she had figured that he must be proportionate, and it wasn't like she hadn't thought about it.

She was human.

She often pondered, in a passing sense, the penis size of the men around her.

She was curious by nature.

But this was visceral, and it was real, knowledge that hit her deeply and was extremely relevant to what would be happening to her soon. Very soon.

His body was so beautiful, sculpted, perfect, and she had the desire, almost overwhelming, to worship it.

So it was her turn to get up on her knees, and when she did she kissed his chest. His neck. Migrating along his hard-cut jaw until she captured his mouth. And when she slid her tongue against his he growled. She could feel the heavy length of him twitch against her hip bone. Reflexively, she reached between them, curling her fingers around that hardness.

So smooth and hot and heavy in her hand.

"You're beautiful," she whispered. "Like art. Like art I want to lick."

A growl rumbled in his chest as she kissed her way down his body, angling herself in front of his masculinity and flicking her tongue over the head of him.

Salty and musky and wonderfully him.

It was such an absurdly intimate thing to do to her best friend, and yet it never felt wrong.

He had been there for her all this time, this wonderful, incredibly beautiful man. And he had existed like this during all those years.

Just this beautiful. Just this incredible, and able to give her pleasure that no other man ever had.

And she felt nothing but wonder at that. And what was there to do but take him in deep and express that wonder with everything she had.

He pushed his fingers through her hair, holding on to her tight, and the hollow ache between her legs intensified. Grew. Expanded.

How was it that pleasuring him only increased the desire in her?

She didn't understand how it worked.

And she wondered if he felt this last night, felt it and then had to leave without any kind of satisfaction.

It made her believe what he'd said about walking away.

That he'd really done it because of her.

Because he was worried that she was afraid. Because he hadn't wanted to take advantage of her or the moment.

And that only made her want to pleasure him all the more. But she was feeling restless.

She pressed her own fingers down between her legs and tried to ease the ache as she worked him with her mouth.

"Don't," he said, his voice rough.

He grabbed hold of her hand and took it away from herself.

"That's for me to do. You have to wait."

She was ready to call him out on his extremely unfair behavior, but the problem was, he probably had a point considering she was one up on him in orgasm land.

Though he was probably a great many up on her when it came to having them with someone.

But not with each other. That was the thing.

This whole thing that was happening with each other was singular and different, and she didn't want to sully it by bringing in other people. Not at all.

So she obeyed, which was uncharacteristic of her, but felt right in the moment.

And she continued to pleasure him with her mouth until he moved her away and lifted her against him, kissing her mouth and sliding those rough fingers down between her thighs as he kissed her deeper and deeper still. As he stroked her, light and teasing, then firm and intense, pushing the pleasure that centered there into a white-hot inferno. One arm was wrapped around her like a steel band, pressing her breasts against his hard chest as he continued to kiss her; the other hand relentlessly teasing her between her legs. And when he pushed a finger inside her, his eyes were blazing into hers.

She couldn't breathe. And for a moment she felt like splintering glass. The cracks growing and expanding until she shattered completely. And when she did, he caught her in his strong arms and laid her down on the bed.

He was poised above her, positioned between her thighs.

And suddenly, she couldn't breathe.

The blunt head of his arousal pressed against the slick entrance to her body, and he began to fill her. Ryder.

Him.

Inside her.

And it was like the air changed between them, like he

could feel the difference, too. Like the whole world had tilted on its side, and whatever roots she had been so certain were there only a few minutes before were twisted and gnarled and unfamiliar to her.

Like she didn't know who she was or where she might be going. Or which way the world spun or why.

He was *inside her.*

And it was almost too much to take. Too big to breathe around.

He was over her, in her, breathing her same air. And when he lowered his head, a shudder racking his big frame, something inside her cracked.

Because he was shaking.

Her mountain.

And if even her rock could tremble, she didn't know if they could survive.

She had been so certain that neither of them would break here in this bed, but suddenly she wondered if this was the very place they might.

But then she couldn't think at all, couldn't breathe.

Because the pleasure that she felt was so deep, so all-consuming. And it was something other than pleasure. Something more. And it was something different than sex in the way that she understood it. And it wasn't just because he was so large, so big that he seemed to touch every part of her. It wasn't just that the way he moved seemed to touch her in amazing ways that she hadn't realized existed.

It was more. It was him.

They were skin to skin in a deep and real way she had never been with anyone, because of course she had always used protection in the past, and they weren't using it now. But it didn't feel like it was part of the whole baby situation. Instead, this felt entirely separate. Like it was something just between the two of them and whatever happened after would simply be.

Because maybe when this was all finished they would know.

Maybe it would shift everything, change everything, and maybe then she would understand. What to do and where to go from here, what it meant for them, meant for everything.

But then he began to move. And there was nothing. Nothing but the moment. Nothing but him. Nothing but this.

It was impossible to think that she could come again, so quickly after she had the first time. But as he thrust into her, slowly pulling back out, pleasure built inside her like a thunderstorm, building and growing, waiting for the heavens to release. And when they did, when her release poured down on her like rain over the land, she wanted to weep. As her internal muscles pulsed around him, pulled him deeper, she understood something.

He became part of her in a way that no one else ever had.

It was so deep and intimate. Such a peek of all that they were.

When she thought it couldn't be more, he shivered. Shook. Thrust hard into her one last time and filled her with himself.

She clung to him, breathing hard, holding his shoulders and fighting to keep tears at bay.

She felt altered. Shifted. As if the very makeup of what she was had changed. But then, the roots of the world had become something new since Ryder Daniels had touched her, so why wouldn't she be different also?

She moved away from him, swinging her legs over the side of the bed, clinging to the mattress as she breathed hard, trying to collect herself.

"Sammy," he said, and she heard the rustle of the covers behind them.

Suddenly, it was like the room tilted. And she could see clearly the past, when she would come in here as a girl, running away from life, and the present.

Dammit.

She was just the same.

She was running away from something in her life. Pursuing this whole idea of a baby because she wasn't happy with what had happened with herself. And… And then she had done it. She had climbed through his window, and she'd had sex with him, and they'd done it without a condom.

She was always doing this. To herself. To him.

Running and using him as a shield, and she had flung all those things at him, and she had been defensive when he had flung things at her.

But the problem was she suspected that from the beginning she had wanted it to be him.

Because she was using him.

The way that she did.

She squeezed her eyes shut, regret washing over her.

What if she had ruined them? What if she had ruined this forever?

"I…" She started to collect her clothes off that familiar bedroom floor. That scarred wood that she had walked across so many times. Just a few days ago she had followed him in here and seen him get out of the shower in a towel.

Had that been only a few days ago? It felt like a lifetime ago. And that everything between them was so unutterably altered that she could never get back to that person. That moment.

All the moments ever that had come before.

She had thought she'd known what sex was. She had thought she'd understood what she was asking him.

She was asking the man to let her carry his baby.

A piece of Ryder. A piece of her. All of it growing inside her. And the way they had...

She got dressed as quickly as she could.

"Don't run away," he said.

"Why not? You got to run away last night."

She didn't face him when she said that. Instead, she just wrapped her arms around herself and stood there, waiting for him to argue. Waiting for him to push. Waiting for him to say more, because he got to be stubborn and unhappy whenever he wanted to be, but he would never let her do it.

Except no reprisal came. He didn't push. He didn't tell her she was silly. He didn't tell her she was wrong.

She didn't know what the hell to do with that.

What was she supposed to do if not even Ryder would push? Did that mean that they were broken? Did it mean that this was a mistake? In ways that she couldn't have fully anticipated? It all felt a lot like he knew things that she didn't. It all felt a lot like dying.

But she believed in rebirth, she really did. The problem was, she'd been trying to force one, and she didn't know what came from that.

If the phoenix lit herself on fire, did she get to rise from those ashes?

Sammy feared the answer might be no.

And she feared that she had turned her best friend to ash right along with her.

She had no perspective, and she needed it.

She went over to the window and pushed it open.

"You're not climbing out the window," he said, his voice hard.

"You want me to take the stairs?"

"Don't break your neck on top of everything else, please."

She was going to argue, but he had a point. The window had been a gesture.

She walked to his bedroom door and opened it, walking out into the hall. And as she closed the door behind her, she felt the sense of change settle over her.

Because Sammy, his friend, would've always climbed in and out the window.

He was sending her out the door.

Like a lover who was on a walk of shame. Like someone altered, changed and broken.

Broken.

She felt *broken*.

She walked slowly down the hall, down the stairs. And she heard the clicking of nails on the hardwood floor, and suddenly the three farm dogs were swirling around her, silly, excited beasts barely able to contain themselves.

They didn't bark. She had a feeling Ryder had trained them to keep quiet at night.

But she could tell that they wanted to bark, curious about why she was here when it was so late.

She patted them on their heads.

"At least you still like me," she whispered. "But you're dogs. So I suppose you always will."

She wasn't sure what their owner would think of her right now.

As he lay in bed.

He hadn't tried to talk her into staying.

She didn't know what that meant.

And it was good, because she didn't want to. Because she didn't think she should.

Because they needed to regroup and think, or at least she did.

She gave the dogs one last pat, then sneaked through the living room and out the front door. And when she saw a figure out of the corner of her eye on the front deck, she startled.

So did the figure.

He looked at her, and when she could see him more clearly, she recognized that it was Logan.

"Huh," he said.

Oh, screw him and his speculative sounds.

"Don't make that noise at me," she said.

"Rose doesn't know shit."

Sammy rolled her eyes. *"Obviously."*

"I figured you guys would eventually. And based on the way he's been acting the past few days... I thought it might be soon."

"I'm the one who instigated it," she said.

"I'm not really that surprised by that, either."

"What are you doing out here?"

"Thinking."

"What about?"

"All the shit I shouldn't do," he said, leveling her with a look.

Only a few months ago Iris and Rose had introduced the idea that Logan might have feelings for her, but she had been certain that he didn't. She didn't know why she was so certain. Only that she was.

And something about the way he was sitting out there brooding confirmed it.

"You want to talk about it?"

"Not any more than *you* want to talk about it." *It* being her current parade of shame, she supposed.

"Fair enough. Though right now I would argue that there's a case to be made for *inevitability.* Whatever your issue is."

"I think there's a bigger case to be made for self-control," he said. "But then, what do I know?"

"I don't know. But right about now I don't know much of anything."

"He's a good man," Logan said. "Better than me, that's for sure."

"Better than me," Sammy said.

"They had that foundation. Losing their parents was hard. But your parents are scum. My mom was great. I don't even know my dad."

"You really don't know who he is?"

He paused. And that told her everything she needed to know. "Good night, Sammy."

"Good night." She stood for a moment and listened to the crickets. Breathed in the warm air. "Aren't you going to warn me not to mess this up? I mean, as the other non-blood relative, aren't you going to warn me not to tear my square out of this crazy patchwork life of ours?"

"Don't mess it up," he said, but there was no heat or heart in it.

"That's unhelpful to me."

"I don't know what you want me to say. Life is hard, and it's lonely sometimes. And I'll tell you this. I do know what it's like, like you, to have a living parent that you still can't see or touch or have a relationship with. They lost everyone, and that's tragic."

"Yeah, ours just don't want us."

"So all I'm saying is…well, nothing. I don't have anything to say. Not about this."

"Well, good night, then." She started to walk down the steps.

"He was different before you came."

She stopped and looked over her shoulder. "Huh?"

"Ryder. He was different. Before he met you. You taught him to smile."

She laughed. "Not well. He still doesn't do it often."

"Before you he didn't do it at all." He stood then. "Good night."

And she nodded, and fled across the driveway, letting her hair fly wild in the breeze, running until she thought her heart might burst from her chest.

She'd had sex with Ryder.

Everything felt changed.

But he hadn't smiled until she'd come to the ranch seventeen years ago.

So maybe, just maybe, there was hope all this wasn't broken after all.

And neither was she.

CHAPTER TWELVE

WHEN RYDER GOT UP the next morning his whole body ached. Like it was punishing him for the pleasure that he'd found last night inside Sammy.

Sammy.

If he didn't feel the effects of last night so keenly on his body he would be tempted to imagine that it had been a dream.

A fevered dream that blended the past with the present, reality with fantasy.

But no. It had happened. He was sure of that.

His skin felt different. Hot. Because of her.

Because she had touched him that way. All over. Because she had kissed him, taken him into her mouth.

Because he had…

He gritted his teeth, walking into the bathroom and turning only the cold water on in the shower. He stepped beneath the spray, bracing his hands on the wall and gritting his teeth. He waited. Waited for the cold water to do something. To make him numb so that he didn't feel any of this anymore.

She had left.

They'd had sex without a condom.

But she'd left.

And he hadn't fought to get her to stay.

Those facts rolled around inside his brain, and they effectively distracted him from the cold shower, which ultimately did nothing. Absolutely nothing.

He didn't feel better. He didn't feel fixed.

He felt changed.

And not necessarily in a good way.

He got out of the shower and dried himself off, making certain to scratch his skin with his rather cheap and threadbare towel. Just as a continuation of the general physical punishment he felt that he deserved.

He got dressed and jerked open his bedroom door and stopped. Right there in front of the door, between his bare feet was...

A sugar cube.

He bent down slowly and touched the top of it, looked down at the bright white shape on the scarred wood floor. Picked it up, rolled it between his thumb and forefinger.

Sammy.

He walked down the hall toward the landing, and there was another one, just before the first step. He picked that up, too.

There was another in the middle of the staircase. And another.

And Sammy was lucky that he got up earlier than anyone else in the house, or he was sure that the sugar cubes wouldn't have remained.

As he got closer to the kitchen he could smell bacon cooking. And on the dining table was a plate. At the center of it was of course—a sugar cube. His lips twitched.

He sat down in front of the plate, but left the sugar undisturbed.

A blond head poked around the kitchen doorway, a sheepish look on her face. "Good morning."

"I didn't expect to see you here," he said.

"You walked right into my trap." She had a bright, triumphant look about her that seemed more hopeful than actually happy.

"Don't I always?"

Their eyes met, and held.

There was a weary look on Sammy's face this morning, and he swore he could feel an extra line carving its way into his forehead.

If he'd aged ten years last night he wouldn't be surprised.

Apparently, she felt the same.

"Yes," she said softly. "Which makes setting traps for you fairly low risk. But I had my questions this morning."

"And what inspired you to set one in the first place?"

"I wasn't going to leave it like that. We both deserve a little bit better than an awkward walk of shame and waking up alone. Don't you think?"

"In fairness, I'm used to waking up alone."

"Well," she said. "I don't walk of shame."

"I didn't want you to."

He hadn't asked her to stay, either. But he hadn't wanted her feeling...that. Not in a million years.

"I know," she said slowly. "The shame was all mine. But it doesn't need to be there. Not with us."

"Why was it?"

"Because," she said, sighing. "I... I'm afraid that I was doing something terribly me. And I got you caught up in the middle of it."

"Something terribly you? What does that mean?"

He had a very solid feeling that he wasn't going to like the answer. Whatever answer it was Sammy came up with. He didn't know why.

"I used you as a lifeline," she said. "Because I felt like I was drowning. And I don't mean to do that to you. I know you've got enough on your plate, and enough people to take care of. I do. But something in me has always known that you would take care of me. That you could help fix me. And I've always wanted it. Craved it. And I just… I think I did that here. I'm really afraid that I did. It wasn't fair. I lied to myself about how big it would be."

"What are you talking about?"

"I wanted to fix my life. I wanted to feel better. I wanted to feel like I could be different and prove my mother wrong. And I thought that maybe having a baby would catapult me into a new phase of life. Just like moving here did. Like becoming part of your family. And I think that…"

"You weren't planning on having me be the father of your baby. Not initially."

"Wasn't I?" she asked. "Because I asked you. It just blurted out of my mouth."

"Don't you trust yourself, Sammy? Even a little bit?"

"Sure. I trust myself to have extreme powers of denial and…and to be…sometimes completely and utterly willful when it comes to what I want versus what other people want. And I know what it comes from. Being raised with a father who genuinely didn't care about my well-being. Quite the opposite. I think sometimes he just wanted to hurt me. Because he attached a lot of the rage in his life to my existence. And I got tired of apologizing for existing. So I think sometimes I go too hard the other way. And I'm afraid that without meaning to I…"

"That's an awfully big step back from you shouting at me about making light of your feelings."

"Well, I'm afraid that I…" She pressed a palm over one eye before releasing it. "Not that it was light. And I'm not saying I don't want it. But… I got hung up on you calling me selfish. And what I really should have looked at wasn't the word *selfish* but whether or not I was doing this for a bad reason. And I think maybe I was. Am. And look, the minute I thought of you being the father of my baby you were the only one that I could possibly… And on some level I must have known that, right? That you were the only one I would've been happy with."

Something in his chest froze. Because it was so very close to the right thing. But it wasn't. Not quite. He didn't even know what the right thing was in this case. Because he wasn't supposed to want any of this.

Not a baby. Not…her. In whatever capacity he was imagining he might have her.

He'd offered to marry her.

And he'd never wanted any of that.

Because he hadn't wanted to do any of that all over again.

"I just don't want this to ruin us."

"I already told you," he said, the words coming out gruff. "Nothing's going to ruin us."

"You said that," she said. "And I believed you. Until… I didn't know, Ryder. I didn't know it would feel like that."

He felt like she'd just set a ton of bricks on his chest.

He did his best to shove them off. "Of course you didn't. You've never had decent sex."

"It's more than that," she said.

"What's the point of it being more than that?"

She sighed heavily and then disappeared back into the kitchen, returning a few moments later with a platter of bacon and eggs.

She retreated one last time and came back with mugs of coffee. Then she sat across from him and started to fill her plate. He just sat there looking at the sugar cube.

"I don't know what the point is at all," she whispered. "But I'm not going to go out and have a baby with somebody random."

"You aren't?"

She shook her head. "No. I need to figure out what my problem is. Because it's something to do with me. It's something to do with being unhappy with where my life is, and I don't know what that is. I mean, I'm happy with my business. It's going pretty well. Is it as simple as being jealous that Pansy found a way to be normal?"

He didn't quite know what to say to that. "I don't know. Is Pansy normal?"

"She's getting married. She fell in love. I told myself that I didn't ever want to be normal anyway. But the problem is I kind of suspect that I just can't be. Because nobody ever attached to me, and I had to force my way into this…quilt."

"We were always happy to have you," he said.

"I know," she said. "But you can't erase the early memory stuff."

"You can't?"

"I talked to Logan last night."

He curled his hands into fists, a strange sensation raising the hairs on the back of his neck. Jealousy? Was he genuinely jealous of Logan because she talked to him?

Well, yeah. Because she talked to him after she left his bed. And what the hell was that?

"I ran into him on my way out. So he may have figured out that something is going on between us." She sighed. "He's like me. I mean, we're not really family, are we? And we both want to be. We both... We both have parents that are out there. They don't want us. He got me thinking. About how much you all mean to me. And about the things that I try to avoid. Namely that however much I might want to be, I'm not part of you guys. Not in any way other than this kind of enforced way. And sometimes... Sometimes that hurts me. The reminder of it hurts me. And..."

"And you think that maybe you wanted to have a baby with me to become part of the family?" Just saying it was bitter.

"No!" She shook her head vigorously. "No. That's not it. I wouldn't... I would never do that. But I do think I wanted to use you to try and fix me. To make me normal, and that wasn't fair. Not to you. Not to any potential baby. It's just not... I'm done with that. I'm not going to do it anymore. That's what I wanted to say."

"So now you don't want to have a baby?"

"It's not that I don't want to have one. I mean, not that I don't want to ever have one. I do. I just think that I need to sit with this for a while. And deal with myself."

"You know," he said, working to talk around the gravel in his chest. "It might be too late."

"It was just once," she said.

But her words were thin, and he had a feeling that she knew as well as he did they didn't mean anything. It was just once. Once and it had changed everything. It had changed the way his skin felt. Changed the way the world was. It was just once. It had changed everything.

"So you're telling me that you're happy enough to have been in my bed once. And to never be in it again?"

"Ryder…"

"I don't know that I'm ready to be done, Sammy."

"I love you," she said. "So much."

He felt those words resonate in his body. In the back of his teeth. Like a shock wave. Except that he knew what she meant. There wasn't even a question.

"I'm so afraid that that might undo what we are. This is the strongest, best relationship I've ever had in my life. The closest thing to family. And I just don't…"

"You came to me," he said.

"I know." And he might have been confused before the two of them had actually made love. But he felt a lot less uncertain now. Like he knew exactly where he was supposed to be. Because she might be abandoning her pregnancy plan, but that didn't mean he was ready to release her so that she was free to be with someone else.

And he knew Sammy. She wasn't going to be with someone for the long term, not any more than he was.

They were the longest term relationship the other one had had. That was true enough.

Whether or not they were functional was another story. But they were in each other's lives.

And whatever happened after this…

They had to see it through. That he knew. He was sure of it.

"I'll tell you what," he said. "Maybe instead of making pronouncements you see what happens."

"I don't think I can do that."

"You? Spontaneous, bohemian Sammy? I thought thy name was spontaneity."

She leaned in, a sad smile on her lips. "It's a lie," she whispered. "Don't you know that? I keep everybody around me guessing. But that's how I make sure I'm never guessing. I do something, you all react. And I stay one step ahead. I'm not spontaneous. I'm a control freak."

And suddenly, some things crystallized for him that he had never realized before.

All the way down to the sugar cubes.

Sammy liked to take the lead so that she knew what was going to happen.

Of course.

And he hadn't seen it because he was happy enough to labor under the impression that he was protecting her. That he was standing sentry, that he was the steady one. The rock. And by the very nature of those words, that he was in charge.

But it was her. And those careless dances she had done clearly had more intricate and carefully plotted footwork than he ever realized.

He took the sugar cube from the center of his plate and held it up. She looked at him quizzically. "Hold out your hand," he said.

She obeyed, and then he held the sugar cube out just over her palm, hovering over the skin there. But he didn't drop it in. Instead, he took her hand in his and lifted it to his lips, kissing the tender skin on the inside of her wrist gently, knowing full well that his stubble scraped across her skin there. He felt her shiver. Her blue eyes were wide, full of questions, but she didn't ask any of them. And then, he set the sugar cube in her hand.

"You're not the only one who knows how to lay bait, Sammy Marshall."

He took the cup of coffee off the table and lifted it as he stood. "I don't need any bacon this morning. I have work to do. I will see you later, though."

That was a promise. Both to him and to her.

And he knew Sammy was a smart enough woman to know that he always kept a promise.

He didn't know exactly what the end goal of this game was. But what he knew for sure was that they were finally playing his, and not hers.

And that was a victory he was going to take.

CHAPTER THIRTEEN

SAMMY'S WRIST STILL burned hours later where Ryder had kissed it.

She had the sugar cube in her pocket, and her head felt fuzzy.

She had been filled with resolve this morning. She had laid a trap, very calculated. And she had spent all night planning that. She hadn't even slept. Because she needed to make sure that she was in the house before anyone else got up, and she had needed to be sure that she was on hand to cook their bacon. A way to get back on the right footing. Almost a restart, she had purposed.

Because she had a lot of apologizing to do. And she was very good at apologizing. Because when you lived your life using spontaneity as a weapon you often had casualties, and she was just used to that.

Overstepping, stepping back, saying she was sorry. And as long as she smiled broadly enough people tended to be okay with it.

But he wasn't… He wasn't doing what he was supposed to do.

He was a rock. And he was hardheaded. But he was a smart man, and she had been certain that he would see sense.

She shifted where she sat, all her jewelry laid out in

front of her on a blanket outside her camper, and her top scraped against her nipples.

Arousal coursed through her body and she let out a frustrated growl.

He had turned her into some weird sex fiend.

She had always considered herself *sensual*. Somebody who liked touch. Somebody who was completely relaxed about it, in fact. And until he had gotten in her face about orgasms she had thought that she was neatly organized on that score.

That she knew where to have them and when, and that sex itself served the kind of spiritual function of creating human connection.

But Ryder had taken it and he had melded those things, and when he had done that he had stolen her control. Her neatly ordered way of looking at things.

She felt absolutely vile about it. And she wasn't someone who normally kept things to herself. But her confidantes were all deeply tied to Ryder, or they were Ryder himself.

If there was anything more annoying, she couldn't think of it.

She heard the sound of footsteps and looked up. But it wasn't Logan or Ryder, and for some reason she had expected it to be either of them. No, it was a red-faced and angry-looking Rose, picking through tall grass.

"What's wrong?" Sammy called.

"Did a calf wander this way?" Rose asked. Her cowboy hat was askew, her dark hair falling out of its braid. Her white tank top was dirty, and so were her jeans.

"No," Sammy said. She scrambled to her feet, setting her jewelry fixings down. "But I can help you look."

"You look pretty," Rose said, not as a compliment but in kind of a regretful tone.

Rose was dressed for practicality and sweat. Sammy wasn't. But she always dressed like this and all of her clothes were machine washable anyway, so it didn't matter.

"Oh, I wear skirts every day. I'm not particularly dressed up."

"Well, fine," Rose said skeptically. "But at your peril."

"What happened?"

"A calf must've gotten through the hole in the fence, and I'm just really hoping that that's what happened, and a predator didn't take him. But I went charging down the hill back there, and I fell on my face, so now I'm just mad."

"Where's Logan?"

Rose waved a hand. "Oh, I told him to go look in the other direction."

"You know, it's not a crime to take help," Sammy said, feeling every inch the hypocrite as she spoke those words.

It was so easy for her to fall into a role of giving advice, usually advice contrary to what Iris would give when it came to Rose and Pansy.

She had installed herself in a kind of counterbalance position. One that was a little bit more loose and free than their older sister. And every so often she gave advice to Iris, as well, but really, they all did try to help each other.

She had a fair amount of unvarnished honesty between her and the sisters. But right now she couldn't be.

She couldn't ask for help.

Because the source of her issues was their brother.

And she knew that they wouldn't want to hear about the fact that he was the best sex that Sammy had ever had. And also…

It felt too personal. For the first time in her life she didn't want to share details. Didn't want to get into anything like that. For the first time sex felt intimate. And she just… She couldn't bring herself to speak any of it out loud. Like it was a sacred verse that she had to hold to her own chest. A wish that might not come true.

She didn't know what she was wishing for.

"I just didn't need any," Rose said.

They weren't all the same. For some reason that revelation hit her hard and real as she looked at Rose's red face. It was easy to think that Ryder, Iris, Rose and Pansy were the same because they had been raised by the same parents, whom they had lost.

But Ryder had assumed a parental role, and Iris had taken a somewhat secondary position to that. Pansy and Rose had been children. Pansy had taken on the mantle of preserving her father's legacy to an extreme place. And Rose…

Rose was such a little, vibrant thing. Brimming with life and vigor. Almost as if she was daring the world to come at her. Except, she also stayed in her very safe space.

It was easy for Sammy to think of Rose as being a child, but of course she wasn't. Of course she was a woman now, and she was still here. Working the ranch. Staying in her place that she had carved out for herself.

Sammy had to wonder if Rose ever felt like she did. If she ever felt like she was stuck behind a wall that she couldn't break through.

Of course, Rose was twenty-four, not thirty-three. So whatever Rose had to work out it was a little bit less sad than Sammy.

"Is this your dream?" Sammy asked.

Rose wrinkled her nose and cast Sammy a strange look. "Is what my dream?"

"Staying here. Working on the ranch."

"I love what I do," Rose answered simply.

"I know." Of course, Rose was always making suggestions for other people's lives. Meddling in the kindest and sweetest way possible. And it made Sammy wonder why she wasn't quite so active in her own life.

So good at psychoanalyzing other people, Samantha.

She ignored that mean inner voice.

They started walking down an informal path, beaten by the cows, through the field. They moved the cows all around, and currently they were in a pasture across the property.

The calf they were searching for was so small, there was a serious concern about him being separated from his mother for too long. And she knew that Rose's real concern was that it had been taken by a cougar. Which, in this area, wasn't an unfounded concern.

"Wait." Rose stopped, putting her hand out. "Do you hear something?"

Sammy strained to listen over the sound of the rustling plants, and the breeze moving through the trees. And then just faintly she could make a plaintive sound out.

"Yes," she said. "I hear it."

They moved quickly toward the sound, picking through brambles and trees, and making their way into a thicket on the edge of the wood.

And that was where they found the little calf, tangled around thornbushes, looking desperate and thin and dehydrated.

Poor little thing.

Sammy knelt down next to the tragic creature. She put her face on his, listening faintly to the sound of him breathing.

"Oh, dear," she said.

"I'll text Logan," Rose said. "We need him to bring the pickup truck out here. And call Bennett Dodge. He'll need help."

"Of course," Sammy said.

She kept her hand on the pitiful animal while Rose sprang into action. Sammy appraised the situation as best she could, looking at the brambles wrapped around the little creature.

"Trust me," she said, her voice soothing. He began to thrash as she grabbed hold of him where the stickers were buried in his skin.

"Trust me," she said again, knowing full well that the cow couldn't understand her, but hoping that he would somehow get her intention.

He was horribly tangled and she tried to help get him undone, sticking herself every few minutes with one of the terrible thorns. At least the animal tired after only a few moments and didn't struggle anymore. Although, she wasn't sure she should be relieved about that or concerned. Concerned, likely. If he didn't even have enough energy to fight for himself...

She swallowed a lump in her throat, unsure why this was affecting her quite so deeply.

But the calf didn't know any better. He was innocent.

And he had wandered off and gotten himself into trouble. And she just wanted… She wanted to help.

She wanted to do something good and make a difference.

She fought harder with the brambles, her hands a bloody mess.

Rose was finally done with phone calls and turned her focus back to the spot, back to Sammy. "Holy hell, Sammy. What did you do?"

"Nothing intentional," she said. "I just wanted to help."

It sounded so feeble when she said it out loud.

"The boys will come with something to cut all this with. And Bennett will be here soon with his whole mobile unit."

"Good," Sammy said.

But still, she sat with the calf and worked at the thorns. Because she couldn't stand for him to be in pain.

By the time the truck rolled up with Logan and Ryder, her hands were a disaster, and Rose was pacing angrily.

She had asked Sammy to stop several times, but Sammy wasn't listening.

"What did you do?" Ryder approached her directly, sinking down to his knees beside her and taking her hand in his.

A bolt of electricity shot through her.

"I couldn't stand him being stuck," she said.

When her eyes caught his shamefully, her throat started to close. Tears welled up in her eyes, and she didn't know what had her feeling so emotional. She wasn't normally like this. But there was something about the tender fury in his gaze that struck her deep.

"Come here," he said, hauling her to her feet, bringing himself with her. "You're going to have to make sure you get medicine on these. And Band-Aids."

"I know," she said, feeling stubborn and grumpy. Like a little kid getting scolded in the too-hot sun, and the worst thing was she sort of felt like a petulant kid.

Plus, her hands hurt.

But Ryder's hold on her was firm and masculine, and the feelings he created under her skin made her feel like a woman and not a child at all.

The contrast of the two warring sensations made her want to sit down on the ground and cry. And why on earth she should feel so emotional over her *best friend* touching her arm she didn't know.

It had been sex.

Just sex.

Sex didn't have to matter.

It could just be nice.

It didn't have to change you.

As she looked into those whiskey-brown eyes she wondered though if you didn't get a choice on when it *might* change you.

"Sammy…"

"Hey," Rose said. "Break it up."

And Sammy knew that Rose thought she was being funny. Because Rose had no idea what had happened between her and Ryder last night. But Logan did. And he was giving her a hard, appraising glance.

She scowled in return.

She would not be accepting the judgment of Logan Heath, thanks so much.

"Let's see what we've got," Logan said, hunkering

down by the animal. Ryder joined him, and Sammy stood back, pressing her thumb against one of the particularly deep gouges on her palm. Now it hurt. When before she had been able to ignore it a bit.

"Fool," Rose said.

"I just wanted to help."

It didn't sound any better the more she repeated it. And standing there she couldn't quite articulate why she had to.

It was just… It was all part and parcel to this weird feeling of uselessness inside her. That sense that she was adrift in some way.

There was something incomplete about her. Something that needed filling and fulfilling. Which was how she'd arrived at the baby.

At Ryder. At everything.

Using tools, Logan and Ryder got the little calf free much more quickly than the progress that she had been making. They got the calf loaded up into the back of the truck, and Logan got into the driver's seat, Ryder getting into the bed. Rose got into the cab with Logan, and that left Sammy with the decision to make. Squeeze into the cab, or climb in with her friend.

She got into the back with him, because if she didn't, it would be weird. And the fact she was thinking about it all was weird, but there was really nothing to be done for it.

She crouched beside him, beside the animal.

"Your heart is too big, Sammy," he said softly.

"Really?" She looked at the wound on her hand. "Here I was just thinking it's not big enough. That's part of my problem. Feeling like what I'm doing is so… That everything in my life is about me and it's not really enough anymore."

"You take care of us," he said.

"Do I? Because it seems to me like you're always taking care of me."

He shook his head slowly. "I was drowning," he said, his voice rough. "When my parents died… You know I don't really remember that night very well. Except I remember Pansy's old boss, my dad's friend, Chief Doering, coming to the door. Except he wasn't the chief then, he was just another officer. And I answered it and he looked so grim. I knew enough about my dad's job to know what those kind of visits meant. But all of them… Sammy, all of them. My mom and dad, my aunt and uncle. Logan's mom. Everyone. I just remember… It was like being shot. This burst of pain and impact like you don't think you could possibly survive. And then silence. Nothing. Just numbness while you wait to bleed out. And then the strangest thing happened. Sugar cubes started showing up in my barn." He lowered his head. "You know, it's embarrassing, and I never told anybody this but at first I thought maybe it was…my mom's ghost or something. Not a ghost. I never had the sense she was a ghost. Her soul. An angel. Because I couldn't figure out where else sugar would come from. It was just so strange and funny. And that night I found you."

She blinked hard, trying to keep from dissolving into tears right there in the back of the truck with an injured calf between them.

"Were you disappointed? I mean, I'm not exactly a brush with the supernatural."

He shook his head. "I always thought you might be. It took me a while to be sure that you were real. And not…"

"Don't tell me you thought I was an angel."

He huffed a laugh. "A fairy. Not an angel. You are too damned pretty and not in the heavenly way."

That compliment, delivered with a slightly wicked smile, made her stomach turn over.

What did he mean by that? Did he mean that he had wanted her even then? He'd said as much. That when she had come to his bed he'd wanted her. But this was still slightly different.

Because for one, it was easy to imagine that he just wanted her because she was a woman and she had gotten into bed with him. And he was a man, and it was a very basic response for that to become sexual.

"Why wasn't I an angel?" she pressed.

"Because the things I wanted to do to you would've got me thrown into hell."

She felt both satisfied and unnerved by the response. "Oh."

"But you know, that wasn't the important thing. The thing was… It felt like everything was dark until you. You were something else. Sunshine coming through the darkness. And all that was more important than wanting you. So I forgot about that quick. Especially… Especially when I found out that you didn't just come out from behind a flower in the garden one day and decide to join the family. When I found out about your dad."

"You have taken care of me," Sammy said.

They never talked about that night. Ever. It was as unspoken between them, as well… All of this was. Except, this was spoken now.

They had touched each other.

Things had changed.

The truck continued to rumble, the calf between them occasionally making a plaintive bleat. It was a ludicrous time to have this conversation, which made it about as good a time as any.

"I wanted to kill him," Ryder said.

"You almost did."

"No less than he did to you, Sammy. I'll never get over seeing those bruises on your face. Knowing he put them there. Dammit. I still wish I had killed him."

"He's dead now anyway, and we've had all this time. And if you'd killed him then you'd be in prison. And we wouldn't be here."

He shook his head. "No, we wouldn't be."

That felt loaded right about now. Because where exactly were they? She didn't know.

They rode in silence after that, until they reached the barn. Bennett Dodge was already there, his mobile unit fully equipped to handle any sort of emergency.

"Hi," Ryder said, getting out of the back of the truck and shaking the other man's hand. "How are things?"

"All right. Kaylee's got some wicked morning sickness but other than that…"

That was the first that Sammy had heard about the veterinarian's wife being pregnant. His wife, who was the other veterinarian.

Bennett Dodge was one of the least scandalous people in the entire town of Gold Valley. But he had one of the more scandalous things from his past pop up to haunt him. Well, not haunt him, she supposed. But one day three years ago a fifteen-year-old son he hadn't known he had had ended up on his doorstep. That was when things had changed between him and his coworker and friend Kaylee. Sammy wasn't privy to all the details; all she knew was that they had been the best of friends, and then the next thing she knew she heard they were getting married. And now apparently having a baby.

"Congratulations," she said.

"We were empty nesters for all of two minutes."

He said it with a lot of humor. Bennett was only in his midthirties. She doubted he was ready to be an empty nester anyway.

Plus, he'd missed the first fifteen years of his first child's life.

"I'll never be an empty nester," Ryder said, looking around. "I can't get these people to leave."

"It's overrated anyway," Bennett said. "Having been one for most my life."

"I never have been."

He'd never lived alone. And neither had she. Not really. But it struck her then how funny that was.

Was that what she needed to do? Did she need to get back to her original thought of being independent? She wasn't really sure.

"Let's check this little guy out."

For the next half hour or so Bennett gave the calf a thorough once-over and dressed his wounds. Primarily, his issue was dehydration. But Bennett was hopeful that with the minor injection of fluids and a speedy reunion with his mother, he would pull through quickly.

He left them with instructions on what to look out for, and then left on another emergency call.

"I better get back to… I was making jewelry, actually."

"No, you don't," he said. "We need to go in the house and get your hands patched up."

"I'm fine."

Rose appeared from around the front of the truck. "You're not fine. You're bleeding like a son of a gun. *A stuck pig.* It's awful, Sammy."

"I'm fine," she protested.

But she found herself being grabbed by said hands and propelled toward the house.

It took her a moment to realize it was only she and Ryder who had gone inside.

"Where's Iris?" Sammy asked.

"Don't know," he said.

He opened up the cabinet in the kitchen that housed all the medicine and the first-aid kit and dragged it down. It was an old, metal thing that could probably be used for a weapon. She was sure that they'd had it since they were kids. Probably something that their parents had bought and they had just continued to restock.

Ryder got out an antiseptic ointment and some Band-Aids, and she leaned against the counter, watching his movements.

His dark head was bent low as he opened the Band-Aids and put medicine on them, one lock of hair falling into his face.

She fought the urge to reach out and push it back off his forehead.

A casual gesture that she might have engaged in thoughtlessly before last night. But now she just couldn't. She couldn't do anything like that casually.

Because touching between them was no longer casual.

It hurt her to realize that.

That last night they might have found something, but they lost some things, too. And she wasn't sure that they would ever be able to get back to a place where they had them. She wasn't sure if you could have everything after all.

She never had been.

It was one of those big promises that you saw trumpeted everywhere and she had always been naturally suspicious of it. As she was naturally suspicious of all things that sounded slightly too good to be true.

"Give me your hand."

She did, and remembered this morning when he had kissed her wrist after he demanded her hand. But he didn't kiss her wrist this time. Instead, he started putting a bandage on it, followed by another. "You should have waited."

"It just felt really important," she said. "I couldn't stand to see him suffer like that."

"I know. It's one of the things I like about you."

He began to position a Band-Aid over a particularly deep one and she winced, air hissing through her teeth. He paused, leaning in and blowing cool air over the wound. She shivered. His breath against her skin was a whole revelation.

No. They couldn't touch casually anymore. But his touch had transformed into magic, and right now she wasn't sure she would trade the two things.

Sunlight filtered through the window and illuminated his face. Spiked the tips of his lashes with gold, those brown eyes looking more whiskey in the light. It even highlighted his stubble. Then she noticed. For some reason now every little detail of his face—it all seemed to matter so much.

She swallowed hard. He licked his lips and looked up at her, met her gaze. Her heart started thundering. Hard.

And she was feeling pretty glad that they hadn't made any kind of decisions or thrown down any gauntlets or anything earlier in the day. Sure, that had been his suggestion, but it was seeming like a very good suggestion right about now. She was about to ask him to do something naughty. About to open her mouth and flirt with him. Ask him if he wanted to kiss it and make it better. When Iris breezed into the room.

"Sammy. Are you okay?"

She and Ryder jumped, like a pair of startled raccoons that had been caught getting into some feed.

"I'm fine," she said, jerking her hand away from his and lowering it to her side. "I was trying to rescue a calf."

"She was," he grunted.

"Okay," Iris said.

She was carrying a bag of groceries, which she set on the counter and began methodically taking out. And of course, she had no idea what she had interrupted, because it would never occur to her that she might have interrupted something like that between Ryder and Sammy.

Each piece that she pulled out of the bag was like torture.

Sammy felt like she was made of sexual frustration. And as the seconds ticked on she found a sort of gratitude for it. Because maybe Iris had to save them from doing something stupid.

She was in a weird space. Feeling obsessed with Ryder and what he could make her feel when she should be dealing with the fact that she had nearly had an emotional meltdown and gone off and had a baby with a stranger.

Yes. At some point she was going to have to deal with that.

"Can I help?" Sammy asked.

Iris looked at her like she was insane. "No. Your hands are all messed up."

She looked down at her Band-Aid-covered paws. "Sure. I suppose they are."

"There's no suppose about it. I don't want you touching any of the food."

"She *is* disinfected," Ryder pointed out.

"Gross. It doesn't matter." Iris looked at him. "You could help, though."

So he did, rallying and getting all of the food put away. Iris cast them both a long look before she walked back out the door.

"It was always like that," Sammy said. "Wasn't it?"

"I was never even tempted to bring anyone home," he said.

"But we were always just…in your stuff, weren't we?"

"It doesn't matter. It was for the best that I never did bring anyone. I wasn't looking for anything permanent anyway. And bringing somebody into this family… You all would've jumped on her. Asked if I was going to marry her five seconds after she walked through the door. No, thank you."

It hit her then just how much of his life actually was kept a secret from her. And she probably knew more about him than anyone else in the family. But she had tended to let him keep separate what was separate, too. Maybe on some level because it might bother her.

The truth of the matter was it had always suited her that he didn't have girlfriends in a traditional sense. Because they would've been jealous of her. And it would have been an issue. Sammy had never wanted to compete with another woman for his attention. He was hers in a way that none of them ever could have been anyway. It would've been foolish for them to try to compete with her. At least, that was her humble opinion on the matter.

"Still. I just guess I didn't really appreciate... I mean I understand that you were basically being the parent while everybody else still got to be a kid but sometimes I think I still don't fully get everything that you did. For me. For us. For them."

"I wanted to do it," he said. "Don't go acting like I did some kind of great sacrificial thing. I didn't. When I lost my parents...the idea of being away from anyone else in my family was pretty much unbearable. Taking care of them, making sure that they were okay, that gave me a purpose. And if there were some sacrifices in there... I don't mind. It was part of it."

"Well. It would be nice if you could get some privacy now."

He looked at her far too meaningfully. She felt herself blushing, and she couldn't remember the last time she blushed before this. Ridiculous.

"Anyway," she said. "Thank you. For helping with my hands."

She wanted to thank him for some other things, too, but she didn't know if it was appropriate. He picked his hat up off the counter and put it back on his head, and damned if the man didn't tip it at her like some old-fashioned movie cowboy.

"I'll see you later, Sammy."

"See you," she said, and when he left the room, she was almost certain that he had taken the air right along with him.

CHAPTER FOURTEEN

WHEN THEY ALL went out for drinks on Friday night, Rose acted scandalized when Sammy ordered a beer.

"What about the baby?" she said.

"I'm on hiatus from that," Sammy said.

Logan looked at Ryder, and then back to Sammy.

"I decided it wasn't a good idea," she said.

He could feel his friend's eyes boring a hole through the side of his face.

"Why not?" Iris asked.

"You didn't think it was a good idea," she said. "Why are you suddenly asking why I don't want to do it?"

"Because you don't normally change your mind. At least, not unless there's a particularly shiny whim off somewhere, and I haven't seen any."

"Maybe because I was trying to fix a problem with something that isn't supposed to be a Band-Aid." She looked down at her hands.

Putting Band-Aids on her earlier had been some sort of weird torture. It shouldn't have been sexy. But it was. Maybe because she was, no matter what. Still, he hadn't realized quite how sick he was until he had wanted to make out with her while putting ointment on her hand.

"And what gave you clarity?"

The look Logan was giving him sharpened, and Ryder

nearly choked on his beer. It was like Sammy had taken her thoughts and planted them into his brain. *Ryder's penis. Ryder's penis gave me clarity.*

It had to come from her. Little witch. Because he would never think of such a thing. It was her. Prolonged exposure to her and her ridiculousness.

"Well, Iris, I went out into a field sky-clad and asked the earth to tell me the answers. Then I went to a pond and knelt by the water. I reached in, and when I pulled my hand out there was a stone in it. And on that stone was written the word *idiot*. So yeah, then I figured maybe I shouldn't go have a baby with a guy I don't know."

"I was asking you with sincerity," Iris said.

"I don't think you were. Anyway. Not doing it. So we never need to discuss me or pregnancy again. Sorry I exposed all of you to it in the first place."

A muscle in his face twitched. Because of course that was a great reminder that what the two of them had done had the potential for consequence.

He should talk to her more about that. Of course, that would mean talking more about it when what happened next was still up in the air.

So maybe he would give that a pass.

He was momentarily distracted by the arrival of Pansy and her fiancé.

They sat down at the table and Pansy launched into a story about how West's half brother Emmett, who lived with them at their house, had gotten into an epic scrape with a bull on the Dalton family ranch. Hank Dalton was West's father. Not his half brother Emmett's father. But he had other half siblings through Hank. It was all pretty complicated, and a whole lot of mess as far as Ryder was concerned.

Logan and West tipped their hats in greeting to each other at the same time, and not for the first time it occurred to Ryder that the two of them shared more than a passing similarity.

And given who West's father was, and given the fact Logan didn't know his…it was enough to make a man wonder. If he were the kind that wondered about things like that.

"And how are you?" Pansy asked, tapping him on the forearm.

"Good," he said.

Pansy had always been independent. She was a lot like him. And it felt good to be in her presence. Because half the time he felt like they were the only two people in the room who could fully understand each other without the use of words. Well, Sammy understood him. But that didn't mean that she agreed.

The same things that resonated in him resonated in Pansy. And that was a gift he didn't take for granted. He figured it was a piece of their dad that they carried around inside them.

"You neck deep in wedding plans yet?"

"Actually," she said. "That's something I wanted to talk to you about. West and I would like to get married at Christmas. At Hope Springs. It means a lot to me. I want to get married in the old barn, and decorate it with some of Mom's old Christmas decorations."

"I like that idea," he said.

"I was hoping you would. It's important to both of us. West is learning a lot about family. I think it means a lot to him to have the wedding at a place that's so meaning-ful to me."

"Well," he said, suddenly feeling a bit tight in the chest. "That's…great."

"I know you're deeply uncertain about me marrying him."

"No," he said, shaking his head. "I just can't believe you're getting married. That you're the police chief. That you're grown-up, and not just grown-up, but grown up well."

"Because you didn't think I could?"

"Because I didn't think I could pull it off."

"You don't get all the credit," she said, but her smile was good-natured.

"I get some of it," he said.

"Sure," she said.

Suddenly, the family conversation was broken up by someone approaching the table. "Hey, Sammy," the in-truder said.

Ryder recognized him as one of the guys that Sammy had been dancing with the last time they were all here.

"Care to dance?"

"Not right now," she said.

"Come on," the guy said in a cajoling tone that made Ryder want to rip his voice box out straight through his throat.

"I'd rather not," Sammy repeated, her voice firm.

"I think you just need a little convincing."

"I very much don't," Sammy responded, her eyes going icy and glittery.

The guy leaned in, like he was about to say some-thing again, and Ryder stood up. "She said she'd rather not," he said, feeling the bubble of murder start simmering in his blood.

"She can speak for herself," the guy said.

This guy. He hated *this guy. This guy* that Sammy always seemed to attract. Such a *nice guy.* Who wore slouchy beanies and pants that were too tight. Who acted like he read tiny little books full of poems written by dead guys and made a business of turning his compliments into knives, guaranteed to slice beneath the skin so sharp the target wasn't even aware of it until they'd been slashed all over. Guys who acted enlightened and said all the right things but didn't seem to follow any of it up with action.

"She *can* speak for herself," Ryder said. "And as a matter of fact, she did speak for herself, and you didn't listen."

"We're friends," the guy said.

"*I'm* her friend," Ryder said, taking a step toward him, barely stopping himself from reaching out and grabbing him by the shirt. "And I know all of her other friends. You are not among them. And if you would like to continue to be among your friends here in the bar and not thrown out on your ass, I suggest you turn around and walk away."

"I was just asking her for a dance. I didn't realize you were going to pull some kind of alpha caveman bullshit and act like you own her."

"Well, your use of the word *man* in regard to me is correct, as I'm the only one standing here. You're just a boy playing at being smooth. And that's the kindest description I have of you. At worst you *are* a man. Which means you know what you're doing. Twisting up somebody's words and trying to point them back around at them. Smiling so nobody will call you out. Well, I will. And I did. Now, get the hell away from here."

Everyone at the table looked stunned, but the guy turned around and walked back.

"Little bit of an overreaction," Rose muttered.

"It wasn't," Ryder said.

"I told him to go away," Sammy said. "He didn't. So…"

"That's ridiculous," Rose said. "Why should Ryder have to step in and say something when you said it?"

"Because men like that only listen to other men. And they like to pretend that's not what they are, and you saw him, trying to act like I'm some kind of problem because guys like him make it so I have to be."

"It would've been funny to watch Sammy handle him," Rose said. "Because she would've ended up kicking him in the balls."

"It's true," Sammy said. "If I had to, I would have."

"Excuse me," Ryder said, getting up from the table and heading toward the bar.

Sammy intercepted him halfway. "That wasn't really necessary, was it?"

"Don't start with me."

"What? You can't go acting like that just because we…"

"I would've done that either way," he said.

"No, you wouldn't have. You were far more inclined to let me fight my own battles before you saw me naked. And maybe you don't remember it accurately, but I do. The blood is all down in your penis. I, however, remain clearheaded."

He snorted. "Do you?"

"Yes," she said, but her voice wobbled on the word.

"Well, every time some asshole hassles you, that was what I always wanted to do and since I'm in a space of wish fulfillment, why not do that, too?"

"Wish fulfillment," she repeated.

"I told you. I wanted you for a long time."

"I know," she said, hushed. "I just find it kind of hard to believe."

"Well, believe it," he said. "If Iris hadn't walked in earlier... I would've had you naked in two minutes."

Her face turned scarlet.

A smile made the corner of his mouth twitch. "Sammy. Are you blushing?"

"No. I don't blush. There's nothing to be ashamed about. Sexual appetites are healthy and normal. And I am sex positive. So there's no embarrassment that resides within me. And any that I may have felt I rooted out when I confronted my feelings about the poorly named walk of shame."

"You're just human, Sammy. Shame is part of being human. Shame is what makes some things fun."

"That can't be true," she said.

"Sure it is. A little bit of guilt amps up the heat."

"I don't... I don't think that's true."

"Clearly you were not raised Catholic."

"I wasn't."

His lips twitched. "You're missing out."

She made a strange huffing sound.

"What?" he asked.

"This is weird," she said.

"Why?"

"Because we are talking. We always talk. And I'm

distracted by the fact that I know how you look naked. And that I would like to… There's not really a delicate way to say it."

"Don't say it delicate, then," he ground out.

His whole chest was tight. His body primed for her. It didn't take anything. A side-glance. The brush of her fingertips against him.

This.

She bit her lip. "It's messed up."

"Is it?"

"Yes. Because you're my friend. You're my friend before you're anything else. And being so distracted by the fact that I want to climb you like the tree outside your window is a problem."

"Not for me."

"You're a man."

"That's stupid. When has what we had together ever been based on something that simple? I've been a man the whole time. It was never that simple. It was never like that. And you know it. What happened between us isn't about just a simple chemistry between a man and a woman."

He didn't know why he cared about that at all. He didn't know why he felt the need to belabor the point. It was fine to let her think that it was just that simple. Why did he need to make her understand what he couldn't?

He didn't know. Only that he apparently did.

She looked over her shoulder, and then back at him. "They're staring at us," she said, indicating the table full of his family.

"They are not," he said, directing his focus to them. Well, hell. They were.

When his eyes connected with Iris's she lowered them quickly, going back to her beer and playing like she hadn't just been staring. But she had been.

Which meant they really were giving off some kind of a weird energy, because he and Sammy talking to each other shouldn't draw attention. Not from his family.

They were too used to them.

He was certain the whole town figured they slept with each other. Most people would never understand the kind of relationship that they had. Hell, at this point he didn't understand it, either, but that was what happened with introducing sex into the mix.

It made less sense. Not more.

A funny thing, because he knew that a lot of people thought that men and women couldn't have that kind of connection.

Now he was beginning to question it. Since theirs had exploded so brilliantly. "I've half a mind to drag you into that bathroom over there."

"You wouldn't."

"Carve our names on the wall."

It was a well-known Gold Valley tradition that when people hooked up in the bathroom at the saloon they carved their names there as a memento of the occasion.

"They would *know*," she said.

"I thought you didn't feel shame."

"I don't," she said. "But I am a little bit worried about what will happen with my place in your family if…"

"It's fine," he said. "Nothing is going to happen to that."

She nodded slowly, her eyes full of skepticism.

"Hey," he said. "One thing I know for sure in this

life is that there are certain things you just don't get through if you don't have your family. And you are family, Sammy."

"Not the same, though," she said softly.

He couldn't even figure out a way to argue with that, because obviously it wasn't the same. If it was the same then he wouldn't have been able to make love to her the way that he had. If it was the same, then he wouldn't have spent the past seventeen years caught in a strange place that existed somewhere between desire and duty. Between his intention to be like a knight guarding a maiden, a man who would never take advantage of the woman who depended on him the way that she did. And his desire to have her. Hold her.

Lay her down on the bed and press himself inside her the way that he had done only the other night.

His desire now to let things go back to the way they were, and to absolutely cave the face in of that bastard who had come and hit on her. Like she didn't belong to *him*.

He knew that was messed up. He didn't much care.

That was the problem. He was somewhere out in the middle of a vast field where he couldn't find a single *give-a-damn*. Not a one. And every bit of intent that he felt as far as not making a scene, doing what was right, all that—he couldn't access it anymore. It was gone. Even looking over there at his family giving them far more than a cursory bit of attention… Yet, he found he just didn't care like he should.

"Samantha," he began. But she darted away toward the bar. And he followed, feeling a little bit irritated by her avoidance.

But when she turned to face him there was something slightly impish on her face, and he had to wonder if he was…being treated to Sammy's version of flirting. Damn. He didn't really know what to do with that.

"Two beers," Sammy said.

Laz looked between the two of them. "Glad to see you worked it out."

"Worked what out?" Ryder asked.

"Whatever it was the two of you were stewing about the other night."

"Were we stewing?"

"She was," Laz said, stepping away from the bar and going to grab what they had ordered.

"I might have maybe propositioned him slightly," she said.

Ryder nearly growled. "You did?"

"We hadn't done anything yet. And you were being possessive. And irritating me. And I was trying to prove that I didn't need you to complete my objective. It didn't work."

"You're a little witch, you know that?"

"Not the first time I've heard that."

"What exactly are we doing here?" Ryder asked.

"Aren't we just playing it by ear?"

Laz brought the beers back and Sammy took one, lifting it to her lips.

"I've got them," Ryder said, handing the cash over to Laz and watching as Sammy brought the bottle of beer up to her lips again. The whole thing felt deliberately sexual.

"You don't have to buy me a drink."

"I think I do."

"I'll just go over there," Laz said, excusing himself from the middle of them.

That didn't really bother Ryder, either. If the other man read the sexual tension between them that was all the better for his purposes.

He found that he wasn't all that invested in hiding what had happened between them at all. Because Sammy seemed to thrive as a sunbeam shining through the trees. A little bit winking around the shadows here and there, but not shining full out.

It left her the opportunity to be coy. To be a little bit ambiguous and naughty. And she enjoyed that. It was obvious enough to him.

He wasn't going to allow it. Not caring who was watching her, what they might think, he reached out and stopped her beer bottle as it began to make the journey up to her mouth again. "Don't look at me like that while you take a drink, Sammy, unless you plan to make good on that little promise later. If you want to use your lips and tongue on me, go right ahead and keep teasing. Otherwise...rethink."

That earned him a shocked expression. And it was a hell of a thing to have managed to shock Sammy. But then, that was becoming more and more normal as he stepped outside the box that he had built for himself. As the two of them began to forge new territory. Where he was someone he didn't recognize and sometimes she was someone he didn't know, either. He didn't know that he liked that part of it. Redrawing those boundaries and setting foot onto uneven ground. But it was part of it. And there was nothing that could be done about it. Not now.

Her lips twitched. "Yes, sir."

And that bratty little comment sent a lightning bolt of heat straight down to the part of him that craved her the most. His gut went tight, his blood running hot. "You think I'm safe," he said. "Because you've only known me as your friend. Because I had myself on a leash every time I was ever around you. Because I decided a long time ago not to be this when I was with you. But you don't know all of me, Samantha, so if I were you I would tread a little bit more carefully."

"So many threats," she said. "So many promises. And we're still standing here."

"Do you want to go?"

"Maybe we should."

"Are you going to leave me again tonight?"

"Are you going to let me?"

He gritted his teeth. "I only let you because I couldn't think straight. And yeah, that was me retreating. Not knowing how in the hell to handle what had just happened between us. I was being a coward."

"I thought you told me to quit messing around with cowards."

"Yep. And I'll quit being one. You come to my bed tonight, you're staying all night. Understand me?"

"Well, then I guess I know where I'm sleeping."

She walked away from the bar and headed back toward the table.

She was intent on tormenting him tonight, and he wasn't even all that mad about it.

No. Because she would be in his bed tonight. Something had changed. From the sugar cubes to this moment. And maybe it was just good old-fashioned temptation and neither of them were doing a very good job of turning away from it. But then, they didn't want to. He didn't want to. Why the hell should he? Really, why? There wasn't a damn reason in all the world to deny what they wanted. So why should they?

Sure, she didn't want to do the baby thing now, and that was probably for the best. Because he didn't want to do the wife and child thing.

He didn't.

But a chance to explore some of the heat between them? Yes. Now he knew one thing for sure. There was no halfway with him. And he knew that was going to take some doing for Sammy to accept. It made sense to him. A kind of sense, anyway. That they would keep each other in this regard the way that they had kept each other before. But this time, they would share a bed.

He couldn't care about Sammy any more than he did. And this was… It was new. But he wasn't going to go ahead and throw that on her now.

She wanted to play it by ear; that was fine.

She wanted to pretend like it could be casual; that was fine, too. As long as in the end she understood that he wasn't a man who could be casual when it came to her.

He took his place at the table beside Sammy and everyone acted casual like they hadn't been watching the interplay between the two of them. He got a strange enjoyment out of the fact that they were all clearly slightly more embarrassed that they'd been watching him and Sammy than he and Sammy were by being watched.

He didn't know why the hell they should care what anyone thought.

That was one thing about living life the way that he

had. He had no illusions that his world would ever look like anyone else's.

He had given everything up at eighteen to take care of his siblings. There was no keeping up with the Joneses. He couldn't see their yard over his overgrown hedge and dilapidated fence anyway.

There was no worrying about having a life that looked like any kind of particular thing. Because there wasn't a blueprint for what they were.

And maybe that was the lesson with Sammy and him. There was no blueprint. So he didn't need to worry so much about where the boundaries fell. They just needed to see. Just needed to follow what felt right. And all right, so going with the flow wasn't usually his thing. Usually, he was more about trying to find a set of rules so he could make sense of the situation that he was in. But maybe it was time to take a little bit of sunshine and carry it with him. Do a little bit of what Sammy would do.

Hell, it was probably the only way to really be with Sammy.

He had to grit his teeth through the rest of the evening, and when it was all over, though Sammy had ridden over to the bar with Iris, she made a show of leaving with him.

There was something about it that made him want to beat his chest like a gorilla. He didn't know what this thing was doing to him. Unless sex with Sammy had caused some kind of strange testosterone surge in his body. Which seemed possible. The minutes ticked by in the car, as did the silence. And he suddenly was overcome by the fact that he was going to go home and bury himself inside Sammy.

Sammy Marshall.

His deepest, most forbidden fantasy.

And yeah, he'd had her once. Yeah, he'd tasted her, but it didn't mean anything in terms of it being old or over now. No. He wanted her. He wanted her so badly he couldn't see straight. And he wasn't going to wait. Not anymore.

He couldn't wait.

He pulled the truck off the main highway, up a gravel drive that led into the mountains.

The kind of thing he'd gotten up to in high school, but never, ever since.

He didn't do things like this. He wasn't spontaneous. He wasn't crazy.

He was the kind of guy you could depend on. The one who would always help you move. The one who would make a plan then stick to it. See that everything went well. According to that plan. He wasn't the kind of guy who did spontaneous sex.

Hell, for him, hookups had become pretty thin on the ground because he just couldn't be bothered half the damn time.

But he couldn't wait for Sammy. He had to have her. He had to have her now.

"What are you doing?" Sammy asked.

"I have to have you," he said. "Right now."

He pulled the truck off to the side, into a slight outcropping of trees. It was still there. He remembered it being there.

"What is this?"

"You know exactly what it is."

"Oh, this is where you got into trouble in high school."

"Damn straight. I'm about to get in some trouble with you."

"Ryder…"

"Don't," he said. He unbuckled his seat belt, scooted away from the driver's seat, then hauled her up onto his lap. She was straddling him, her blond hair covering both of them like a curtain. "Don't make a joke out of this. Don't make light of it."

He pressed his thumb against her lips. "I can't wait," he ground out. "I have to be inside you. I waited for you for seventeen years, and once wasn't enough. It's never going to be enough."

She blinked, surprise and something else glistening in her eyes. "Ryder…"

"I'm sorry," he said. "I know this isn't you. I know you do things a little bit different. But I can only be me. And I'm… This is why I let you leave. Because I'm not cool. I don't have any chill when it comes to us. When it comes to this."

"I'm glad," she whispered. "I've never… No man has ever looked at me the way that you do."

"Because no man has ever felt for you what I do," he said, the words a vow of certainty. "I know it."

"How?" she whispered.

"It's impossible. Nobody could ever feel this." He wrapped his hand around her wrist, pressed her palm against his chest. Let her feel the way that his heart was raging, utterly and completely out of control. "Nobody," he said.

"Ryder…"

"Kiss me," he said.

CHAPTER FIFTEEN

SAMMY WASN'T BIG on obeying commands, and he knew it, but she did obey this one.

Those lips made contact with his, feather-soft at first, until he angled his head, and she seemed to sink right into him. He could feel the heat between her thighs blazing against his arousal, could feel the desperate need as she slid her tongue against his. He could feel it in the little whimpers that she made, the way that she arched her body against his.

And he was wild. Wild in a way he could never remember being, because nothing had ever been this. Nothing had ever been her.

Sammy.

He stripped her top up over her head, pushed her skirt up so that her thighs were exposed.

She didn't have a bra on.

It drove him absolutely crazy when she did that. And he had spent years pretending not to notice.

"Do you know what a damned achievement it was to be around you when you were like this?" He pressed his thumbs against her nipples and slid them over the tightened buds. "And not spend the whole time staring at you. For years, Sammy. For years I wanted nothing more than to touch you here. Like this. To taste you." He pressed his palm against the center of her back, brought her body closer to him and sucked one nipple deep into his mouth, proving his point. She gasped, wiggled restlessly.

She was panting, tugging at his shirt, trying to get it up over his head, but she couldn't because he was latched onto her.

"Wait," he said, sliding his thumb over her wet nipple. "I'm not done."

"Please," she said. "I have to see you. I have to touch you."

"You weren't the one dying to do this for years."

"Because I didn't know," she said, helplessness in her voice. "I didn't know."

He leaned back in the seat, and she pushed his shirt up, tugging it over his head. Her breath hissed through her teeth as she moved her palms over his body.

"You're so sexy," she said. "And it was killing me tonight. Talking to you and knowing that. That guy who was trying to pick me up was like an indistinct blur. I couldn't even really see him. I just kept thinking about you."

That level of intensity coming from Sammy was something else. And he hadn't thought that his arousal could get turned up another notch. He didn't think it was possible. But that did it. Oh hell, that did it.

He pushed one hand between her thighs and shoved her panties to one side, stroking her while she continued to explore his body with her fingertips. She whimpered, moving her hips back and forth in time with his strokes. Then with fumbling fingers she undid his belt, his jeans, and he lifted his hips so that she could pull them down partway, expose him. Delicate fingers wrapped around his length, and she squeezed him.

Even in the dim moonlight, he watched her face. Made sure to look down where her hand met his aching flesh. Because it was Sammy touching him like that. Sammy with her hand on his body this way. He was ready to shift, ready to plunge inside her body when he remembered. He cursed, then struggled for his wallet, which Sammy took out of his fingers. She went pawing through it, digging until she produced a condom. She tore it open.

She made a slightly regretful expression as she rolled it onto his body. "I need you inside me," she said. "And this is the right way to do it. But I have to say... I liked having you with nothing between us."

"I just need to have you," he said, but her words burned through his blood. Because there wasn't a hell of a lot that was sexier than a woman saying she wanted you with no barrier.

Well. Sammy wanting him at all was damn sexy. Barrier or no.

Sammy.

Her name was like a banner stretched across the whole of his mind as he positioned himself at the entrance to her body and flexed his hips as she sank down onto him.

Her fingertips digging into his skin as he filled her.

"Ryder," she whispered, his name on her lips as the tight, wet heat of her surrounded him, the most erotic and heady experience he'd ever had in his life.

Yeah, this was why he'd let her run away. Because he couldn't breathe through this, much less think. Because she was too beautiful for him to see past. Because the scent of her, the feel of her, filled his senses entirely, and he didn't know what that meant for him. What it meant for them. Because he wanted her. And he was having her, and still wanted her, so he had no idea what that meant for his sanity. For the whole rest of his life.

But it didn't matter. Not right now. Because all of his doubts, all of his concerns, were washed away by sunshine. By her. Her heat and warmth and everything else. Lighting him up from the inside out. That was a truth that was with them, whether it was seventeen years ago or today. When things were dark, there was Sammy. When he thought he would never smile again, there was Sammy. Beautiful, constant. The one thing in the world that made sense, even when she didn't.

There was nothing outside this truck. There was nothing outside the space they'd made with just the two of them. And there was no space between them. Not at all. He held her as she rode him, as she arched her back and let her head fall back, ecstasy rolling over her like a wave. A wave that he could feel. As if it were his own. Her pleasure was the most erotic thing he'd ever experienced.

His own didn't matter, not half as much.

She reached her peak, panting and shuddering out his name, and then he reached between her thighs and stroked her until she reached the peak again, until she went over.

And again.

Until she was begging him to stop. Until he couldn't keep it going anymore. Because he had been pushed to his breaking point.

He lost himself. Thrusting up into her and never once losing sight of the fact that it was Sammy. His Sammy. That this was different. But it was more.

He held on to her shoulders and slammed into her one last time, his pleasure a roar in his blood, in his chest, his head.

He could hear it reverberating in the cab of the truck, and he knew that it was outside him, too. That he had lost himself completely in a way that he hadn't ever before.

She collapsed against his chest like a wilted flower. He pushed her hair back from her face and kissed her cheek.

"You killed me," she murmured, her breath hot on his chest.

"I hope not," he said. "Because I'm not done with you yet."

He found her top and put it back on her, and then put the rest of her to rights before taking a moment to step out of the truck and engage in condom disposal. Then he got back inside and turned the engine on.

"Let's go home."

And he meant *his* home. *His* bed.

If she was bothered by that, she didn't protest.

CHAPTER SIXTEEN

THE NEXT MORNING Sammy woke up with her body tangled all around Ryder's. He was so beautiful. And the way he made her feel…

Last night had been…intense.

Intense on a level she hadn't known she was capable of feeling.

She extricated herself from his hold and hunted around the room. It was late. Much later than he normally got up. And later than she typically got up for their bacon day. She didn't want to wake him. Instead, she stood there, staring at him. The gray light was filtering beneath the crack in the curtain, casting his face in a glow. He looked so much more relaxed. Usually, even in sleep his face held tension.

But of course, now she knew that all those years he had been holding himself back. Because he wanted her.

And last night he'd had her. To his heart's content. And hers.

It had been incredible, and so had he. So had she, for that matter.

She had never, ever, had a guy lose it with her like that, and she had loved it. She would have said that she wouldn't have. She would have said that things like that—desperation and roadside sex—were for other people. People who were more into it from a physical, sweaty standpoint, rather than the spiritual connection she had always claimed.

But it turned out that pleasure and sweat did not preclude spiritual connections. Because she felt transformed. Turned inside out.

She tried to breathe around the heavy pressure in her chest and found that she couldn't. She also couldn't find some of her clothes.

They were somewhere. She knew that. She had dressed before coming into the house, and then he had proceeded to strip her as soon as they'd gotten behind the door of his bedroom, after which he had done things to her body that she would have said she wouldn't have any interest in.

But he made her insane. He made her beg for what she had thought she might actively ask a man to not do.

His tongue was wicked. And it was wonderful.

And she had known him all this time and hadn't realized he was capable of such things.

She had called him steady. She had called him boring. She hadn't had any idea he knew places to touch inside a woman that could give her the kind of orgasm that made her scream.

She curled her toes inside her sandals and proceeded to hunt around the room. Giving up, she went over to his dresser and grabbed a T-shirt and a pair of sweats out of there. They were way too big. She had to cinch the sweatpants up ferociously to make them stay up. But it was fine.

Then she tramped downstairs, barefoot, and started to hunt around for their breakfast. He would follow soon enough, and she would take the moment to engage in a little bit of self-examination.

Or maybe, just think about what had happened the night before.

Maybe this was part of the key.

This exploration with him.

Because yeah, she was a control freak, and she had a feeling that it was that control freak part of her nature that had made it impossible for her to orgasm with a man until this moment. Only with Ryder had she been able to let go of that control. And only because she knew him so well. And he knew her.

He knew how to get her there. How to put her mind at ease. Didn't they say that a woman's most important sexual organ was her mind?

Of course, it felt like somewhere a whole lot lower. Felt like every inch of her skin.

Every inch of her.

He did things to her...

She began to look in the fridge for eggs and bacon and found them, then found some leftover French bread, which she sliced up to make toast.

The eggs this morning, she decided, would be over medium and on top of the toast. Maybe she would even make sandwiches. That might be nice. She wanted to watch him eat.

Wanted to watch his mouth close around a sandwich.

She was going crazy.

Really, the man was her friend. She should have a little bit of...something. Self-control. She didn't have any. She had nothing but a kind of intense, satisfied hum that, all things considered, she might take in lieu of self-respect.

She hummed to herself as she cooked, and then she heard footsteps behind her. She turned and saw Ryder standing in the kitchen doorway. He was wearing nothing but a pair of jeans, slung low on his lean hips. His hair was disheveled, his whiskers looking deliciously feral and scratchy.

She liked Ryder feral, she realized. Perhaps because she had spent most of her life as a somewhat feral creature and had felt like she had been the odd one in their midst. But uncovering those pieces of him, that bit of uncivilized that was apparently a lot closer to the surface than he pretended, was…exhilarating. Somehow, that change in him was liberating for her, and she couldn't quite put her finger on why.

On why it made her feel a whole lot more like she fit. In this house. In her own skin. Against his skin.

"Good morning," he said.

"And a very good morning to you," she responded.

She turned back to the pan and flipped perfect eggs onto the toast that was already laid out on the plate.

And then one big strong arm wrapped around her and pulled her against his hard body. She shivered, and he angled so that he could kiss her neck.

"Good morning," he said again.

His voice rumbled in his chest, the feeling so intimate between them.

Everything inside her fluttered. Between her legs, and her stomach. Her heart. All of it.

She had never fluttered in her life. She had just assumed that she was the kind of person who didn't. She had thought that maybe her father had broken something fundamental inside her with his fists. The ability to be excited about people. About the possibility that could exist between her and someone else.

That was the problem. Fundamentally, romance had never really excited her that much because she felt like she had seen too much of the negative outcome. The potential for disaster.

She had never really engaged in *romance*.

She had all these words for what was simply a desperate attempt to deal with the loneliness inside her heart.

Yes, she had connections with Ryder and his family. Had all kinds of different emotional needs met through them. But it wasn't being held by someone. And so she had gone out and had physical relationships, as well. Had played at light romantic connections that she knew weren't going anywhere so that she could fill the different gaps in her life, in her soul, without anything becoming all-consuming.

And wasn't that the same thing she was trying to do with the baby? It had been. An attempt to get herself something without hoping for everything.

She didn't know what this was, this thing with Ryder. Her making breakfast, him kissing her neck. Then he pushed his hands underneath her shirt, brought his rough palms up to cup her breasts.

"Hey," she said, wiggling out of his hold. "We're in public."

"We're in my kitchen. Early in the morning."

"Not as early as usual."

"No," he said. "I overslept. Some wicked woman kept me up most of the night."

"That's funny. Some asshole guy did the same thing to me."

"It's kind of funny," he said. "Knowing after all this time just how sexy that body of yours is. I had my suspicions…"

"You know," she said. "I was thinking the same thing. How fascinating it is to know that you can do those things with your fingers. And your tongue." She shivered in memory. "All this time I didn't know."

She started to pick up the plate of eggs and toast, but he stopped her, bracing her hand down on the counter with his over the top of hers and kissing her deep on the mouth.

She kissed him back. She could have kissed him forever. And she couldn't recall ever feeling that way about a kiss.

He was a fascinating study in textures. His whiskers scratchy, his lips hot and firm, his tongue slick. She wrapped her arms around his neck, and he brought his hands down to her hips, her body pressed hard against the countertop as he arched himself into her, letting her feel the full force of his erection nestled there between her thighs.

"Oh… Oh, *holy shit*!"

They jumped apart and turned, and Rose was standing in the doorway, her mouth wide open.

"You… You… Why do you have *her tongue in your mouth*?"

Fear was the first emotion that Sammy felt, and she wasn't really sure why. Only that her throat felt like it was getting too tight.

"Rose…"

"You two are practically…brother and sister."

"We are not," Ryder said. "Practically or otherwise."

"I thought that Logan liked you," Rose said, clearly agog.

"He doesn't," Sammy said.

"Did you…"

"I'm not answering questions," Ryder said. "I'm a grown-ass man, and I have a sex life. You may not want to think about it, but I've had one since you can remember, okay?"

"I'm… I'm emotionally scarred. My eyes are bleeding. It's like seeing siblings make out." She frowned. "Or like seeing my parents make out."

"Get out," Ryder said.

"I don't know what to do with this." Rose covered her forehead with her hand.

"I didn't ask you to do anything with it."

She slapped her hand back down at her side. "Am I supposed to keep it a secret?"

"Well, you may have noticed that we didn't exactly make an announcement about it."

"Are you…"

"There are no good answers to any of your questions," he said. "Shout it from the high heavens for all I care. I don't. But don't embarrass Sammy. If you can't talk about it without being embarrassing, or being awful, you're going to have to keep your damn mouth shut, kid."

"I just…"

"I made bacon-and-egg sandwiches," Sammy said. "Why don't you sit with us and have one."

"No, thank you," she said. "I have to go…bleach my brain."

"Well, why don't you take a sandwich on your way." Sammy held it out and Rose looked at it skeptically, like it might have cooties. "The sandwich was not used for anything untoward," Sammy said.

Rose blanched. "Honestly. That doesn't make it better. That didn't help at all. Because now I'm wondering about what you could have possibly done with the sandwich that would be considered… No. I don't want it. Enjoy your sandwich. I'm not going to…say anything. To anyone. You're right. You didn't tell anyone. I just had the bad luck of walking in while you were…well, eating each other's faces."

"Eloquent," Sammy said.

"Charming," Ryder added.

"I try to be both," Rose said. "As often as possible. The opportunity so rarely presents itself. And yet, here we are."

"You're mostly mad because you got it wrong about Logan," Ryder said.

"Well," she said, her visible deflation at that confirming Ryder's statement. Rose didn't like to be wrong. "I'll have to think of someone else for him."

"Will you?" Ryder asked, his tone dry.

"Yes. He is actually like a brother to me. And one of my dearest friends in the entire world when I don't want to punch him in the face. So yes, I've been scheming a little bit to make him happy. And I thought maybe it might help Sammy to…"

"Or, you could just give up meddling," Sammy said.

"Well, that would be boring," Rose said, brightening. "At least this isn't boring."

"So glad we could entertain you," Ryder said. "Now, go on. Get out of here. Get." He said the last one like he was trying to get rid of a perfectly ridiculous dog.

Rose didn't have to be asked again.

That left just the two of them, and four sandwiches.

"Well. That was…"

"Who cares?" he asked.

"Don't you think it will be awkward when… I don't know. This runs its course?"

"I'm not sure that I'm thinking of it that way," he said.

"You're not?"

"There's no point thinking that way," he said. "You're in my life. The way that you've always been. And sure, things are a little bit different with the way that we're… with all of this. But you're going to be in my life, Sammy. That's just the truth of it. You can count on it. Count on me."

"I do," she said. "I mean, I trust you. I do."

"Then don't think of it that way. I'm not ashamed of anything we've done. I'm not ashamed of you."

"I'm not ashamed of you," she said.

"I didn't mean to imply that you might be. But I just wanted you to know… I'm not. And I don't care if they know."

There was a lot underneath that, she was sure.

He'd spent so many years sacrificing for them. She could see why he didn't want to do it now.

"How many women have you been with, do you think?"

He drew back, snorting. "What the hell kind of question is that?"

"I mean, you've spent a really long time just kind of… being good to everybody. And going out of town to hook up and whatever. I know you haven't had relationships…"

"I don't know," he said. "I mean… I hook up. I have since high school. I don't count them."

She nodded. "All right. Same. But like…those things

were different than this. But all those guys I sort of knew, but I didn't know, you know?"

"I expect that has something to do with it," he said.

"I thought I understood sex but this feels like a totally different thing."

"Yeah," he said. "Because it is."

Then they set about to eating their food, and she had to agree with him. This was different. Like a different thing entirely.

So yeah, maybe they didn't have to try to see it through to the inevitable conclusion. Maybe all they had to do was be in the moment.

She really, really liked the moment.

In fact, she liked it more than any other moment she'd ever been in in all of her life.

And that was something to hang on to.

CHAPTER SEVENTEEN

THEY WEREN'T ALL that careful over the next few weeks. If people in the family other than Rose had figured out something was going on, Sammy wouldn't be all that surprised.

It was impossible for her to keep from giving Ryder lingering looks during the day. Impossible to keep from sharing secret smiles with him. There were so many secret things to smile about. Truly, she felt like she was in some kind of weird haze of bliss she hadn't known was possible.

If her moment of insanity regarding pregnancy had led here, then she was happy to have had her small psychotic break.

It was well worth it.

And today she was engaging in one of her favorite pastimes. In fact, she might have called it one of her top two favorite pastimes until she had discovered sex with Ryder. But today was canning day. A day that she and Iris looked forward to every year. They would make all kinds of things. Jam and preserved lemons. Pickles and peppers.

It was a lot of work, but it was fun. And today they had managed to enlist the help of Rose and Pansy. She was happy to see Pansy—who she had seen a bit less of since her relationship with West had gotten started.

She understood.

It was normal to separate often to make your own thing. It was. Exceedingly and wonderfully normal.

And she was working very hard at not resenting it at all. Because she didn't have any call to. Pansy had a right to a normal life.

Anyway, Sammy didn't need normal. Not as long as she had Ryder.

"I want spicy pickles this year," Rose announced when they had everything set out in front of them.

"We have to have regular ones, too," Pansy said. "West can't tolerate that kind of heat."

"Bless," Iris said.

"I thought he was a tough ex-convict!" Rose hooted.

"Well, he doesn't like spicy food."

"He's…mostly a Texan. That's kind of shameful."

"That's not why I love him," Pansy said.

"Why do you love him?" Rose asked.

Pansy's response was to blush to the roots of her hair.

Sammy grinned. "See. Good for you. And it all happened because you took my advice."

Iris scowled. "Yes, and it could've also backfired. In fact, it very nearly did."

"But it didn't," Sammy said cheerfully. "Love prevailed in the end."

As she said it, the word caught in her breastbone. Then she realized… She realized just what awful advice she had given to Pansy. And so cavalierly. Because she hadn't really understood. Because for her, sex had never been intimate. Because she had worked so hard at compartmentalizing all of her emotions. And it had been helped by the fact that none of it had ever been terribly physically satisfying.

She could have ruined Pansy's life.

She started fiddling with all of the canning supplies, blinking rapidly.

"What?" Iris asked.

"Are you okay?" That question came from Rose, and the fact that it was sincere made Sammy slightly concerned that Rose was connecting some of the issues that Sammy was currently having with the situation with Ryder. True to her word, Rose hadn't said anything. It surprised Sammy a bit that Rose—who was a notorious loudmouth—had kept her counsel quite so well. But she had.

Sammy wasn't really sure why she cared if Rose told. Ryder clearly didn't. But it did come back to that intimacy thing. A funny thing. Because she would've thought she'd have been the first one to share. Of course, it was awkward because it was Iris, Pansy and Rose's brother. And they certainly didn't want to hear about his prowess, but still.

She didn't want to share about it anyway. No matter what. Whether it was weird for them or not. She wanted to keep it to herself. She wanted it to be her secret. She wanted it to be her thing to marvel at.

Suddenly, she felt oddly emotional. And the vinegar in the room smelled too strong. She didn't like it.

"I don't know. I want to do the jam," she said. She wrinkled her nose. "Something smells off."

"Nothing smells off," Pansy said.

"I think it does. And no offense, Pansy, but I don't necessarily trust your culinary sensibilities over mine."

"I don't think anything smells off," Iris said.

"Well. It does," Sammy said. Suddenly, she felt resolute in that.

"Fine," Iris said. "I'll check everything over."

"Dammit," Pansy said, grimacing. She clutched her side. "Do any of you have any fem pro?"

"Pads or tampons?" Iris asked.

Sammy blinked.

Pads or tampons.

Pads or tampons.

Neither of which she had used for longer than she ought to have not used them.

Holy. Shit.

She just stood there while the sisters moved around her, while Iris gave blithe directions as to where Pansy might find her tampons. Pansy, who was engaged. And in love. And who would probably find it positive news if she didn't need feminine protection.

"What's wrong?" Rose asked, her expression far too insightful.

"Nothing," Sammy said vaguely.

Except now she felt nauseated combined with the fact that she didn't like the vinegar smell. The vinegar, which smelled weird. Which was definitely a symptom of something she didn't much want to think about. But one that connected very much to a missed period.

"What's wrong?" Rose asked again.

"I just… I think that I… I…"

"You look like you're going to be sick."

"Oh, my gosh," Iris said, crossing the kitchen. "You're white as a sheet. Sit down."

And suddenly, Sammy did feel light-headed, and she swayed. She found herself being propelled by Rose and Iris, out into the living room, where they sat her down on the couch. Pansy reemerged only moments later, her expression filled with concern.

"What's going on?"

"Sammy isn't feeling well," Iris said.

"No," Rose said. "She's not."

And she didn't want to talk about it. She really didn't. And she didn't want to do this on her own, either. And didn't want to talk to Ryder unless she was absolutely certain.

No. She couldn't let Ryder know. Not unless she knew for a fact. Thank God he wasn't home.

"I think I need a pregnancy test," Sammy blurted out.

"You what?" Pansy and Iris asked in unison.

Rose, however, was still.

"I'm late. When Pansy asked for tampons it reminded me. I should have started my period like four days ago."

"Oh," Iris said. "Are you usually regular?"

"Pretty regular. I mean, it could be nothing. But on the other hand…it definitely could be something."

It was just all very suspicious that she would suddenly be late when she had also had unprotected sex just the right amount of time ago.

"One of us can get it for you," Rose said.

"That's going to cause serious issues," Iris said.

"Pansy can do it," Rose said. "Pansy is engaged."

"Pansy is on her period," Pansy said. "It's ridiculous."

"No one else will know that," Rose said. "Anyway,

it's the most reasonable. If I go buy one, Ryder is going to start roaming the town looking for someone to beat up. And if Iris does…well, people will start wondering about virgin births."

"Excuse me," Iris said. "And wouldn't they wonder the same thing about you?"

Rose shrugged. "I'm a wild card."

Iris's brown eyes went narrow. "Not as much as you think."

"I can get my own pregnancy test."

"You don't need to," Pansy said. "I'll be back in fifteen minutes. None of you move. And I'm going to have to call my fiancé on the way and make sure he knows that whatever rumors he hears…aren't true."

"Pansy…"

"It's fine," Pansy grumbled. "Exactly what I want. Rumors about the chief of police being knocked up."

She was gone for thirteen and a half minutes, and when she returned she also had a box of pads and a box of tampons. And a bottle of wine.

"I thought I would throw them off my scent."

"Super sneaky," Iris said, rolling her eyes.

"Well," Rose said. "Go take it."

"You seem very keen to get the answer," Iris said.

"Well, aren't you?"

But Sammy knew why Rose was so keen. It was because she knew who the father was. Or at least suspected.

"I'll go," Sammy said.

Rose followed for a moment, and Sammy turned to her. "Don't say anything. Not yet."

Rose shook her head. "I won't. Would it be… I mean… Is it his?"

"It would be," she said.

"I didn't think you were going to do the baby thing."

"I wasn't," Sammy said. "And I need to know before I say anything to him. I need to know for sure."

"We're here for you," Rose whispered, squeezing her arm.

She had never known her friend to be quite so mature, and she really appreciated it. Because she was going to need all the support she could get.

And by the time she opened up the pregnancy test and took it, and got the results, she really knew she was going to need all the support she could get.

Because she was going to have a baby. Ryder's baby. And everything should have seemed all right, but instead she felt like the world had been turned upside down, and she didn't have any idea what she was going to do.

CHAPTER EIGHTEEN

HE WAS IN a good place today. Both physically and mentally. Spiritually, Sammy would probably say. Not that he gave much thought to that kind of thing. But she made him consider it, because there was something to the connection the two of them had, and it was deeper than anything he could see. So maybe she was on to something after all.

It was his favorite kind of day. Out in the middle of the field, having just moved the cows from one pasture to another. The kind of day that reminded him why being a rancher might have chosen him, and it might not have been where he imagined his life going, but he was happy with it.

Yeah, maybe he would have gone to school. And he would've played football longer. His coach had been upset about his quitting. About his not going on to college to play. But by now he would be done with football anyway. He had worked this land since he was eighteen years old. Had cultivated this herd. The animals changing as the years rolled on, the landscape staying much the same, but there were slow changes that he could see. Changes that he had forged with his own hands, and changes that had been the result of nature pushing right back at him.

He loved those losses as much as he loved the victories.

Because in the end they were what reminded him that he was alive.

He heard the sound of a truck engine and turned around, shocked to see Sammy driving across the field toward him in his sister's truck.

That was unusual. To say the least.

She parked and got out, all fluttering pale pink summer dress and wild blond hair. And he had the irresistible image of laying her down on the grass and stripping her naked underneath the sky.

Yeah. That was what he wanted. And bad.

He moved quickly, closing the space between them, but she stopped him with one look from wide blue eyes.

"I have something to tell you," she said.

"What?"

He was immediately struck by terror. Because she looked afraid, and anything that scared Sammy struck him deep.

"I… I just took a pregnancy test."

It was like the mountains all around the horizon had tipped in on themselves and crumbled. Like the world had gone concave, leaving only the place they were standing on. His boots were rooted to the ground, that same ground that he had worked all these years. That familiar, unchanging earth. And yet, it was all new now. Everything was. It would never be the same again.

"It must've happened that first time," she said.

"I know when it would have happened," he said.

They had used a condom every time since.

"I know I said I wasn't going to…"

"Look, I wasn't opposed to getting you pregnant," he said, because there was nothing else to say. It was true. That first night he had fully intended for the sex they'd had to result in the pregnancy she was looking for, because the alternative was that she was going to go find it with another man. He had been happy enough that she had decided to put it off. But that chance had been there.

And he knew what had to happen next. As sure as he knew the sun would rise tomorrow and that he'd work this ranch like he'd done every day for the past seventeen years.

"We're getting married," he said.

Her face popped up, her hair swinging with the movement. "No," she said. "No. We don't have to do that. I mean… Why can't we just live here? Live here in this place and… I don't know. I can be in the camper. And you can be in the house and we can be together sometimes and…"

"Because it's not enough," he said.

"Why not?"

"That's not how families work."

"It is how families work. It's how our family has been for the past seventeen years."

He gritted his teeth. "We're not family, Sammy."

She jerked as though he slapped her. And he hated the look of pain that crossed her delicate face. "No. Of course not. I mean, not that way. I get it."

"That isn't what I meant. I just meant that we can be family. The way that my parents were family. That's how it should work."

"I'm not going to do something like that just because that's how it should be."

"Why the hell not?"

"Because believe me, marriage is not just the answer to everything. I lived in a house with a horrible dysfunctional marriage and will not raise a child in an environment where two people are stuck together."

"Are you comparing us to your parents?"

"It's just… Look, I know how bad it can get."

"Are you scared of me?" he asked.

She looked horrified by the very thought. "No," she said. "I'm not afraid of you. But I'm afraid of what that forever stuff does to people. I'm afraid of the misery that you'll expect because you signed a piece of paper. Because you stood up and made vows in front of everybody and said that you would. And we are happy. We're happy like we are."

"We are not going to stay like we are. There's going to be a baby. And that changes things. It changes things a hell of a lot, Samantha. We can't undo it. We can't undo what is."

"But why not?" She blinked furiously, the terror rolling off her and turning into something else inside him. It was one thing when she was afraid of something and it wasn't him. He wanted to fight that battle for her. He wanted to fight every battle for her. But he didn't know what the hell to do when he seemed to be the battle. When she was looking at him and acting like his proposal of marriage was the worst thing that could possibly happen. "Why can't we make a new reality? That's what you did here. And all right, maybe you don't consider me part of the family, but I've always considered myself part of it. I wanted to be here. So badly. Because I lived in that life that was supposed to be right. A mother and a father who were married. And I was miserable. Every day I had to apologize for being. And when I left there, when I came to you, I promised I wouldn't do that anymore. And I haven't. I got to grow up in the most amazing place in all the world because of you. Because you rescued me. And because you were all brave enough to make a family out of something else. To sew it together using leftover pieces, and I've always felt lucky enough to be one of those pieces."

"But we are not left over," he said, his voice rough. "You and me, we're something real. We get to make a choice, Sammy. What we are, what we're going to be. What we want to be. For our baby. Our baby."

He had feared this moment. All of his life.

That he would get to this stage where he was finally free, and then he wouldn't be. But the reality was if he didn't have Sammy with him, he wasn't all that free. If this child was out there in the world and he didn't have access to him, he wasn't all that free.

It was a new version of freedom, that was for sure.

But then, he never felt more himself than when he was in bed with Sammy, so being with her could never be a prison.

"I'm scared," she said.

"Of me? I'm not your father," he said, his voice rough.

"I know," she said.

"No," he said, "you need to understand. Not just know in your head. You need to feel it in your heart. I am the man who would destroy someone for touching you like that. And anyone who would come after our baby. I would destroy him, too. I will never hurt you. And I will never hurt our child." He brought her close to him, put his hand on her stomach. And he felt a sense of awe wash over him.

Because they had created something between them. They had created a life, and he had experienced so much loss of life over the past thirty-five years. To have there be life, created new because of them…

"It's a damned miracle, Samantha. That the two of us made something like this."

She looked up at him, fear and tears in those blue eyes. "What if I'm a terrible mother? And a terrible wife. What if what we have is broken by this?"

"We will never be broken," he said. "Didn't I promise you that?"

"Yes," she said. "But that doesn't mean I'm not afraid."

He nodded slowly. "I understand. But can you trust me? Marry me. Move in to my house. Sleep in my bed. Be my family. Make a family with me."

He had never seen things going this way with Sammy. Not for all those years. But there was no other option now. She was his. She was his and the baby was his. And that meant that it had to be this. Hell, that had been the case from the moment they had first kissed. Because the alternative was that they would go their separate ways, be with other people. Continue on the way they'd always done. Occasionally hooking up with strangers in bars, making sure that they ignored any heat between the two of them.

So it had to be everything. Because it could never be that.

It was suddenly all he wanted. Sammy as his bride. Walking toward him in white.

"Marry me," he said again.

It wasn't joy on her face, but it wasn't fear. It was more a slow acceptance of what had to be. And that was it. There was no other route. She could see it, too.

"All right," she said. "I'll marry you."

"We can have normal," he said.

He took her into his arms and held her. He didn't kiss her, even though he wanted to. He just held her there. "We can be normal," he repeated again. And there was a strange sort of giddy feeling that washed through him, because he had never imagined that this moment would be for him. Getting married. Having a child. It was right there. He could taste it. And he wanted it. He found in that moment, he really did.

"Okay," she said.

It wasn't *yes*.

But after the lifetime they'd both had, he would damn well take *okay*.

CHAPTER NINETEEN

SOMEHOW, SHE WENT back to canning after that. When she walked into the room, Rose, Pansy and Iris all craned their necks. Iris and Pansy didn't know yet. Rose hadn't told them. She'd simply offered up the use of her truck, and Sammy had taken it.

And now she supposed was the time for the explanation. Especially when he had gone and proposed. Or made demands, as it were. But she couldn't refuse him. And he had said…that they could be normal. Maybe nobody else would understand what that meant, but he did. And she did. A deep desire in her heart that warred in many ways with that fear of being trapped. But it meant they weren't broken. And that was a miracle she hadn't expected.

Of course, that meant explanations. It meant bringing other people into their secret thing. She didn't like that. If only it could just be them. Their world. Their bubble. But then, she was back to the little fantasy she had spun out in the field. When she had asked him why they couldn't just be without labels or papers or vows. But Ryder was a man of paperwork and vows. She knew that. And who he was mattered. What he wanted mattered.

"Well, I'm engaged now," she said, making her way purposefully over to the canning things.

The reaction was deafening.

"I didn't think that was the whole point of your… baby thing," Iris said.

She sighed. "This is sort of separate from the baby thing. I mean, the initial endeavor. It's just something that happened." She looked at Rose, who was gazing at her with wide eyes. And she figured it was as good a time as any.

"So I'm marrying your brother."

The response was, yet again, deafening, but this time there were expletives.

"Is he the father?" Pansy asked.

"Yes," Sammy said.

Iris and Pansy were utterly agape. Rose was still.

"I don't even know how to…approach that," Iris said. "I thought that the two of you were…friends. But maybe that was a little bit naive of me. To assume that you weren't…"

"We weren't," Sammy said. "I mean, not until the past couple of months."

"I knew you were acting weird," Iris said. "That night at the saloon I knew the two of you were being strange. And frankly, I knew you've been strange much of the time since."

"Well. We were. And it wasn't supposed to be this. But it is this. So we are… We care for each other. There's no reason in the world we can't make it work. And nothing much is really going to change. Except, I guess I'll be your sister somewhat legally."

It was Rose who closed the distance between them and wrapped her arms around Sammy. "You're my sister already," Rose said. "But I'm really glad that you're going to be my sister-in-law. It just seems delightfully official."

"Yes," Sammy said. "It does seem official."

"You don't like official," Pansy said.

"I don't really. But Ryder does. And I like him. An awful lot."

"Are you in love with him?" Pansy asked.

That word struck a strange sort of terror into the center of Sammy's chest.

"If ever there were such a thing as soul mates, I think he's mine. I think we knew each other before we met. I don't know if that makes sense. I'm sure it doesn't. We're that. Whatever *that* is."

"That's nice," Iris said, far too mildly.

"I don't know," Pansy said. "I think you should be in love with the person that you marry."

"Just because that's how things worked for you, Pansy, that doesn't mean that's how it works for everybody."

"I know," Pansy said. "But… Sammy, you're wonderful and you deserve everything."

Sammy brushed the feelings off her that settled like an uncomfortable cloak. "Anyway…there *can't* be anyone else. Honestly, there never could be. He's…" They were all looking at her, sadly, meaningfully. And so she twisted her lips into a strange sort of impish smile. "He's a damn genius in bed."

"No!"

Pansy threw her hands up and doubled over like she was retching, and Iris put her palm on her forehead.

"He's ruined me for other men," Sammy said, nodding gravely to underscore the point.

That was true. More than true.

"Well, I'm very happy for you," Pansy said, making a mock retching sound again.

"We'll be fine," Sammy said. "Nothing is going to change, really. I mean, nothing has changed. Yes, there's a new…dimension to our relationship."

"I don't want to hear about my brother's dimensions," Rose said.

"Oh. Big, just so you know. But also, we care for each other. We care deeply. And that is very important. And that's what's going to see us through all the changes in life. Anyway, I can't imagine anything better than being here with all of you, and you being my baby's aunts."

That did seem to make everyone happy, and make them forgive her for what she had said about dimensions.

And it gave her the confidence to hope that whatever happened from here would be all right. It had to be. There really wasn't another option.

CHAPTER TWENTY

EVERYTHING WAS FINE until the vomiting started. And once it started, it was pretty intense. And lasted from the very early hours of the morning, where it woke her from a deep sleep, and Ryder, as well, and carried her through until lunchtime.

It was awful. Truly awful.

And enough to make it so that planning the wedding felt more or less impossible.

Anyway, she felt kind of guilty about the fact that they were going to end up getting married before Pansy and West. They had gotten engaged first after all. But they were having a shotgun wedding.

Of course, she wasn't sure she was going to make it down the aisle in her present condition.

That, though, was its own gift. This illness. Because she felt horrible. And all of this wasn't going according to any plan at all.

And she still knew.

That she would protect her child with all of herself.

When it woke her from her sleep that morning at 3 a.m. she wanted to cry. She reached for the sleeve of saltines that she kept beside the bed and chewed on one, feebly, hoping that it would do something to counteract the horrible, cramping nausea.

It didn't. She rolled out of bed and ran into the bathroom, just making it to the toilet before she lost the meager dinner she had managed to consume the night before.

She rested her head against the cool porcelain, sweat beading on her brow, tears streaming down her cheeks. She knew that she wasn't going to be able to move, not for a while. It always held her captive for quite a bit of time.

She felt miserable. And small. And a whole lot like the vulnerable girl she had never been allowed to be while growing up.

Had she ever been like this? Had she ever just sat down and cried?

There had never been the choice.

She had been around her father, who would use that weakness against her, and her mother, who hadn't really cared. Not as much as she said.

She scrubbed her arm over her eyes, feeling completely beset by her misery now.

Ryder was right. Her mother had never really cared that much. Not about her. She had used her as an excuse.

Suddenly, she felt strong hands on her shoulders, felt the warmth of a solid body behind her.

"Can I get you anything?"

She shook her head miserably. "No. My body hates me."

And with the way she felt, it was difficult for them to have much in the way of a sexual relationship at the moment, so she felt disconnected and useless. Less like a sacred vessel of life and more like one of agony.

A wife he would be sorry to have before he ever had her.

He pulled her back against him, cradling her in his arms, and she went limp, resting there.

He was where she had always been able to be vulnerable. He had always been strong for her.

But it reminded her of that night. That night that he had come to her rescue. The one they didn't much talk about.

She closed her eyes, a tear sliding down her cheek. "Did I ever thank you?" she whispered.

"For what?"

"For saving me."

"Sammy…"

"I mean, we don't really talk about that night so much as talk around it. I think he was going to kill me," she said. "I really do."

"I can't think about that," he said, his voice rough.

"All I did was…" She had never told him this. And he had never asked. Of course, he never would. Of course, in response to her father beating her mercilessly he would never ask what she had done to earn that, because of course he would never believe that she had.

Not Ryder.

But she had done something. She had wanted something.

"He was…doing what he did. Angry and drunken… He started in on me, because he found condoms in my backpack. And he asked why I was such a slut. He backhanded me. He said that he didn't want any daughter of his going around acting like the town bike. Said that what I was doing was wrong. That I was dirty. And I looked him right in the face and I asked him… I asked why he couldn't love me. Why he couldn't love us. I asked him what was wrong with him."

Tears blurred her vision, her throat so tight she

couldn't speak. She had to let them sit for a moment. Had to let it all settle.

Ryder didn't say a word. He simply tightened his hold on her. She had thought they couldn't possibly have any secrets between them. But they did. There was this. This big, looming thing that had created her, transformed her into the person who had moved into Hope Springs Ranch. And what she had been every day since.

"He hit me," she said. "He said there was nothing wrong with him. It was just all the stupid, stupid women in his life. And we made him do it. I made him do it. Because I made him so angry. And I had to be my mother's fault. He said he never hit her until me. It was me." She blinked furiously. "He just said that. Over and over again. And then you came for me. You came for me, Ryder. And you stopped him. And you were the one who sat with me at the hospital. You were the one who got him arrested. You helped me. My own parents hurt me. But you… You rescued me."

"You never told me any of this," he said, his voice rough.

"I know. And you never asked because you're too good to ask. Too good to ask what I had done. I just asked him why he couldn't love me."

And she had emerged determined never to feel shame about what she did. About her body. About who she was. She had emerged determined never to be that girl who asked in such a small, frightened voice why her father didn't love her.

To ask for love and to look up and see only a violent void was a nightmare. *The* nightmare, perhaps.

The most awful, wrenching thing that she could ever

imagine. And she had endured it. She had come out of it. And she had been determined to learn from it. To never feel like that again.

Ever.

And here she was, vulnerable now, but not afraid. Not afraid because of Ryder. Because of everything he was and everything he always would be.

She had landed somewhere safe at least. She could be confident in that. Her child would never have to look at his father and ask that question.

That was a gift. One that she would never, ever undervalue.

"He was broken," Ryder said. "The reasons you can't love come from inside you."

There was something hollow and empty in his voice, and it made her want to ask another question, but she feared the answer far too much. So she didn't ask. Instead, she kissed his forearm, and rested herself more deeply against him. No good came from asking questions you didn't want the answers to.

She had done her best to make a life where she didn't need to ask those kinds of questions. And she didn't.

She didn't need to.

She had him. He was committed to her. To taking care of her, to taking care of the baby. There was no reason ever to ask for more. No reason to hope for more. So she wouldn't. And she would be all the happier for it.

She had his arms. And they would always protect her.

What more could she possibly need?

THE FAMILY FOURTH of July picnic was interesting this year. West and his half brother, Emmett, made for a fascinating new addition. West was the subject of much interrogation from Colt and Jake, who had come back from the circuit for the event.

But they took a break from interrogating West just long enough to corner Ryder and shove a beer in his hand. "Getting married, huh?" Colt asked.

"To Sammy," Jake added.

"And having a baby," Logan added.

"Are you congratulating me or accusing me of something?" Ryder asked.

"Both," Jake said, looking at Colt, who nodded in agreement. "Definitely both."

"Seriously?"

"If you hurt her," Jake said.

"We will tear you apart," Colt added.

"Limb from limb," Jake finished, then took a swallow of beer.

"I'm sorry," Ryder said. "Have I stepped into an alternate dimension? I have been taking care of Sammy for the past seventeen years. I'll keep doing it now."

"She doesn't have a father who will threaten you. She doesn't have brothers to do it. She has us."

"I'm your brother, you assholes."

"Technically our cousin," Colt said.

"No relation," Logan said.

"This is the thanks I get?" he asked. "For taking care of you fools for all those years?"

Colt shrugged. "Sammy's a nice woman."

"I'm nice," Ryder said.

Colt shook his head. "You're a lot of things, but *nice* isn't really one of them. Decent. Good. But not nice."

"Ungrateful fuckhead," Ryder grumbled.

"See, my point," he said.

"I'm taking responsibility," Ryder said. "Doing what any good man would do."

"Oh, I hope that you used that in your proposal," Jake said. "Height of romance."

"I didn't say it was romance." He and Sammy were deeper than that anyway. He didn't need to put labels on it. Wasn't Sammy the one who was so averse to labels anyway? It all made sense. It really did. There was no point being a fool about it.

He remembered what she had told him this morning, in the early hours, as he had held her on the bathroom floor. About how she'd asked her father why he didn't love her.

What he'd said to her then had been true.

People didn't not love you because of something wrong with you. It was always something with them.

And there was something with him.

That was the thing.

What he felt for Sammy was some kind of sickness. An intensity that made it so he couldn't breathe, couldn't think clearly. Not like the sweetness shared by his parents. Damn it all, he worried. He worried what it would be like, over the course of years, for anyone to be in a house with them.

He looked at her and it felt like bleeding.

He felt love for his family. Though it wasn't an easy thing. More like a bonding that couldn't be undone. Forged in the kind of fire that you would never walk through on purpose. He didn't have it in him to love, not the way that he watched his parents do it.

Theirs had been something wonderful, had brightened

up the whole house. Easy and companionable and the kind of emotion he didn't think he had the ability to feel.

For him, connections to people would always be double-edged, because the more you care, the more you feared losing them.

And yeah, having this baby was a miracle, but it was a burden, too. Because there was a burden to caring. To having something that small and vulnerable be your responsibility. Yeah, it was something.

But he was handling things the way that he knew to do it. Taking control. Taking ownership.

It was what he did.

It was how he made it better. How he made it work.

"We're happy for you," Colt said. "But are you happy for yourself? Because Sammy deserves someone who thinks this is happy."

"She's got me," Ryder said. And somehow, he felt like that was a metaphor for everyone's life that was here.

They had deserved something else. They had gotten him. Maybe he was supposed to have something else, but he'd gotten them.

Not that it was... Not that he resented it. Especially not Sammy.

Because God knew there was nothing else.

No one else but her.

But it was just that... Well, maybe they'd all deserve to feel a whole lot differently. To love a whole lot more differently. To live a whole lot more differently. But they'd gotten the parents they'd gotten; they'd lost them when they had.

And in the end they'd been left with the things they'd been left with. Sammy had come to him because he was next door. Not because she had an endless array of saviors to choose from. But because he was the only savior on hand. It was all well and good, but it wasn't the same as…people who went through life with the support group you were meant to have. The parents that you were meant to have. Parents who lived. Parents who loved you.

Not parents who would hit you for asking where that love was.

His blood burned.

Now that he knew. Now that he knew what Sammy had done. Dared to ask for what should have been hers by birth.

"We did all right," Colt said.

"Yeah," Ryder agreed. "You did okay."

His relationship with these men had shifted over the years. They were more like brothers now.

But they'd been something more than that to him for a long while. He had known what it was to be an older brother, and that did come with feelings of a certain amount of responsibility. But it was different when it was you the school had to call when grades were down, or they'd gotten into a fight. It was different when you were the final word, when you were the one who had to lay down the law over underage drinking. When you were still underage yourself.

It was all just different.

And he didn't need them trying to throw down guilt trips about Sammy and what he could be to her and what he couldn't.

He was aware of his shortcomings.

He was well aware.

But he was offering her something. Not nothing.

And maybe it wasn't everything, because he didn't possess the ability to give a whole lot more than what he already offered. But he offered what he had. That was going to have to be enough.

"Come on, let's stop talking about our feelings," Ryder said. "Football."

The guys went out onto the field and a rough game ensued. It was tradition for them to throw the ball around, but Ryder always got overly competitive. Which his almost-brother-in-law seemed to love.

There was only a mild amount of bloodshed.

"Dammit, Ryder," Colt complained, wiping his palm over a bleeding scuff on his face.

"We don't do touch football. I'd think a big, bad bull rider could handle that," Ryder goaded him.

"Bulls have more honor," Colt muttered, walking to the cooler and getting a beer, which he promptly pressed to the side of his face.

They dispersed after that, making their way over to different food stations. Sammy and Iris had made amazing side dishes. Macaroni and cheese, baked beans, homemade rolls. Pies, cake. Rose—true to her own nature—had provided chips and beer, along with some soda. Ryder had a soft spot for off-brand soda, since that was what they'd had often when he was in charge, and they were living off a shoestring. Nothing wrong with bottom-shelf cereal and grape soda; not in his opinion.

Logan fired up the grill, putting on steaks and hamburgers for the group, and Colt picked up his guitar and started to strum a halfway decent country tune. He would never be one to perform anywhere but in the backyard, but he had a decent voice and passable skill, and he did fine enough for entertainment at family gatherings.

In the middle of all this familiarity, there was still something that stood out.

Bright and different even though she was the same.

Sammy was laughing, the dogs swirling around her, overly excited blurs of fur. Looking at her made his chest hurt. The sun shone down on her like she was an angel of some kind.

Like the light was finding its own and gathering together, creating something so brilliant he could hardly bear to look at it straight on.

Sammy.

Something shifted in him, something deep, and he couldn't find a name for it. Except all of a sudden a whole bunch of truths tumbled in on him. That in a couple of years he would be watching his child run around at this very same barbecue. That he would be about his father's age when he'd died.

It was such a strange milestone to move toward. A part of life that his dad hadn't even lived.

And he would be a father.

The idea of leaving his son behind, his son or daughter, to face the kinds of things that Ryder and the rest of them had had to face alone…

The kid was barely bigger than a lima bean at this point and he was already making him insane. Making him think about things that just about brought him to his knees.

Dammit, this was tough stuff. And he couldn't quite find the words to say why.

He never had to find the words for his particular pain;

all he had to do was figure out how to shove it down and deal with it. Because he was the oldest. So there was no one for him to talk to. He hoped that they had talked to each other. That Colt and Jake had found ways to give their grief a language. That Iris and Pansy and Rose had bonded with each other. And he had Sammy. Beautiful and bright, and he hadn't wanted to put any of his pain onto her. He had only wanted to enjoy her particular brand of beauty. Her particular brand of brightness. That had been everything he wanted.

She saw him, and smiled.

"You look better," he said, moving to close the distance between them.

"I feel better," she said. "But then, this is a good time for me. And sometime in the early hours my enjoyment of this barbecue will rebound on me. I feel like our child hates me already."

"He doesn't hate you," Ryder said, not even sure why he was engaging in this strange line of conversation.

"He?"

"I mean, I don't know," he said. "I'm just saying. You're talking like you know its emotions. Me knowing its gender seems weirder?"

She laughed. "Not weirder. But maybe we're both a little bit weird." She shook her head. "Is this what it does to you?"

"I guess so," he said. "I don't have another frame of reference."

There was a strange threat of awkwardness between them, and that was never the case for him and Sammy. Because Sammy was never awkward. And he had never taken her for someone who held things back, but he could feel it now. Feel himself doing it, and her doing it in response. Could feel a strange threat of tension between them that just wasn't them. Not usually. Not them.

But he had a feeling that getting rid of it would take sorting through some of that shifting that had happened inside him, and he didn't know how the hell to do that. Didn't think he wanted to, either. And he was pretty damn sure that Sammy wouldn't want to anyway.

Because all he could do was think about that emotion in her voice when she had told him that story about her father. There had been no small amount of fear there.

He never wanted to be the cause of fear.

The day wore on and faded into evening, and he watched Colt and Jake set off fireworks and come damn near close to blowing their fingers off. Laughing like oversize teenage boys.

Ryder was grateful they did laugh like that. That they had come through everything with a sense of adventure. That they had grown into themselves. Gone off and joined the rodeo and all of that.

"What?" He looked over at Sammy, whose face was illuminated by the golden pink of the fireworks that were going off around them.

"Nothing," he said. "Just watching the show."

"And thinking so loud I can practically hear the gears in your head grinding."

"I'm happy for them," Ryder said. "I'm happy that they went and found their dream."

"What about you?"

"I have more than I imagined I would," he said.

But when Sammy smiled up at him, it seemed forced,

and he didn't like that, either, because Sammy didn't do forced, not usually.

"You know, you can always find out if there's a coaching position available at the high school," she pointed out.

"I don't need to coach," he said, a strange, bruised feeling hitting his chest. "I'd be retired from the game by now anyway, even if I had gone on to play for real. And I wouldn't have."

"You don't know that."

"I mean, I pretty much do."

"Everything is going to be okay, right?"

She was looking up at him, hopefully, and the problem was, he knew that you couldn't make guarantees like that. That you couldn't just say it would be fine, because you didn't really know. But what he did know was that you could stay standing even when dark stuff went down. He knew that you could withstand a hell of a lot more than you thought you might be able to.

And that you could take broken pieces and turn them into something. Not necessarily something that was just as good as what you had, and not even something that would make it all okay. But if you worked at it, if you tried, you were never left with nothing.

He knew that much.

"It's going to be," he said. "That I know. The sun always rises and sets, Sammy, no matter what's happening in other parts of the world. No matter what's happening in your life."

"So you're telling me the world's not going to end, and that's about all you can guarantee."

"That's about all any of us have."

"A great comfort."

"You know," he said. "It's not different for anyone else. Really. No one has guarantees. It's just that you and I know it. We know that sometimes life is not kind, and you're born into the wrong family. Two parents who should never have had children."

"That's awfully cheering," Sammy said.

"I've always thought so."

But as they sat there together, together like they'd always been, and different than they'd ever been, he had to hope that it really would be okay.

Because they weren't like anyone else. And they weren't like they'd ever been before.

He reached out and took Sammy's hand in his, brushed his thumb over her ring finger, which was bare because she'd told him she didn't need real wedding things. Because she'd acted like rings and dresses would scare her away from the aisle.

And it felt wrong.

He knew how to be friends with Sammy. He knew how to protect her.

He had no real idea how to be a husband to her.

And if he was going to promise her it would all be okay, he was going to have to figure out exactly what to do.

CHAPTER TWENTY-ONE

SHE HAD BEEN married to the idea that they would do this casually and unconditionally. But she was out shopping with Pansy, Iris and Rose one afternoon, and they passed by the small bridal store that occupied the end of Main Street.

"We're getting married outside," Sammy said. "In two weeks. It's not like… It's not like I can wear an actual wedding gown."

She didn't even have a ring yet. But of course, she could make her own, and she had told Ryder as much. She didn't want diamonds or anything like that anyway. She preferred to work with more unusual stones. And for some reason, everything about what she said rang hollow in her chest at that moment, as she looked through the store window. And, at the gown in there.

She was being ridiculous.

"Why don't you go see what they have?" Pansy asked.

"Are you going to wear a wedding dress?"

Pansy laughed. "I'm going to be a bride, aren't I?"

"You're getting married at the ranch, too."

"Yes," Pansy said. "In the barn, though. With the fall wedding, the weather is a little bit too much of a gamble."

"Yeah. I mean, we're going to get married in the field. Because it feels very me. But…"

"Sammy, why don't we go look at dresses?" Pansy said.

"Can you imagine me in a wedding dress? It would be silly."

"I couldn't imagine you marrying my brother, either, but you're doing that," Pansy said. "And it makes sense now. So maybe if you go in to try on wedding dresses, it will make sense."

She had not expected Pansy's particular brand of practicality to extend to wedding dresses. But lo.

She would have thought that Pansy would say there was nothing practical about a wedding dress. Because there wasn't. She didn't need one. She didn't need to pretend that this was normal. That they were normal.

"I don't…"

"If you really don't want one, then you don't need to fear them," Pansy said, maddeningly logical. "The only problem seems to be that you don't want to want one."

"You don't know me," Sammy grumbled.

But on that grumble the four of them walked into the bridal store.

There was a young woman behind the counter in the front, who treated them to a smile. The whole place was oddly polished for this part of town, and so was the attendant.

"Welcome," she said. "I'm Miriam. Are you looking for a wedding gown today?"

"Actually," Pansy piped up. "Two of us are."

It was as if her friend knew that somehow it would be more acceptable if the two of them did it together. And that was how Sammy found herself only a few moments later stuffed into a dressing room with an endless parade of gowns being brought to her by Miriam and Iris and Rose.

When she emerged in the first one, Pansy was already standing there, boosted on a stool. The dresses were cut for women who were even taller than Sammy, so Pansy herself was swallowed up by the length. Without the stool, the fabric ballooned around her and it was impossible to tell if the dress looked nice or silly.

"All of it can be hemmed," Miriam said. "It's sort of cut in a default state. But all wedding gowns are made to take any number of alterations."

"I don't have a lot of time," Sammy said, looking at herself in the mirror. "So it's okay if I can't make one work."

"Nonsense," Miriam said. "I'm sure we can find something for you." She looked at her enigmatically. "You don't like this, though."

Sammy looked at herself, and the insane, princess-like confection of tulle around her body. "No," she said.

"Do you know what you like?"

"No," Sammy said. "In fact, I was absolutely opposed to having a wedding dress until we walked by your window. And now I'm not really sure what I'm doing. Considering that I'm just getting married in two weeks and it's a whole backyard shotgun situation."

"I see." Miriam looked her over and then went into the dressing room for a moment. It took Sammy a second to realize that the other woman was looking at the clothes that Sammy had come in wearing.

"Just give me a minute," Miriam said, and she disappeared back into the racks of dresses.

She reappeared shortly after with three other gowns in bags, and thrust them into Sammy's hand.

"It's okay," Sammy said. "I probably won't find one.

You should help Pansy. She's much more likely to walk out of here with the full meal deal. *She's* having a real wedding."

"Isn't yours real?" Miriam asked, her voice low.

"Well. Legal."

"That sounds…"

She cast a glance over at Iris, Pansy and Rose. They weren't paying attention to her. They were too busy putting veils on Pansy's head, and she was grateful for it.

"Ridiculous?" Sammy asked. "It's not. I mean, he's my best friend. He's literally my best friend. But we're having a baby so… He's very traditional."

"And you're not," Miriam said.

The other woman was probably about Sammy's age. But there was a gravity to her that Sammy certainly didn't possess. Her black hair was tamed into a bun, the deep rose-colored lipstick she wore matte and perfect and sophisticated. Her brown skin glowed with the radiance of someone who had the patience for a daily skin regime, something that Sammy didn't think she would ever have.

She was probably very traditional. Though Sammy noticed she didn't have a ring on her elegant finger. She did, however, have a very nice manicure, which also spoke of patience and attention to detail.

"Not really," Sammy said. "I've never believed in doing things for the sake of tradition. That's how people wind up miserable."

"And, often they wind up miserable bucking tradition for the sake of it, too. Nothing should be done just for the sake of it."

"A good point," Sammy said.

Of course, she didn't know what the point of the point

was. She was committed to marrying Ryder and everything was going to be fine. No matter what. There was no other option. Which was great, as far as she was concerned, and she didn't need some polished-looking woman with better fashion sense than she had to start talking about her situation like she knew. She didn't know. Nobody did.

She and Ryder weren't like anyone else. There were no comparisons to make. No precedent set. Maybe that was a little bit egotistical, or something. But it was true. She knew that Pansy and her fiancé, West, had found some kind of amazing manic version of true love, and she was happy for them.

She and Ryder knew each other. They had the benefit of years of caring for one another. They... They practically were married. And had been long before they had ever slept together. If any two people knew what to expect from a lifetime commitment to one another, it was them. He was right. They knew each other too well to let themselves break apart over something as simple as sex. It just wasn't them. It wasn't in them.

"I'll just go try the dresses on."

She was feeling sulky and resolved to find nothing by the time she stripped the poofy confection off and put the new dress on. But then, something really unexpected happened, and when she stepped out of the dressing room and caught a look at her own reflection in the mirror her breath got trapped in her throat. She didn't know she could look like that. The dress was simple, made of lace and beads, clinging to her body, rather than adding any volume to it. The kind of simplicity she hadn't known could come with a wedding dress. It made her feel traditional and herself all at once.

And suddenly, she could see it. Really see it. Walking down some sort of aisle toward Ryder. As his bride.

His *bride*.

And he would be her groom. Was he going to wear a suit? Suddenly she wanted him to. Suddenly, she didn't want it to be the same kind of day that they'd had a hundred times before, only with vows instead of a barbecue. Suddenly, she wanted a whole lot more.

She looked over at Pansy, who was stunning in a dress made from soft, flowing fabric that didn't dominate her petite figure, but made her look like an absolute princess.

"That's wonderful," she whispered, looking over at her friend.

Pansy looked back at her. "Sammy, you look…"

That earned her the attention of all the women, and suddenly, she was being swarmed by her friends, each clucking and touching pieces of her dress and she unexpectedly felt part of something. Traditions and a family in a way that touched her down to her soul. She hadn't thought she wanted any of this. But to her surprise, she did. They were going to be her sisters-in-law, and that was significant. Sharing this with them was significant. She just hadn't expected it. Not at all. She had expected… She didn't know. To feel above this. To feel like it didn't matter. Not when she knew that he didn't… That he didn't love her. Not really. Sure, as a friend, but it wasn't the same. It just wasn't. And that was fine; it had been fine. All of this had been fine until she had come in here.

"Get the dress," Iris said, her voice soft.

"Yes," Rose agreed. "Get the dress. You're going to absolutely knock his socks off."

And she could see it. Hearts in Rose's eyes. Because she wanted to matchmake everyone and anything, and she seemed to truly believe that anyone could have a happy ending. It was more than Sammy could believe. But somehow, even though she didn't believe that she could have normal and love, even though she didn't believe this whole wedding thing was going to work, and didn't think that it would be a marriage in the real sense, and didn't want to have all the feelings she would need to have to get those things anyway, suddenly she wished that she did. Suddenly, no matter what she felt, no matter what made her afraid, she wished that it could be more.

But mostly, it made her wish she were different. It made her wish that she were the woman in the mirror. A girl getting ready for her wedding day. A bride.

Well, she could be. For one day. So why not embrace it? Pretend that she was a normal girl. Pretend that she was living the kind of romantic fantasy that she had never imagined she could.

Why couldn't she have a fantasy for one day? Pretend that she was a normal girl. Pretend that this was the fantasy. Her throat ached with it. Her whole body ached. Well, in one way he was right. She did want this. She wanted this whole thing. The family. His family. Yes, she did want them to be her family, too. She couldn't pretend that wasn't the case. She wanted to dive headfirst into this whole thing all of a sudden. And maybe that was what she had been afraid of all along.

"Thank you," she said faintly.

"Do you want a veil?" Iris asked.

It was uncharacteristic to see even practical Iris alight with pleasure over something as inconsequential as bridal fashion. But it added to the well of feelings building in her chest. It added to it quite a lot.

"Probably not," Sammy said.

She had so much hair, and that was one thing she had no desire to change much for her wedding. She wouldn't feel herself with her blond hair tamed in any fashion. She was accustomed to it as it was. Out of control and a bit on the feral side.

Plus, Ryder liked it. He liked to run his fingers through it. Liked to hold on to it while she pleasured him. Liked to pull it sometimes, quite frankly, and the idea of leaving it loose for him felt...

"You're blushing," Rose said.

"No, I'm not," Sammy said. "I don't blush."

Except, she found that with him, she did. For him, she did.

He was responsible for a whole lot of firsts. A whole lot of things that she would have said weren't her. Weren't possible or real.

And yet, here she was.

"I have to try on the next dress," Pansy said. "This one isn't quite it, either."

Iris and Rose disappeared into the dressing room with her, a gown that elaborate apparently requiring multiple people to get off her.

That left her alone with Miriam.

"I think the dress might be too much," Sammy said. "I mean... I don't want him to think I'm taking this... more seriously than he is."

"But you like it," Miriam said.

For some reason Sammy's throat got tight. "I do. I like it a lot but… I don't want to want this." She blinked away tears. This poor near-stranger had not asked for Sammy to cry on her. "I don't want to care more than he does."

"He's marrying you," Miriam said gently. "He must care an awful lot."

"I'm afraid it won't be enough."

Sammy ended up being the only one who left with a bridal gown. And the gown felt heavy.

She didn't want to be in love. Not at all. Love was such a weird thing. The kind that you wanted to give and get back. Friendship was different. You didn't wander around wondering if the people you were friends with loved you. Telling them you love them and hoping for a reciprocal response. At least, not her friendships.

You did that with parents. You did that with husbands. In a traditional sense. She didn't want to do that. Not ever.

As a friend, she had never wondered if Ryder's feelings for her were real.

Heading into a love situation…

She ignored the pain in her chest when she thought of it. Because that was… It was so nothing she wanted to get involved in. Not in the least.

Why add a worry like that to her plate? Why, when in the context of friendship the two of them were so solid?

Unbreakable.

Suddenly, in her mind the scale of what they were appeared, and it seemed so much more precarious than she would like. Like if something was added to it that brought them out of balance all of it could crack, crumble and dissolve.

That if love was added to it, the hope of it, the demand for it, it finally would destroy things.

Good thing she didn't want it. Good thing she found no security or satisfaction in it.

Good thing her father had broken her of the desire to ever enter into a conversation about love.

Miriam was a nice woman, but she sold wedding dresses, and she didn't have a ring on her finger.

Sammy realized again that she didn't, either, and felt irritated about it.

You told him you wanted to make your ring.

Well, suddenly, she didn't. Suddenly, she wanted him to choose one and give it to her.

She squeezed her eyes shut, her whole face feeling scratchy for some reason.

Everything was fine, and she was not going to allow a bad case of bridezilla fever to infect something that she was so certain about otherwise.

She simply wasn't going to.

Wanting a wedding, and what their marriage was, were definitely two different things and she needed to be careful not to get them twisted up. She would have a wedding gown, and that was fine. She had wanted one, so she had one. If she wanted to have a little dress-up and glamour situation happening, that was fine.

She rationalized as they wandered from the car to Sugarplum Fairy's, the bakery that had opened a couple months back across the street from their favorite coffee shop.

She decided that she was far more likely to find answers in the cupcake she ordered than she was in the tangle of thoughts whirling through her mind.

She didn't need to untangle them, either.

Because if one thing was certain, it was Ryder. He was always certain, and he was always steady.

She could count on him if nothing else.

And that made her feel relieved indeed.

CHAPTER TWENTY-TWO

RYDER DIDN'T TAKE asking for advice lightly. In fact, he never took advice, so the fact that he was doing it at all spoke volumes about how out of his depth he felt.

But he'd never been married before. And it had hit him at the barbecue that he had to figure that out.

He didn't start a workday on the ranch without a plan. He'd never gone out onto a football field without knowing the plays.

He needed to figure out some husband plays.

West was in love. West was marrying Ryder's sister. And West was also a degree removed from Sammy in a way that Logan and the others weren't.

And that was what brought him to his future brother-in-law's side at the Gold Valley Saloon that evening, only a couple of days before his wedding.

"She says that she doesn't want a ring," he said. "But it doesn't feel right to me."

"She says she doesn't want a ring?"

West repeated his own words back to him, and Ryder found it astonishingly unhelpful. "Yes," he said. "Well, I mean, she said she doesn't want me to get her one. She wants to make it. You know, she's into all that artisan stuff. It's kind of her thing."

"Sure," West said. "But…a woman shouldn't make her

own wedding ring. That's like making your own birthday cake or…hell, buying your own Christmas presents, I guess. It's dumb, essentially. And I would think that most women would actually be not okay with it at all."

"But she said she was."

"Danger, Will Robinson. That sounds like *one of those things*."

"Sammy doesn't do that stuff. She doesn't play games."

"Maybe she didn't when she was your friend. But now she's your fiancée. The future mother of your baby. And that means games come into play."

"Are you telling me my sister plays games with you?"

West lifted a shoulder. "We play games with each other. Even if we don't mean to. That's how it all works sometimes. Because suddenly when you've got your feelings in the mix it's easier to play games than outright say it. Half the time I'm convinced the game is with your own head. I bet she's not tricking you on purpose, but she's probably afraid to ask in case you don't want to do it."

"Look. That's all fine for you two, but she and I have been friends for about a thousand years."

West leveled a serious look at him. "But now you're more."

"Not really," Ryder said, ignoring the tightness in his chest.

"Seriously? You got the woman pregnant, and you're marrying her, and you're still going to say that there's nothing more between the two of you?"

"Okay, it's more. But I guess more accurately it always has been. It's not love. I mean, not in love," he clarified. "But it's… She's always belonged to me. And that doesn't make sense. I know that. It sounds like a whole asshole caveman thing. And it isn't. It's more than that. I'd… I've spent the past seventeen years protecting her from the world."

"And now you have to protect her from you, too. Because I don't care if you think you're in love with each other or not, there's a hell of a lot higher stakes when it comes to feelings than there were before you were engaged. Than there were before you were having a baby. That's just a fact."

Ryder turned that over in his head for a moment. And he supposed that was probably true. And some of it was that it hadn't really occurred to him since he had wanted Sammy for quite some time, so the shift for him had more uncovered things he had already known existed, rather than treated him to anything new. But he was sure that Sammy herself had never thought of him that way and so for her it was an entire sea change.

And maybe that did require something different on his part. Maybe it did require a shift. Except…

"I mean, we have great sex," Ryder said.

West looked at him like he had grown a second head. A second head that was dangerously stupid.

"You know," West said. "I'm not an expert *necessarily* on the finer feelings of women. Being that I've only successfully managed to carry on a relationship with one. I mean, my relationship with my ex-wife was fine until she framed me for fraud and had me sent to prison. But I'm hoping for better with Pansy. So you know you can take what I say with a grain of salt. But great sex isn't enough."

"It's not?"

"No," West said.

"Even if…" Ryder was not the kind of person who shared things like this, but he really did need to make sure. Because for the first time in his life that he could remember he had a pretty delicate situation he needed to talk over with someone, and Sammy wasn't available to have a discussion with. He could say anything to her. He always had. Though the conversations had never strayed into advice about sex or anything of that nature, because the two of them had never really had relationships. And when it came to the actual quality of the sex, he was good. Thanks.

"Even if," he started again, "you're the best sex she's ever had?"

"Bro," West said. "I am the *only* sex your sister has ever had. And I still got her a ring."

Ryder bristled up the back of his neck. "Didn't need to know that."

"Hey, you brought it up. And you're being pretty dense for a guy who essentially raised three girls. I would have thought you would know better."

"Yeah, but it feels… It feels like something."

"Sure. Sex is like that. It feels like something. In the moment. And it takes things inside you and twists them up and makes them all feel bigger and deeper. Gets its hooks in you, and links you to another person in a way that can't be undone."

Yeah. That was definitely true. And he would have said it wasn't, because before Sammy, it never had been.

But then that was the other thing. She had wound herself around his life, around all that he was, way before they had ever started sleeping together. There was a permanence to who they were that had always existed.

Sex had deepened that for him, but…it wasn't the thing that had created it.

"So I should buy her a ring," he said. "That's what you're saying."

"Yes," West said. "As big of a diamond as you can find, because you're not just sleeping with her and marrying her. She is pregnant with your child and she probably feels like crap."

"It would have to be an ethical diamond, or whatever they call it," he said, racking his brain to figure out how he would find one of those on short notice.

"I imagine for Sammy, it would."

"She's very aware of everything to do with shiny rocks and stuff. It's what she does. Okay. I bet there's a place in town I can go to. I bet Willow Creek will have something."

"Excellent. I suggest you get your ass over there bright and early."

"Definitely."

"And you should propose to her."

"I did," he said. "I proposed to her, and that's why we're getting married soon."

"Did you get down on one knee? I know you didn't give her a ring. Sounds like a pretty half-assed proposal."

"Well, it's different."

"Quit making it different. Give her both. Give her the different that you are, but give her the tradition, too. Because isn't she worth that? Who else is going to do it, Ryder? You think some other bastard is going to propose to her in a couple of years? He won't. Not if you don't screw this up. So if I were you, I would make sure that I was the man that gave her absolutely every damn thing, or expect that someday she'll go find somebody else who will."

That stuck deep in his chest, lodged in a place that he couldn't access. Couldn't shake it free.

"You don't like that," West said. "Good. So I suggest you make sure it's a nonissue."

Ryder nodded and lifted his beer bottle to his lips. "Okay. I can do that."

Romance wasn't really his thing. Never had been. But for Sammy, he would do anything.

And if West thought she needed some trappings in order to make this all feel real, he would give her whatever the hell trappings she needed.

He had never intended to propose to a woman in his life. And now he was fixing to have done it about three times. Because the first time she had refused him. The second time she had accepted. But it hadn't been real. So now he was going to set about to make one as real as he could.

And he knew exactly where to source the help. "I hope that you and Logan aren't busy tomorrow afternoon," he said.

"What do you have in mind?" West asked.

He could see her suddenly, so clearly. His Sammy in a flowing dress under a beautiful arbor. Lots of flowing. That was Sammy. She was a fairy and she should have a fairy wedding, and he didn't know why he suddenly knew that, only that he did.

There's nothing sudden about it.

No. Knowing that was seventeen years in the making. And so was this marriage.

"I'm going to need some help with some building."

"I think I've created a monster."

"With any luck, a monster who's going to be able to hang on to his marriage."

CHAPTER TWENTY-THREE

THE WEDDING WAS TOMORROW, and Sammy was starting to feel jittery. Worse, she was starting to avoid Ryder because whenever she was near him she felt enervated. Like all of her anxieties had twined together and left her feeling completely drained and flat. She hated that. It had never been like that between them.

She would have never thought that a friendship that had spanned seventeen years, her ridiculous rebellious phase where she had basically kicked back against everything in the world just to test her freedom, his grief and the stress that he felt over ensuring that all of his siblings and cousins made it into adulthood, could possibly become complicated.

But it had.

They had survived raging teenage hormones only to be completely overtaken by the heat between them in their thirties.

Now they were getting married because of a pregnancy that had made exploring that heat difficult, and it forced them into another new space entirely. They weren't just friends. They weren't just lovers.

It was all blending together. And it only got yet more blurry when he held her through bouts of morning sickness, his touch intimate but not sexual.

It made her chest ache in good ways she didn't want to explore.

She returned, somewhat triumphantly, to her camper for the evening, and stopped when she saw a note pinned to the door. She pulled it off, recognizing Ryder's blocky handwriting immediately.

Follow the trail.

She looked around and didn't see anyone there. It was getting dark out, the sun sinking down below the mountains, the sky illuminated with gold. The trail...

She looked down, and right next to her foot was a sugar cube.

A small smile touched her lips at the same time her heart crashed hard against her breastbone.

He was baiting her.

And in all their years of friendship, she couldn't recall that happening.

She picked up the first sugar cube, then the next. Then started leaving them behind, because the silly man had put a surplus through the field, and they became more difficult to follow as the grass got taller, but she managed.

Then in the distance she could see it. A big wooden frame wrapped in light suspended high above everything else on the near horizon. White swathes of fabric were wrapped around the frame, with flowers and lights entwined all around.

Magic.

A fairy house right there in the field, just for her.

But they hadn't talked about doing anything like this. In fact, they had basically committed to standing out in a patch of dirt while Pastor Michael came and said all the right words. She quit looking at the sugar cubes and started to run.

Her long skirt whipped against the grass as she did, her hair flying in the breeze behind her. And then she saw him, standing in the center of that big bright creation. She was glad that she had run, because when she stopped about ten feet away from it, from him, she could pretend that the sickening thud of her heart was from physical exertion, and not from wondering what this was.

He was standing there in a black T-shirt, black cowboy hat and jeans, and suddenly she didn't even want him to wear a suit for their wedding. She wanted him like this. Her cowboy. So stalwart and perfect.

Her every cowboy fantasy, which, if it wasn't for him, she wouldn't have at all.

For the first time she wondered if the real reason she had gone for men who were so opposite to Ryder was that anyone who wasn't Ryder would have only ever been a poor substitute.

In reality, that was what they had been. Poor substitutes for the kind of man she had never let herself want. No. Not the kind of man. *The* man. Because… Oh, she had never wanted to want him. Even now, looking at him standing there like this, she felt so stripped bare. So vulnerable. Like he would be able to see all the soft, needy places inside her. Places that she had vowed she would never show anyone ever again.

"You made it," he said.

She nodded wordlessly. She was unable to find a way to get speech through her tightened throat.

"Well, you left a pretty clear trail."

"I tried," he said.

"What is this?"

The light was continuing to ebb, and that made the glow around the structure that Ryder stood beneath all the brighter.

"Did you *make* this?"

He shrugged a shoulder. "I had a little bit of help."

"It's beautiful," she said.

"Come here," he said.

She found herself hesitant to do so. But then he reached out his hand, his eyes intense as they stared into hers. She reached out slowly, and she took his hand.

He pulled her beneath the lights, against his chest, and then he did something she didn't expect. He started to sway, like they were dancing. His hold on her possessive and expert. Then he twirled her, her skirt and hair flying around her in a circle, before he brought her back to his chest. She laughed breathlessly, and he continued to move with her, to no music at all. But she could feel the rhythm between them. The one established by her heartbeat, moving in time with his. Yes, she could feel it.

Could feel it coursing through her like a current. This was something else.

It wasn't friendship. It wasn't sexuality, attraction. It wasn't logical. It wasn't built around doing the right thing, or looking the right kind of way.

He was simply holding her, dancing with her. Like he wanted nothing more than to exist in that moment. In that space. She didn't know when they stopped spinning, because her head still was. Because her heart was still beating out of control, and it wasn't because she was out of breath. Not from the dancing anyway.

She whispered his name, and he kissed it off her lips,

pulling her in and taking it deeper. She felt wrapped in him completely. Those strong arms all around her, big hands pressed firm between her shoulder blades. She loved this. Being utterly and completely surrounded by him. He had always made her feel safe, but now she felt invincible. With her guardian, her rock, wrapped around her like this it felt like there was nothing that could hurt her.

Nothing but him. That thought chased through her like an errant lightning bolt streaking across the dark sky, and she shuddered.

He pulled back and looked down at her. "Is this okay?"

"It's beautiful," she said. "Is it for the wedding?"

"It can be, if you want. But mostly it's for right now. For us, and no one else."

She couldn't understand that. That this was just for a moment. A moment, and not appearances. Not forever. A moment for them.

It all chased around in her head like foxes going after their own tails, and she couldn't grab hold of any of it long enough to make sense of it.

"I need to ask you something, Sammy," he said.

"What?"

Hope burned bright and fierce inside her, and she couldn't quite say why. Or what for. All she knew was that it was blinding and all-consuming. Terrifying.

It filled her, made her want to float into the air, to burst into a million sparkling pieces, because her human body couldn't contain it all. She needed to become something else. Something new.

Something his, maybe, or something more her own. She didn't know.

That was at the heart of all of this. This journey that she had been on from the moment she had opened her mouth outside the Gold Valley Saloon and told Ryder that she wanted to have a baby.

On some kind of journey to herself, and she knew that she hadn't quite found it yet.

And then, suddenly, that big mountain of a man dropped down to his knee in front of her.

She couldn't breathe. She couldn't even think around it. She had never imagined… Had never wanted to imagine him doing such a thing. Because he was the kind of man who had to stand strong and tall for all of his life. A man for whom absolute certainty was essential. And something like this, getting down on his knee with a question in his eye would never and could never be him. At least, she would have said so.

But there he was, on his knee for her. It was something kind of mind-blowing.

Then he reached into his denim jeans pocket, and pulled out a box. A velvet box. Like on those diamond commercials you saw on TV. Where men always looked hopefully at the woman, and the woman cried. A velvet box that was for normal women, who were cherished and cared for.

Who were normal enough to actually be in a commercial, rather than being somewhere left of center enough that they might never see themselves in anything, except as an eccentric caricature. The friend of the heroine, and never the heroine herself.

It was what she was always cast as, at least in her own mind. What she had always been.

The friend who stood off to the side and gave dramatic

bad advice, that led eventually to the heroine getting a ring, obviously. But never the one actually getting it.

She didn't know what to do. How to react. So she just stood frozen.

Until he opened it.

"It's handmade," he said. "And I've been assured that the salt-and-pepper diamond there is ethically sourced. I don't know what all that means, Sammy, or the full implications of it. But I know that it matters to you. And I thought…if I was going to get you a ring, it had to somehow be all the things that you were. It had to be beautiful, and it had to be unique. But it had to be a diamond, because even though this doesn't look exactly like you think when you say diamond, it's still traditional underneath all that. And it had to somehow be a ring that cared about the world and how it all worked, how it would all connect, because that's how you are. So this was the best thing I could find."

She examined it as he held it out to her. It was made with rose gold, and a beautiful princess-cut diamond with colored flecks in it, which was all very trendy in hand-crafted jewelry circles.

And he was right. If there could have been a ring that came right from her own heart, it would've been this one. She couldn't have made herself one so perfect as the one he had found for her, and that was really saying something.

That was a feat. One that only Ryder could've ever pulled off.

"So I never really asked you, not properly. Not like this. And I thought that I ought to have something to offer when I did. Sammy… Samantha, will you marry me?"

A laugh escaped her lips; it was either that or burst into tears and start sobbing, and she didn't want to do that, because everything was so beautiful. He had made this. And he had gone out and found that ring, and now he was down on one knee. And she had never felt more special or herself in her entire life. She wondered if maybe this was it. If maybe this was the journey she had been on, to this destination. One she had never been able to see, because it ended with this. With being Ryder's wife. And it all seemed joyful now, and not half so frightening or traditional for the sake of it.

Suddenly, she wanted to have that ring on her finger, and she wanted to wear it with her wedding dress more than anything else in all the world. She wanted to see his face when she walked down the aisle toward him, and she hoped that it was filled with...

She blinked hard. "Yes," she said. "Yes."

He let out a breath that she hadn't realized he'd been holding, and took the ring out of the box, sliding it slowly onto her finger. Then he stood up, grabbed her and kissed her hard. "Good thing," he growled. "Since we're getting married tomorrow."

She laughed. "Yes. I guess so."

"Sure am sorry that I went about this the wrong way at first. You know, beating my chest and not exactly being... I don't know. Romantic."

That was it. The word she'd been searching for earlier. For the way he held her even when she was clothed. For the way it felt to lean her head on his shoulder. To be near him. To sleep next to him every night, his strong arm around her waist, his breath on her neck.

"We've never been romantic," she whispered. "Friendly. Sexual. But not romantic."

He cleared his throat. "Well, a wise man pointed out to me that if you didn't get any romance from me, you were never going to have it, or you were going to have to find it with someone else. So I figured… I figured I better make some."

It was an amazing thing. It truly was. Because she would have romance. And she would have friendship. And care. And that was all very wonderful. But somehow, she felt like a piece was missing. Standing there with that gorgeous ring on her finger, and the momentary delight and sense of completion she had felt only minutes earlier dimmed.

What was wrong with her? She couldn't seem to find what she was looking for. She couldn't seem to put her finger on it.

"Thank you," she said, smiling. She rested her hand on his chest, looked at the ring that glittered there on her finger.

This moment felt big and it felt good. It felt right. And for a brief segment of time she was happy to rest in that. Happy to simply be.

Because whatever would happen after this, she didn't know. And the giant well of everything that this had opened up inside her was…terrifying. Terrifying in ways she couldn't quite define.

But it was official now. And it was real.

Tomorrow she was going to become Ryder's wife.

CHAPTER TWENTY-FOUR

THE DAY OF the wedding dawned clear and bright. It was already warm, the sun brutal, baking the ground as early as 10 a.m.

There wasn't a cloud in the sky, though, and Ryder supposed he had to go ahead and take that as a good omen.

He kept replaying the previous night over and over in his mind.

It had been something different for them.

He had proposed, and she had accepted. He held her hand and walked her back to the camper and had kissed her good-night. And he had left her there.

Purposing that they would be a little bit more traditional than they had been up until that point, and going ahead and staying away from each other in the hours leading up to the wedding.

He didn't know whether or not she found that romantic. As far as he was concerned, it was about the best he could do. To show her that it meant something. To show her that it wasn't just a throwaway thing.

It mattered to him.

That they were going to make vows. Vows that were essentially already part of who they were. Already a part of their friendship. But it was going to become official today, in front of their friends and God and everybody. And that mattered.

Given the circumstances, he wasn't having the church wedding his mom would have wanted. Or having a priest. But they were on a tight time frame.

They were going to sign paperwork. Ryder Daniels was the kind of man who never defaulted on a loan, never went back on an agreement. Never shook hands on something he couldn't stick to. That meant for him, the wedding was final.

So it mattered. It really did.

He had put on a suit, too. A suit and a black cowboy hat, and the sun was sort of resting on the top of the fabric, mocking him a bit. He imagined this was what it was like to wear a coffin.

Stuffy and completely and totally constricting.

But he was doing it for her. He wanted to do it for her.

They hadn't gone and gotten official with the wedding party, but Logan was his best man. With Iris, Rose and Pansy serving as Sammy's maids of honor.

Iris had outdone herself baking a cake that had scant frosting and flowers and berries pouring over it, serving as decoration.

It was very Sammy.

She had also worked at making a beautiful lunch, which was absolutely overkill, considering the only attendants to the wedding were their family, the minister, his wife and Pansy's fiancé.

It wasn't like it was a big shindig, and not altogether different than the Fourth of July gathering they'd had only a couple weeks earlier.

But everybody had put on their Sunday-go-to-meeting

clothes, and they all looked damn serious, like this was some kind of momentous occasion.

And it added to that constricting sense that Ryder had been noticing not long before.

But then Logan approached him, not in a suit, but wearing a sport jacket, which he had assured Ryder was the best he could do without disintegrating.

"Be good to her," Logan said.

"I will," Ryder said. "I've been nothing but good to her for all these years."

"Yeah. But it's different now."

"Yeah, so everybody keeps saying. I got her a ring."

"Really?"

"I did. That's why we built this big trellis thing. I have a real wedding band in my pocket, too."

"Did you get yourself a ring?"

"If Sammy cares about that she'll make sure I get one."

He didn't know why he was so sure of that. Only that he was.

"You going to wear it?"

"Of course. When I make vows I stick to them. And I'm not going to have any trouble where she's concerned."

"Not going to be tempted to sleep with other women?"

He laughed, the sound rusty, getting stuck in his throat. "I've had trouble forcing myself to look at other women for the past seventeen years. Now that I have her it's not going to be any trouble to look only at her."

"I knew you were in love with her," Logan said. "All this time."

He shook his head. "I wish. I wish it were that easy and that simple. I just want to keep her forever."

"Isn't that love?"

"No," Ryder said. "My parents were so good to each other. They helped each other. Effortlessly completed each other. Didn't clash with each other. They didn't… I don't know. It doesn't matter. They're dead. They're not here today. I'm about to be a father. And in just a few short years I'll be the same age my dad was when he died." He noticed that Logan's face had taken on a strange expression, probably because he was being strange. But he didn't really care. He felt owed his breakdown.

"Life is a bitch. And I'm not going to worry about what this thing between me and Sammy is. I'll take care of her. I promise that much."

"See that you do," Logan said. "And maybe don't worry so much about what somebody else's marriage looked like."

"You never even saw a marriage. How would you know?"

It was a low blow. Digging at the fact that Logan's mom was single.

"True," Logan said. "But then, if I was ever going to fall in love I suppose I would accept the fact that it was going to be my own particular brand of fucked up. Since I have nothing else to compare it to."

"Well. Aren't you enlightened?"

Logan shrugged. "Yeah, pretty much."

"Leave most of that out of your best man speech, please."

Logan pushed his hat back on his head. "Was I supposed to write a speech? I thought I would just tell everybody to drink."

"Stick with that."

After that the pastor showed up, and everybody began to assemble and take their places beneath the canopy.

He stood there, wondering which direction Sammy would come from. It was part of her charm, that they hadn't done any kind of rehearsal. That she had said that he was just going to have to see what happened.

He wondered if she was thinking about her father, because of course, traditionally, a father gave his daughter away when they walked down the aisle. But her father had given her away to Ryder a long time ago. Had turned over those rights as a protector that he wasn't using.

It wasn't that different. It wasn't really.

Except last night had been completely different. Rings and dancing and romance.

Except it felt different, with him standing there in a tuxedo, unable to catch his breath.

He shook hands with Pastor Michael and then stood, waiting.

Rose, Iris and Pansy came up over one of the little hills, linking arms. The three of them were wearing light-colored summer dresses, smiling, and suddenly they reminded him of themselves as children. Something strange twisted in his chest, and he tried to breathe around it. Tried and failed.

Smiling, they stood across from Logan, and he found himself in between the two groups.

The people he loved most in the world, except for the one who was about to stand next to him.

And she was probably the only person on earth they would kill him to protect.

Which was ideal, because if he did something to Sammy, he would deserve it.

And then, he couldn't pay them any attention any-more, because he was looking at that spot on the hill. Where Sammy would appear. Where he would finally see his bride. And then, suddenly there she was. He saw her hair first. All backlit by the sun, a wreath of flow-ers placed over the top of her curls. It was flying wild, like he liked it.

And suddenly, he was bitterly angry with himself for not taking her to bed last night. Because it might do something now to keep him from having this entirely inappropriate reaction to her.

Because you weren't supposed to want nothing more than to immediately skip straight to kissing the bride, and then go to the wedding night. At least not in front of the minister. No. *Hell, no.*

It took him a moment, because he was so captivated by her beauty, to notice the dress.

A real wedding gown, sleeveless, skimming her curves. All beautiful, delicate lace. She was holding a bouquet of wildflowers that he was sure she had proba-bly gone out and picked herself that morning. Because it was who she was. And this was who she was as a bride.

Every inch herself, still.

The impact of that never lessened.

That she was Sammy, the Sammy that he knew, when they kissed. When they made love. And when they got married.

She didn't transform into something else or someone else. Sammy. His Sammy. In a wedding gown, moving toward him.

She lifted up the front of her gown, one hand still

clutched around the bouquet, and she began to run toward him, and his heart stood still.

She was laughing by the time she got to the canopy. "Sorry," she said, breathless. "That was taking too long."

"I agree," he murmured.

She took his hand, and they began the ceremony. The pastor speaking their vows first, with them repeating after.

For better or for worse.

For richer or for poorer.

In sickness and in health.

Forsaking all others.

As long as they both lived.

I do.

And then, Pastor Michael asked if they had rings. He reached in his pocket and took the box out, producing the band that went along with the engagement ring he presented to Sammy the night before.

A little impish smile curved her lips, and she shifted her bouquet from one hand to the other. And that was when he saw the hammered gold band on her thumb. It was big even for that digit, and thick. And clearly for him.

She slipped it off her finger and held it out to him. Then he took her left hand in his, and slipped the band on her finger. And then he gave her his left hand, letting her put the band on his.

"Perfect size," he said.

"Yours, too," she whispered. "Almost like we know each other."

"By the power vested in me by the state of Oregon, but more important, God," Pastor Michael said, that last part feeling like a warning. God was involved and this better stick. It better be real. "I pronounce you husband and wife. You may kiss the bride."

Wife.

It was real.

Husband and wife.

So he did. He grabbed her, and he kissed her like he couldn't bear to let her go. He kissed her until neither of them could breathe. He kissed her, because he thought maybe it could say something that he didn't know how to say. Put to order feelings that were riding around inside him that he didn't have the vocabulary for.

Or maybe he didn't have the balls for them. He didn't really know.

And when he pulled away, everybody clapped. Cheered.

Everybody who had always been there was there, including Sammy. At Hope Springs Ranch. It was also the same, and yet so completely different. He didn't know how to hang on to that feeling and examine it. Didn't even know what to call it. It was all nostalgia wrapped in a brand-new package. And he was afraid of what he might find if he examined it too closely.

The only pictures they got were on everyone's phones, and when they cut the cake Rose was chanting for him to smash it in Sammy's face. But he wouldn't. He wouldn't do that. He was supposed to take care of Sammy, and he would never in a million years do something to disrupt the reverence that he found today.

She laughed and smeared a little bit of frosting on his lips, then surprised him by licking it off, before laughing and kissing him. Then Logan started to play a song on his guitar, and the demand became for them to dance.

He pulled her against him then, and brought her back underneath that arbor. And he was glad that he had done this with her the night before. A dance that was just for the two of them. Because it was fine doing it in front of his family, but it wasn't quite the same as it had been to hold her against him when it wasn't a show.

And when it was all over he fully realized the change that had happened. The shift. Because when he thought of Sammy now she would no longer be his friend first. She would be his wife. And soon, the mother of his child.

His.

That was the bottom line. And wasn't it what he had always known? That from the beginning she was his?

And when he swept her into bed that night—his bed, their bed—the words played over and over in his head. His wife. His wife. His.

He was living a life that he had never imagined wanting.

One that had actively terrified him for as long as he could remember. To have a woman in his arms, in his bed, his house, his heart, that mattered so damned much. Because life was cruel, and loss could hit you when you least expected it, and he knew it better than most. Because to want to hold on to someone so tight was a terror that he had never, ever wanted to experience. Because he knew that no matter how tight you held, someone could be torn from your grasp. Because he knew that love couldn't keep someone with you. No matter how fierce you felt it.

But he had also lived a life that proved that it could bond people together in the throes of grief. And that you could stitch together new things out of broken pieces.

But it was hard to figure out which truth to take on board. It was hard to figure out which thing to let be largest. It was easier, damned easier, to let it be fear. Fear was so easy. He had learned that early.

Because it let you hide. It was the rest of everything that was so much harder.

But as he lay next to his new wife, exhausted from making love with her, looking at her face, relaxed in sleep in the light of the moon coming through the window she had climbed through as a teenager, into a bed that they now shared, that was now theirs, he knew that nothing that beautiful would ever come easy.

And Ryder was a man who had been built for tough.

So that was exactly what he would be.

THEY HAD BEEN married a week. It was a strange thing. Living in the ranch house. And something that she hadn't entirely thought about when they had gotten engaged. She had woken up late that morning, as she had started to do, and he had made sure that there was a bowl of fruit sitting there on the table for her, covered with plastic wrap and all ready for her to eat.

Insult to injury, their baby did not like bacon. And given that bacon was a big foundation of their initial friendship, she felt somewhat betrayed. How on earth had their genetics combined to make a being that didn't care for the most sacred of cured meats? She didn't have an answer to that. She truly didn't.

But she sat down in front of the fruit gratefully and pulled the bowl to herself. Then she heard footsteps in the kitchen. And in walked Ryder, her husband, holding a cup of coffee. He set the coffee down in front of her, and she inhaled.

"You know pregnant women can have one cup. It's fine."

"You're an expert," she said, reaching out gratefully and taking hold of the mug.

"I'm starting to be. So when do you think we ought to make a doctor appointment?"

She looked up at him just before she popped a grape into her mouth. He was so...conventional. And beautiful. She never got tired of him. Looking at him in this new way. She could still see what she had seen for all those years, but she saw new things, too. Like looking at a drawing that had been traced over another. She could still see both versions clearly. And love them both in different sorts of fashions. Her familiar friend was so dear to her, but her lover, her husband, was...infinitely fascinating.

It was amazing how a man she had known for so long could still be surprising. Except, this question did not surprise her. Not really.

"I want a midwife," she said.

The air around her seemed to skip a beat as he reacted to that, a muscle twitching slightly in his cheek.

"You're kidding," he said.

"No," she said. "I want a midwife."

"I... I don't understand. That was like the kind of thing you had when you lived on the prairie and couldn't get an actual doctor."

"Incorrect. But thank you for dropping your penis knowledge onto this very female subject."

That cheek tick again. "You need a doctor."

"I want a midwife, and I want home birth."

"Absolutely not," he said. "Sammy, that's insane."

"Many, many people have home births," she said pragmatically.

"Yes, people used to have home births back in those prairie days I was just talking about. And they died."

"Do you hear yourself right now? If there's an emergency, the midwife will be equipped with a kit. And, we are not that far from the hospital."

"We are very far from the hospital," he said. "It is forty-five minutes to Tolowa. They would have to airlift you. That's expensive. Ask me how I know."

"I know," she said. "I know that you had airlifted siblings on your watch. But I'm not going to need to be airlifted. Anyway, thank you for showing your concern through your wallet."

"I don't give a damn about my wallet. I would pay to have you airlifted out of here for fun if I thought it would make you more comfortable. I'm just saying I don't want you to be in an emergency. I can't even imagine… Sammy, I could not load you onto a helicopter while you are in labor with my baby and let them take you off to Tolowa, and have to follow behind you in a car. It would kill me."

"News flash," she said. "This whole thing is not in your control. And it's just something you're going to have to let me make some decisions about. Women have been having children for thousands of years."

"And dying doing it for just as long."

She made an exasperated sound. "Is it all death with you?"

"Wouldn't it be to you if you were me?"

She looked at him, at the lines on his face. Lines that he had started earning when he was far too young.

"Okay. I get it. You're scared. You're scared about this kind of stuff, and you want to be the most responsible. But it is my choice, Ryder. I want to do this my way. And I think my way is good."

"I know you do," he said. "Sammy, I know that you aren't intentionally going to do something to hurt yourself or the baby, but I worry that it might."

"You're going to worry either way."

"Sammy, we're married now. We live together. Our lives are part of each other's. You can't just be a free spirit and do whatever you want."

"A very interesting point," she said drily. "Since the same goes for you. You don't just get to tell me what to do all the time. It can't just be about managing your anxiety. I have to be able to live. You're right. Our lives are wrapped around each other's, but that doesn't mean the person with the most anxiety wins."

"Sammy..."

"You have to trust me," she said, putting her hand on his arm. "Remember what we talked about a few months ago? I know that sometimes you see me as haphazard, but I promise you I'm not. I am just as much of a control freak as you are. I want to have the baby at home because I want to be able to do it on my terms. I understand that you're worried about it not being in a hospital, and there not being doctors everywhere. But the last time I went to a hospital it was because my father..." She shook her head. "I don't want to be there to bring my baby into the world. I get that it doesn't make a lot of sense to you, but that is how I feel. You have taken care of me for a very long time. Let me do something for you. Let me…"

She stood up and bracketed his face with her hands, then she moved her thumbs to his forehead and began to massage the lines there. "I don't want to make you more stressed. I want to make you less." She kissed his lips.

"Yeah, that's not how this works," he said. "The caring stuff."

"Why can't you just be… I don't know. You're so worried about everything all the time."

"Because everything has been my responsibility for a long damn time. It's easy for you to say that I worry too much. But if I wasn't around worrying, who would… Who would do everything? Who would have made sure those kids made it to adulthood? Who would have kept the ranch going? Somebody has to worry."

Her heart twisted. "Okay. I understand that. Then can you let me be whatever the opposite of that is?"

His dark eyes were serious on hers. "Sunshine," he said. "It's sunshine. And you've been that for seventeen years. You gave me strength, Sammy. Warmth I didn't have. Without you… I don't think I would have made it."

All of the irritation drained out of her and she stretched up on her toes, kissing him gently on the mouth. "Thank you."

He grabbed her hands and took them from his face, then squeezed them. "You're welcome. And it's true. I will be willing to do extensive research on this home birth thing."

"I guess coming from you that's a compromise."

"It's probably as good as you're gonna get."

"I don't know. We'll see about that."

"Marriage is about compromise," Ryder said.

"And in this case, compromise is probably going to mean one of us just not getting what they want."

"Don't test me."

She laughed. "Honey, there is baby-naming to do. Is this the hill you want to die on?"

"Surely you wouldn't…"

"Rain. River. Forrest. Sunshine."

"Shit."

"Minerva. Severus. Luna."

"No."

"Frodo."

"No."

"You only get so many vetoes in the birthing process, my friend. I'm just saying, use them wisely. Or your son may grow up to believe his one true quest is to throw a magic ring into a volcano."

He narrowed his eyes. "I don't even get that reference."

He was a liar. And she loved it. "The sad thing for you is I know you do get the reference. Because you spent time in my company."

"You can't do that to a child."

"Yes, I can. That's the beauty of being the mother. It will teach him to stand firm in his individuality from a very early age."

"It will teach them how to take a punch to the face."

"Well, one must learn that, too."

"You wouldn't really."

"Wouldn't I?"

"I said I would research it."

"Wonderful. I'll make an appointment with a midwife."

"Sammy…" He took a sharp breath. "I know I can't do this for you. And that's what kills me. I have to let you take the risk and go through the pain. And I'll… I'll trust you to do it how you see best."

Her heart suddenly felt too large, and sore along with it. "Ryder…"

"I know you're strong," he said.

"I never thought you didn't."

She stretched up and kissed him on the cheek. They would be all right.

They had to be.

CHAPTER TWENTY-FIVE

THERE WERE CRYSTALS hanging in the window, and Ryder really would have given anything to be sitting anywhere else. It was like Sammy's chakras had exploded all over the room. Which, he supposed, was why his wife looked so giddy to be sitting there in the presence of the midwife, who had long gray hair and a calming demeanor.

"You don't put crystals on the baby, do you?" Ryder asked.

"No," the woman, who was in fact named Sequoia, said. "I can put crystals on the mother, if she likes. And you can have some, too."

He sensed a faint hint of sarcasm in that.

"I'm good."

He had a feeling Sequoia wasn't shocked by his rejection. Everything in here looked airy-fairy hippie-dippie dipped in incense and essential oils, and he could feel himself standing out against it all, in a black T-shirt, jeans and a cowboy hat. Like some deeply rooted relic of the past in the middle of…well, some relics that were deeply rooted in the past, sure, but one that felt pretty damned alternative to him.

"I might want crystals," Sammy replied.

Ryder rubbed the bridge of his nose. "Okay. So crystals aside. How exactly does this work?"

Sequoia went about explaining the process, and how some women opted for a water birth, and that she could provide the tub for a rental fee.

"So you put a tub in the bedroom?"

"Wherever you want it," she said, "but I think it's best if it's next to a bed in case Sammy wants to move around."

"Okay," he said. "But what about…it being sterile and everything."

"You know, hospitals are sterile, but there are a lot of illnesses and infections in them, as well."

"Yeah, I get that. It's not like you can clear the air." He sighed. "But what if there's an emergency?"

"I have a hemorrhage kit. I have a whole kit for the baby. I used to be an RN," she said. "So I've dealt with emergencies in hospital situations, and I've been a midwife for twenty years. I've seen almost every scenario, and I'm fairly prepared for it. I also won't hesitate to send mother and baby to the hospital if it comes to that. So don't think that I'm going to try to make it all happen at home on principle. First and foremost the important thing is that Sammy and baby come through it all healthy. When and where that happens is secondary. It's wonderful when everything goes according to plan, but often babies have their own whims and schedules. You can't get too married to a plan anyway."

That was like his nightmare. But then, everything about the past few months hadn't gone according to his plan, and if he was honest with himself in general he was much happier than he would have ever thought something like this could make him.

Because it wasn't just a random woman and a random baby. It was Sammy. And it was their baby.

"All right, I take your point there."

"Well, no decisions have to be made yet. My schedule does fill up, so give me a call in about four weeks and let me know if you'd like to have me. I can help with prenatal exams. And I can come to the house. I have a Doppler to check the heartbeat and all of that."

"Right," he said.

After the meeting with the midwife, they drove back into town.

It was teeming with people, which was pretty typical in summer. The influx of tourists who enjoyed getting out and seeing a historic town was necessary for the businesses that were in Gold Valley, but he always found them slightly annoying. It was his town, and he liked that it was small. Liked that he didn't typically have to fight to get a table at the Mustard Seed. Though he did have to do a little bit of fighting today. It was a small building, and it took time for a patio table to open up for him and Sammy. It was later in the day, so she could eat more than fruit, and he was relieved when she ordered a hamburger, french fries and a milkshake. It was a lot more typical of her, and that made him feel better about things in general.

Her eyes lit up as soon as the french fry basket hit the table, and she dove right into them, chewing happily.

And it was like the world turned on its head and suddenly from that angle he could see.

He could really see.

That it didn't matter how his parents had loved each other. It had nothing to do with him. He'd lived through loss. And he'd carried a weight for so many years that everything he felt had teeth and claws.

That he was so aware of the cost of caring it felt like dying sometimes.

But that didn't mean it wasn't love.

No.

It might even be deeper because he was so very, very aware of what it felt like to lose people.

And Sammy… He didn't know what to call that feeling he had for her because it felt like it was as intrinsic to him as the blood in his veins. It was natural, like the beating of his heart, like every breath he took.

It felt deeper than anything.

He'd equated it to obsession. Need. Possession.

Living.

But he'd been too afraid to call it what it was.

"I love you," he said.

In the moment the words left his mouth he knew that he meant them in every way.

That it had been true for a very long time. And it was even truer at this moment.

That he loved her as a friend, that he loved her as a wife, as the future mother of his child.

She smiled vaguely. "You know I love you, too."

And he could hear, in the way she spoke that word, that she only meant it the one way. The way that they had said to each other pretty effortlessly over the past many years.

"No," he said, picking up one of his own french fries. "I'm in love with you."

"Oh," she said and some of the joy seemed to go out of her french fry eating.

"That's not so far away from where we've been, is it?"

"I don't know. You know how I feel about…labeling things."

"Yeah. But we kind of do have labels now. Husband and wife."

She didn't say anything. Instead, she took a sip of her milkshake and then started picking at the top of her hamburger.

"You don't have to say it," he said.

And he found that he really did mean that. He didn't need her to say it. Not now. Someday, it would be nice. But as he looked at her, the chains that had been holding him in place seemed to fall away. And he experienced a kind of lightness that he didn't think he was capable of feeling. And yeah, along with it came some terror. But it was more that he would have felt afraid of losing her no matter what he called it. He'd been afraid of losing her. Had been consumed by trying to find ways to not call what he felt for her what it was. Because he had been in love with Samantha Marshall from the beginning. She wasn't just his sunshine; she was his heart. And it had been beating because of her all this time. She was the reason. His Sammy. His beautiful Sammy. And yeah, he wanted her to love him. The way that he did her.

But if she didn't, that wasn't a tragedy.

He'd lived through tragedy. And he had promised her that nothing would break them. He had promised that he would hold steady. He had promised. And he would.

Loving her could only ever be a gift.

She nodded. "Okay."

This moment was familiar, too. Sitting in the diner. Eating hamburgers. But this moment wasn't recognizing his feelings, giving names to them. He had avoided that for a long time. He didn't know if it was common to have a revelation and a breakdown over a cheeseburger, but he sure as hell was. And he was too consumed by the implications of his own feelings to fully process that she was essentially saying she didn't love him. But he couldn't even get to that place. Not yet. Someday, maybe. But not yet.

"I've loved you for a long time," he said, his voice rough. "I just want you to know that."

Because he wanted to say it. Because he wanted to know it. Wanted to feel it. He had always felt like Sammy was his freedom. The embodiment of emotions and exuberance that he could never inhabit. But the truth of the matter was, she made him feel all those things. She was the key to it, and he had locked it away for all this time because he had been afraid to call it what it was. Because he had been afraid of what it meant. Of the fact that it would mean tying himself down like this. Of the fact that it would mean marriage and kids, or it would mean rejection and heartbreak, and he had already experienced loss that had been like a bullet to the chest and he still had the shrapnel there. He had known that he couldn't take on any more. But it was Sammy, and he couldn't not.

Because he had tied himself down. Lost himself to this ranch, to this life, in part so that he would always be entwined with her. He had made himself a mountain, a rock, a man who felt nothing so that he could handle all that he believed they could ever be.

This was freedom. And now that he knew what it was, it wasn't half as terrifying as the alternative.

"Okay," she said. He was tempted to be hurt by that,

when he looked into her eyes and saw the kind of hollow fear that he had seen on her face that night he had rescued her from her father. And he ached.

"We're in this together," he said. "Either way. No matter what."

She nodded. And then they went back to eating. And he couldn't help but marvel at the fact that one of the deepest, most spiritual moments of his life had occurred at the Mustard Seed Diner, and that it had passed as quietly as it had come on ferociously.

And that it would leave him with an ache in his soul. Because his beautiful sunshine girl was somewhere lost in the dark, and he didn't know how to reach her.

So he would just love her until he did.

CHAPTER TWENTY-SIX

EVERY MORNING SAMMY woke up with a panicked feeling rattling around in her chest. And every morning it took her a little while to identify exactly what it was that had her feeling so panicked.

He was in love with her. Ryder was in love with her. And he hadn't asked her to say it back. In fact, he had told her she didn't have to.

Which made it worse. Because she knew that he wanted something from her he wouldn't even ask for. Or demand.

She'd asked for it once.

She blinked. Trying to calm her heart rate.

Ryder was long gone, up and out of bed and working, and she was in the house alone. But it didn't do anything to help.

She shuffled downstairs, and she found her bowl of fruit sitting on the table. That bowl of fruit that he made for her every morning.

Just one of the many ways that he had shown her that he loved her before ever saying it.

She didn't know why it was terrible, only that it was. She didn't know why it frightened her like this, only that it did.

It didn't have to. It didn't. She could be with him, and it didn't have to be love.

She could still protect herself.

She couldn't eat the fruit, because suddenly her stomach felt off. She went back to her caravan and just sat for a while. Because she thought maybe being there would make her feel… She didn't know. Safe? Back in the role that she was used to?

When she had been his friend who lived next door, and not his wife, who lived in his house and was pregnant.

Okay. She couldn't go back. After a couple of hours in the camper, she made that conclusion.

She couldn't just hide away in here and pretend that nothing was happening. That was impossible, and even she wasn't delusional enough to think it was possible.

None of it mattered. She decided that about the time she had all of her jewelry-making supplies laid out on the kitchen table. It didn't matter what anything was called. They didn't need to get into stuff like that. If he wanted to say that, he could. But in her experience, all those words didn't need to matter quite so much. And they could just continue on as they had been. Bonded together in a really significant way that didn't need words and labels and all of that.

Everything really could be fine. He'd said that it could be. So it could be.

And she wanted… Well, she wanted to find a way to take this little hiccup they'd experienced and turn it into something more.

Because she had been reluctant to make love since he'd said that. And he hadn't pushed it.

He hadn't pushed her at all. Which wasn't like him. He was just letting her sit back and stew. Normally, he was a lot more... Well, exactly the way he had been with the midwife. Encouraging her to make meetings, and then sitting there, asking all the questions, forcing the conversation.

But he hadn't been like that, not since he had told her that he loved her.

Well, she didn't want that. She wanted him to be him. So she would have to be her.

With great purpose she stood up and began to put her jewelry fixings away. Then she went upstairs and found the sexiest white lace lingerie that she had. And she had quite a bit. She liked white, and Ryder seemed to very much like her in white.

He liked her even better out of it, and she intended to go ahead and tempt him.

She tiptoed out of the house, her sexy secret concealed beneath the gauzy white dress, and began to go on a quest to find her husband.

HE WAS WORKING outside the barn, sweat pouring off him, when his wife approached.

Things hadn't been great in the days following his revelation. Not between them.

He had thought that it would be easy to throw the words out there and not ask for anything back. And he could see that no matter what she said about labels and how words didn't change anything, they had. Because for the past few days his Samantha had been running scared from him, avoiding his touch, avoiding his kiss. And he wasn't going to push. Not here, not now. There had been a time when he would have. But not on this.

He couldn't. Because there would've been no pushing him into this revelation, either.

He had a lot of theories about why it had happened, at the Mustard Seed Diner, over a hamburger. Why the words had rolled through his soul like the first rumblings of thunder before a catastrophic storm.

Because love was like that, he supposed.

That it could be there, growing inside you and you wouldn't know. For all that time.

At least, that was how it was for him. But Logan telling him that he was in love with Sammy hadn't made him understand the words for himself. And the first time they'd made love, when he'd known that joining his body to hers had changed the fabric of what he was forever, hadn't spoken those words to him, either.

Wedding vows hadn't done it.

Because there was nothing on the outside that could ever make you see. Not when you didn't want to.

It caught him in the moment she had bitten into a french fry. The most innocuous and normal thing he could even think of.

But every moment, every scent, every sight, was more beautiful because of her. There wasn't a breath he could take that wasn't infused by the loving of her. And the simple truth was it was so deeply a part of the entirety of who he was that the words hadn't formed around it until all those changes had happened. It had taken every last one of them. Sex. Pregnancy. Marriage. Fear. And in those spaces, the words had finally found purchase on his soul.

And now they were imprinted there, he couldn't unknow it. That he loved her more than he loved anything.

He had known that he would kill for her, but now he knew he'd die for her. He had known that he couldn't live without her, but now he knew that he would do whatever it took, change whatever he had to, to live with her, which was an infinitely harder, sharper and more brilliant fantasy than the fear of loss could ever be.

The joy and the challenge of bending yourself and your life around someone else. Finding the better in the worse, the rich in the poor.

Yeah. Realizing that he was in love with her changed nothing. And everything, all at once.

And now she was here, and the breath in his lungs caught and held as he braced himself for what might come next. She looked beautiful. That ray of light she'd always been, streaming into his life and warming him with her brilliance. Lighting the path for him.

"Hi," he said.

Weird now how sometimes it was hard for him to find the words to say to her. They never had that problem before all this. But it was like West had said. The interactions between them suddenly felt heavier. And the potential for pain much larger.

Everything had a higher cost, a higher weight.

"I came to… I thought we might take a walk," she said.

"Okay," he said, putting his pitchfork down. Immediately. Because if she wanted his attention, he was going to give it.

"What's on your mind?" he asked as the two of them set off down the path toward the river that flowed through the property. She didn't hold his hand. And she wasn't looking at him.

"I just wanted to… To be with you."

"All right," he said, knowing he sounded skeptical and cautious. Feeling a bit skeptical and cautious.

But he couldn't deny her. Couldn't turn away from her.

He would follow Samantha Marshall wherever she went for as long as he lived. She had snared him that day seventeen years ago with a sugar cube in her outstretched hand and hope in her eyes and he'd been a goner ever since.

And he wasn't even sorry about it. Not at all.

They made it down to the thick, dense package of trees that was near the water, that protected them from the harshest light of the sun. That was when she turned to him, wrapped her arms around his neck, pressed her breasts against his chest and kissed him.

The impact of it hit him like a sledgehammer. She hadn't touched him like this, not since he'd told her he loved her.

And he was just human enough to be consumed by it. Even though he knew he should find out what was going on. Even though he knew there had to be more to this than she was letting on, he had to surrender to it, because with Sammy, there was no other choice. When her mouth was on his, he couldn't much think.

They pulled back for a moment, and that was when he looked into her eyes. And saw that they were guarded. That she was trying to hide herself from him, and somehow was pretending she was opening up.

Sammy. Being outrageous yet again, trying to control what happened between them.

"Let go," he whispered, bringing his mouth to hers. "Let go, Samantha."

She said nothing. Instead, she squeezed her eyes shut tight and kissed him again. She started to pull at his clothes, quickly, frantically, and he grabbed hold of her wrists, pinning them behind her back and deepening the kiss, taking it slow, achingly so. She arched against him. "Come on," she murmured. "I need you."

"You need to let someone else be in charge," he said firmly. "And don't you give me that *I'm always in control*. It's not true, Samantha."

"Stop it," she said. "Only you call me Samantha."

"I know," he said. "And I'm the only one who ever will. I'm your husband. I'm your best friend. And this is it for me. This is it for me," he repeated. "I want to take my time."

"Well," she said, still sounding petulant and bratty. "If this is it for you, then we have forever."

"Exactly," he said. "So what does time matter anyway? We can make forever this moment if we want." He looked at her, at her beautiful, slight curves, enticing and visible through the thin fabric she was wearing. She had some kind of witchcraft on beneath her top and skirt, and he could barely see what it was, but he was dying to get the view.

He lifted her up off the ground, and she protested for a moment, then gave in, as he carried them both down to the river. He set her down, and she just stood there, looking at him, her face beautiful, glowing, as the sunlight filtered through the trees. Unreadable by design.

"Why are you hiding from me now?"

"You're crazy," she said. "You don't know what you're talking about."

"Maybe not," he said. "Maybe I just want to think I know you. Maybe I never will. Not really."

That idea filled him with despair, almost more than anything else. That he might never get down to the bottom of who she was. That he might never reach her heart.

He wanted to know her.

Every inch.

Inside and out.

He wanted her to know him in ways he didn't even want to know himself.

Something about his words seemed to penetrate, and she registered fear on that beautiful face.

"Does that scare you? That I might not even know?" he asked. "That I might not be able to tell you?"

"Nothing scares me," she said. "I've been to hell and back. I grew up in a house where looking at someone in the wrong direction would mean physical repercussions. My own father put me in the hospital. Nothing scares me."

But he did. He scared her. Not in that way, but he could see it, could sense it.

And he had to wonder if even more than him, Sammy was scared of herself.

He stripped his shirt off, cast it onto the ground, and then he undid his belt buckle, the button on his jeans, kicked his boots off before sliding his pants and underwear down, leaving himself naked there by the river.

"You're always after me to skinny-dip. Might as well give it a try."

He picked her up again and carried her out into the

water, fully clothed. He watched as the river soaked through her shirt, giving him a tantalizing view of her white lace underwear beneath, and the dark shadow of her nipples.

"I've never seen a more beautiful sight than you, Sammy Marshall. And I've been looking at you for seventeen years. The greatest gift over the past couple of months has been seeing your beauty in all these different ways. It's like a miracle. Being so familiar with you and seeing you for the first time. Like a damn miracle."

He kissed her, out in that water, and the cold didn't do anything to dampen his arousal. Her hands were slick on his back as they kissed, and she began to shiver, began to shake. Then she slipped from his arms and beneath the surface of the water, swimming away from him, the white fabric she was wearing floating around her, her blond hair a pale cloud. And when she emerged from the water on the other side of the river, she climbed up the rocks and sat on the edge, her knees pulled up to her chest, her blond hair hanging in limp twists around her face. A bedraggled fairy.

He felt like for the first time he might finally be seeing what she was. Without all her enchantment, without all that magic.

And she was still perfect to him.

Even like this. Frightened and sitting on a rock, reduced by that fear.

But he didn't want her to be afraid.

He swam across the space and climbed up beside her, taking care to avoid the sharp rocks, given that he didn't have the protection of clothing. She looked up at him, and for a moment he saw all that unmasked fear in her eyes. Confusion.

He felt like he was staring down at her like on that night he found her being beaten by her father. When he had carried her out of that house and looked down at her then.

His heart ached. To think that he had caused her pain that somehow echoed back to that.

He wanted to catch her up and protect her. And when she shivered again, that was exactly what he did. He swept them both up from the rocks, and carried her to a patch of grass that sat in the sun. This part of the ranch was generally unoccupied, as it took crossing the river or driving on the road that encircled the place to get back here. So he had no worries about being caught. There was nothing to do but simply lie in the sun on that soft, sweet patch of grass.

He looked at her body, beautiful and pale, droplets of water sliding over her skin, the sun drying her slowly. He put his hand on her stomach, where their child grew, and then he slid it down to her hip, then between her thighs, stroking her as he lowered his head for a kiss. He kept on doing that until she was sobbing, her breath catching on each small noise.

This woman.

This woman had come into his life and burst through all the grief and pain and darkness.

And he wanted to do it for her. It wasn't about her loving him back. He wanted that more than anything. Except this.

He wanted to find her. So that she could find herself.

He wanted her to be able to shine her own light all the way down inside.

To be healed by him in the way that he felt healed by her.

"I love you," he whispered. And then he kissed her, positioning himself between her thighs and thrusting home. Her blue eyes widened, and then she closed them tight.

CHAPTER TWENTY-SEVEN

SAMMY WONDERED IF this was what dying felt like. Being stripped bare. Reduced to a raw nerve both inside and out. It was too much. Her heart felt scrubbed raw, and so did her skin. The feeling was just now returning to it fully from that dip in the water, and it was like icy pinpricks were dotting her skin with flashes of heat in between. And then there was Ryder. Over her. In her. His eyes burning into hers with an intensity that made her need to look away.

Because he could see her.

He could see her, and she couldn't even see herself.

There was nothing but confusion, white noise. Except then he had whispered that he loved her. And he had entered her body. And that noise had quieted, everything centering down to him, to the moment.

And there was something almost more frightening about that quiet, about that calm. Because it had come from him. And it spoke of need.

And something else she didn't want to uncover.

So she closed her eyes, and she tried to hide. Even as pleasure buffeted her. As desire made her mindless, need made her senseless.

"Look at me," he whispered.

And she obeyed. She obeyed because she could do nothing else.

When those eyes met hers again she felt him. All of him, searing her right down to her soul.

And he was… He was the steadiest, best man that she had ever known. Or ever could know. And he wanted something from her. And he would never, ever leave her. He was in it for real. Because that was who he was.

Even if it made him miserable. Even if he never…

He had said to her that he had to be romantic because if it wasn't him it wouldn't be anyone else, because he was marrying her and they were forever. And it was the same for him. He wouldn't have anyone else. Because she was his wife. And if she couldn't give him the words then no one would.

She would make him miserable for the rest of his life. She already had. She had burst in a tangle of complication that a man like Ryder would have never found on his own. Because he was far too good, far too organized, and the universe had dealt its blow to him already. The way that it had treated him taking his parents away…

And that she had just heaped chaos on top of it.

And he was good. He took care of people. It was what he did.

And he thought he was in love with her. Because that was who he was.

He had married her, so now he thought he was in love with her. But he wasn't. And he would go on thinking that for as long as she was his wife, because of course he was a man who would endeavor to love his wife. Of course he was. Because he was good down to his soul. And she was a creature whose own father had been enraged by the sight of her. Whose mother had never once defended her.

She had stitched herself into the quilt of this family, and they had opened their arms and accepted her, but she wasn't one of them. They were united by a common tragedy and she had simply come and covered herself in the protective layer they had created for their own selves.

She was selfish.

Selfish and needy, and she didn't think there would ever be an end to it.

Someday she would look at him. She would look at him and she would ask if he loved her. It brought her to the edge of terror. Because he thought he meant it, he truly did, but someday he would realize that he was in a prison. A prison he hadn't chosen, but one he had been locked in by his own good intentions. And she wouldn't be able to bear that. When he looked at her with disgust, too. She would never be able to weather that.

And she knew then that he could see all of that, that mess of terror, that mess of need, that endless well that would never be filled. That he saw the sad, wounded creature that she was underneath it all.

That girl who couldn't control anything, not at all. Who was helpless and frightened and sad. She hid that girl from everyone.

And she was so confident and sure with her smiles, with her attitude, with the way that she acted around him, and she pretended it was honest. The most honest. That she just said whatever came into her mind; she pretended for him, for everyone, and most especially for herself.

Now that she was the least able to hide, she saw just how much she did. Only when she had become aware of needing to conceal things from him did she realize that she'd been doing it all along.

Because that girl…

How could that girl take what he was offering?

"Sammy," he said gruffly.

She opened her eyes again, and he thrust deep, a spear of pleasure coursing through her. And she gave herself up to him, because she had no other choice. Because when this was over, it would all be over. She had come out here to reclaim something and had found the end.

Because she had found the center of herself.

Selfish and needy and *small*. She wanted to weep with it.

Because she had been so sure that she would find something glorious and brilliant in all her revelation. In her seeking after a new piece to who she was.

But she didn't. Instead, she looked inside herself and found something contemptible.

A woman who had attached herself to a man who had already been through enough.

And she knew that it would be up to her to set them both free.

But she pushed that away for now. Pushed it to the side. Because she could only feel now. And he was in her. He was with her. Making her bright and brilliant and more than she could ever hope to be on her own.

He lit her up.

With burning brilliance.

And that was when she realized that he had always been her sun. Her guiding light. The source of her life. And if she had given him anything it was only because she was reflecting that light back on to him.

He thrust into her one last time and growled, and she found her release on a sob.

Ryder.

Who stood so strong in the wake of insurmountable force.

She couldn't bear him not having everything because he was taking care of her instead.

And she couldn't bear for the resentment that would breed. And what it would do to her. To their child.

She had *been* that child.

Oh, she and Ryder would never be angry fists and abuse. But resentment could take so many shapes, and twist even good people. In fact, she was certain that in some ways it could twist good people in more subtle, sharp ways.

He would stay. And stay and stay. No matter what.

"I have to go," she whispered, slipping away from him and peeling herself away from the wet grass.

"Why?" he asked.

"I don't mean back to the house. I mean… I need to go away."

"What are you talking about?"

"It was my original plan. To leave here. To go and find some adventure. To find myself."

"And you decided the time to revisit that plan would be after you got pregnant with my baby and married me?"

"I'm not revisiting. I'm… I'm remembering why. Why this was important to me. And I've been dealing with all of the… This isn't going to work."

"What do you mean it isn't going to work? We just made love outside. I'm in love with you. I made vows to you. Nothing says more about how well this could work than that."

"Because it's about me," she said. "I can't do this." As soon as the words tripped off her tongue she felt them rebound against her. She tried to take a breath, but found that she couldn't. She didn't know how to articulate all of the things that were rattling around inside her and they would make her feel too exposed anyway. So she decided to lean in to what she let everyone think she was. To what he seemed to think she was sometimes.

"I told you that I wanted to find myself. I haven't yet."

"Bullshit," he said. "You don't mean that. So what is this really about?"

She was naked with the man. With Ryder. Who she would have said was absolutely 100 percent too much of a stick in the mud to ever be naked out in the middle of the woods. Let alone naked and having this conversation. But he had done this with her, because of her.

And he said that he loved her.

Maybe he means it.

How would he know? He'd had every choice in life taken from him from such an early age. And he was...

He was beautiful.

And it reminded her of being seventeen again, to look at him and ache like this. She had wanted so much to join his family. Had watched them over the fence and thought that everything would be perfect if she could just be with them. But it was so much more complicated than that. Oh, how she wished it weren't. Oh, how she wished it could be that simple.

"I don't want to be married," she said softly. "I told you that. But you pushed me and... And backing off when it comes to declarations of love and all of that... It doesn't erase the fact that you pushed me into this part. And it isn't what I want."

His face had gone blank, his whole body tense. "Go, then. Do what you need to do. I'll be here when you get back."

"That's not what I'm asking for."

"And I said that nothing would break us. I said that. And I meant it. I still do. Nothing is going to break us, Sammy, not without our permission. *Your* permission. I won't leave you. I won't forsake you. I've been here for you all this time, and I'll be here when you get back. No questions asked."

"That's the problem," she said. Anger rioted through her. "That's the problem. You don't know what it's like to choose something because you want it, Ryder Daniels. The only thing you know how to do is to martyr yourself to responsibilities. And I won't be one more."

"So now you get to tell me why I do things? What I feel?"

"I know you," she said. "It was never sugar cubes. It was never the sugar cubes. You couldn't resist the pitiful girl folded up in the corner of your barn. And you took me and you made the best of me just like you did every other thing that's been thrown at you in your life. And I can't live in that forever. And you shouldn't, either."

"That's not it," he said. "I was a man...a boy... drowning in responsibilities. Absolutely and completely dragged under the water with them. And you... You were my first glimpse of sunlight in all that time. Sammy Marshall, when I saw you I saw salvation and I reached a hand out. You're right. It was never the sugar cubes. It was *you*."

He cupped her face, his eyes searing into hers. "Your hand. Your face. Your eyes. I wanted you from the moment that I first saw you, and I was willing to love you in the way that I could, in the way that you could take, in the way that it could be for all that time, but it's over now. The time for waiting. The time for holding back."

"I think that you believe that. I really do. But I don't think it's true. I think there's more at play here than that. And I just… It's not the life I want." She sucked in a sharp breath, and she prepared to do one thing that she had never done to him before.

"Why?"

"I never wanted love. I didn't ask for it. Don't keep me caged. You know I can't stand that."

He nodded once. "Sure. But I need you to know something. I'm not your father. And if you look at me and ask me for love, you won't get my fist. You'll just get my heart."

"I know that," she said. "Don't you think I know it? And it doesn't make this any easier. But I won't live a life that I don't want. I was born into one. I'll never stay in one. Our child deserves more than that."

Those last words burned. Because she was lying. And using the baby along with it. And he might not thank her now. He might hate her now. But he would've only hated her later. And that… That would have been unendurable.

The cost.

The cost of waiting for a punch—not to her face—but to her soul. That was the one thing she couldn't fathom.

To take away all her protective layers and to be destroyed later. When her walls were down.

By the one person that she wanted to trust. That she wanted. More than anything.

"I think that later you'll understand," she said. "I'm protecting us."

"I've walked away from you a number of times," he said. "The time I first tasted you in the camper. After the first time we had sex, I let you walk away. And I didn't say anything. I'm not going to walk away now. And I'm not going to let you walk away without hearing this. You're running scared, baby. I know you. Nobody else knows you the way that I do. And I can see it. And that's why you're running. Because you're scared of something. You let me rescue you once. You let me fight for you. Let me fight for you now. Trust me."

"You're right. You did rescue me. And you've done it a hell of a lot more than once. I can't rely on you to do that forever. I have to go out and figure out how to rescue myself. Otherwise… If I lose you I'll be left with nothing. I'll be nothing more than a sad, spineless… I'll be my mother. I can't. For our baby I can't."

"And what about me? Where will I fit? Because I'm not going to be a favorite uncle, Sammy. I am his father, and I will be a father."

His eyes were hard, blazing with emotion, and she couldn't bear to look at him. "No, of course… I'm not… I'll never keep the baby from you, Ryder, but that's not us. I can't do us."

And so she did walk away. And she had to swim across the damn river, crawl out naked and shivering and disgraced, rather than feeling cherished and sensual as she had done when she'd been carried into the river. She gathered her clothes, and she dressed. And he was still standing there watching her. True to his word, he wasn't gone. True to his word, he remained. So damn loyal. So damn fearless.

Not her.

She was a coward.

But she couldn't face the alternative. So cowardice it was.

But as she went back to the camper and looked around at the tiny place she had not called home now for over a week, she knew that it was more than cowardice. Whatever she was doing required that she leave her heart behind.

But she was afraid of it. Because it hurt. Because it was shattered.

But if she left it behind, maybe she could keep on breathing.

CHAPTER TWENTY-EIGHT

IT WASN'T UNTIL Ryder woke up the next morning and saw that the camper was gone that he truly believed what Sammy had said.

She had left him.

She had left him.

His wife. His love.

Sammy.

She hadn't taken all of her things out of their room, but she had taken her jewelry. And as the sun rose up over the mountains, he didn't go out and do his work. Instead, he prepared a bowl of fruit like he had done every morning and left it in her spot. Then he went out to the front porch and sat in one of the wooden chairs. And just sat. Sat until the sun was far too high up over those mountains. Until the sun had lit up the world around him and illuminated it in stark reality, made it impossible for him to pretend that maybe it was a dream.

He'd said that he loved her, and she'd thrown it back at him.

She'd told him that he never had a choice.

But he did. He could've chosen to stay in his fear, to stay in his grief, and he had chosen bravery. But those words hadn't been there. Not then. Because all that had been there was shock. He had believed that nothing could break them. But it turned out that she could.

And he was turning it all over in his head, trying to figure out where he might have let it break.

It was Logan who found him. Damn his friend.

"I was expecting to see you out in the fields."

"Well," Ryder said. "I'm not in the fields."

"I can see that."

"Yep. Now get on with yourself."

"*Why* exactly aren't you out working the fields?"

"None of your damn business."

"Something happened with Sammy, didn't it?"

"And how the hell do you know that? Always so fucking insightful, aren't you? Asking me if I'm in love with her. Telling me I'm in love with her. Now you know something happened."

"Not because I'm particularly insightful, but because her camper's gone. What the hell did you do?"

"Loved her," he ground out. "I fucking loved her. I gave her everything that she could have asked for. But she didn't ask for it. Never once. In fact, she gave it back. She doesn't want me to love her. She says I don't have a choice but to take care of her and I don't know what I want. Like I'm a kid. I haven't been a kid since I was one. You want to talk about dealing with shit? I lost my parents, and then I had to become a parent. I am a hell of a lot more in touch with my feelings than most. And a hell of a lot more in touch with them than I would like to be, I can tell you that."

Logan nodded slowly. "Look. I don't actually know anything about relationships. I'm as bad a bet as there even exists. I know so little about love it's not even funny.

But I know you. And I know her. And I know that she must feel like she's taken an awful lot from you for someone who wasn't blood. Because I know that I sure as hell feel that way. And indebted to you. In a way that... I can't even put into words."

"I don't want you to owe me, not any of you."

"But of course we do. Look at you. This is your life. You didn't do anything else. You didn't go anywhere else, because of us."

"Neither did you."

His friend looked at him, long and hard.

"Well, what the hell, Logan? Is this some kind of indentured servitude?"

"This was the most stable, secure family experience I ever had. Staying in it isn't a hardship. But yeah, I owe you one. I'm glad that Jake and Colt felt like they could move on. But I never did. Maybe because we're not blood. Maybe I thought I owed you a little bit of a stronger oath for that reason. I think Sammy is just scared. Scared as hell."

"Well, she's gone. So I can't ask her."

That seemed to make Logan shut up. But Ryder wasn't sure he liked that any better. Because in some ways it was better if his friend was being relentless. Because at least then the other man had some hope, or an idea. Ryder himself didn't have either.

"Well?" Ryder pressed.

"No," Logan said. "You have a point. She's not here. And you know what? I think that's the whole point. She's going to have to solve this on her own, and you can't do it for her."

"Well, I don't like that at all."

"Of course you don't," Logan said. "You're a fixer who wants to fix everything for everyone. But that's exactly what she's worried about. That you're out there married to her just because you want to fix her problems."

"I love her so much I feel sick. *That's* why I married her. It's not martyrdom or sacrifice or anything like it."

"Sure. But she doesn't believe that. And you're going to have to accept the fact that you're not going to be able to make her. She's going to have to figure it out herself. She's going to have to trust you."

"And if she never does?"

"I think she will. She trusted you enough back when she was a teenager."

"Well, it was me or her old man. I suppose I seemed like the safer bet."

"Sure. Maybe. Though if you think about it, she had no reason to believe that you would be any less dangerous. She didn't know you. And she was taking her chances on her father finding out that she was meeting with you and getting angry with her. This place was enough for her to take that risk. You were enough. You're just going to have to trust that she thinks so again. And the best thing you can do is find a way to show her that you're living a life that you chose."

"But I'm not," he said. "I'm living one without her. And it's terrible. It's damned terrible."

"Sure. Except you're still here. You're still right where you were when your parents died. You didn't choose that. And you chose to stick this out, to take care of us. But now you're still here."

"And what would you like me to do?"

"Move on."

He could only stare at Logan, because he couldn't even begin to fathom moving on.

"Sorry, but it's the one thing you've never really done. Not from her necessarily, but from the past. Figure out what you want. Choose the life that you want. Figure out what kind of life you want to live. And show her that you're not just here out of habit. That you're not with her out of habit, or a sense of obligation."

"Can't I just chase her down and kidnap her and lock her in my bedroom until she sees sense?"

He was only a little bit joking.

Honestly, it sounded more sensible to him. More certain than this relaxed stuff that Logan was suggesting. He wanted to go after her. He wanted to fix it. And he couldn't understand why that bothered her so much. So what if he felt a sense of obligation? That was…

Didn't she understand that that was love to him?

"No," Logan said. "You can't. Because you need to let her figure some things out on her own. She's strong, but she's been in your pocket all this time. She healed with you, around you. So stand apart for a minute. See where it gets you."

"Awfully confident," Ryder said.

"Yeah," Logan said. "I am. Because I know you both. And because I think this place has a little bit of magic in it."

"I don't know," Ryder said. "I always thought it was kind of…the opposite of that. Not a whole lot of magic, mostly a bit of grief and irony. Hope Springs. I tell you what. It made me want to pick the names of things a lot more carefully. Like it was setting us up for disaster."

"That's not how I took it. It's just that even when things are hard… Well, there's still hope, isn't there?"

"I don't know about that."

"Well, if there's not hope, what is there? Maybe think about that. And see where it takes you."

Ryder had no idea what to make of any of that, because it felt to him like his hope had up and driven off along with Sammy Marshall.

SAMMY WAS A COWARD. And she was sneaking around in Gold Valley like the coward that she was. She had gotten as far as Copper Ridge, spent the day at one of the craft fairs there, and had come right back home.

She was currently camped out in the spot that she had used to look down on Hope Springs Ranch when she was a teenager.

And now she was sneaking around in town, restocking her jewelry at the various places on Main Street and in general feeling like a wounded martyr.

She knew that Ryder wouldn't see it that way. That he was currently probably feeling like the martyr. And she understood that. She did. But she was doing them both a favor.

Of course, right now that favor felt like a giant knife wound to her heart. But whatever.

She was just slipping out of Willow Creek when she ran square into Iris.

One of the last people on earth that she wanted to see.

Iris would be furious with her. Absolutely furious. And Sammy expected all kinds of angry words to flow from her friend's mouth.

But instead Iris just stared, and then her eyes filled with tears.

"What are you…"

"Are you okay?" Iris asked.

Sammy took a breath that felt sharp and jagged, sharper than the words that she had expected from her sister-in-law.

"What do you mean am I okay?"

"I'm worried about you. You just disappeared. And you left him."

"I know," she said. "And I understand that means I left the family…"

"You didn't leave the family, you fool. Is that what you think? That it would be that easy? We all feel cut in half, Sammy. Logan, Iris, Pansy and myself. We all feel torn. We love you both. And I hate seeing him like that, but I know that you didn't do it for fun."

"Well, no. But…"

"What's wrong? I mean, I know he can be difficult but…"

"That's not it," Sammy said. "He has taken care of us, all of us, for way too long. And I couldn't… I couldn't stand feeling like I trapped him into it."

Iris simply stared at her. "Really? That's it?"

"Yes," Sammy said, her eyes filling.

"He's thirty-five years old," Iris said. "He chose his life."

"He didn't."

"I assure you that he did. Absolutely and completely. That man is far too stubborn to ever be railroaded into anything. I know that what he did for us when he was younger was out of duty, but this… The way that he works the ranch now, it's not. It isn't. He is absolutely everything that he's chosen to be."

"Well, I don't want him to choose to keep on taking care of me if there's something else that he wants."

"I don't believe you."

"What?"

"I mean, I think that you believe you, but I don't think that's really the problem. I think that you are scared. And you're making it about him."

"I'm not."

"You are. You were asking me if I disowned you in the first thirty seconds of seeing me. Of course you're scared. And I get it. Anyone who's lived the life that we have would be. But I'm still here. Choosing to care for you. That's the thing. We were always making choices. We were never forced into anything. And neither was he. The only thing we didn't choose was losing our parents. The one thing you didn't choose was having the father you had. But we chose each other. We damn well did. Why do you get to decide that his continuing to choose you isn't real?"

"I appreciate where you're coming from. I really do. I just... I can't."

"You're just afraid. And there's nothing wrong with being afraid. Until you let it decide what you're going to do."

"I can't take a lecture from you, Iris. Not seriously. You know I love you, but you've never gone anywhere or done anything."

"Maybe," Iris said, her voice measured. Even still, Iris refused to be angry. "Maybe that's true. But I don't pretend to be anything else. You do. You ran around lecturing and giving advice. You tell other people to be brave when you have no intention of doing it yourself. Again, I love you. But let's stop pretending that you're not running scared."

She began to walk away, and then she stopped. "And I still love you, by the way. You can't push me away. Sorry, I'm not going to let you make yourself safe by trying to get rid of all the people in your life who love you. And you know what? I don't think Ryder is going to let you do it, either."

And when she was gone, Sammy could only stand there. Frozen. And even though she had been found, she could not escape the feeling that she was still in hiding.

That she was still bound up in all she had been.

She'd started this journey to prove she wasn't stuck.

She'd only ended up proving that she was.

CHAPTER TWENTY-NINE

IT HAD BEEN a week since Sammy had left, and he was still coping with intense bouts of feeling like he'd lost his best friend in the world. Because he had. That just happened to be layered on top of the heartache that he felt every time he took a breath. Every time he didn't take a breath. Every time he moved.

He knew that he could survive it. He knew that he could survive anything.

That was the problem, though. Just because you could survive something didn't mean you'd won.

It just meant you were still here.

He knew from the experience of loving lives lost that being here was a victory.

But it wasn't a very happy one, and in fact, it rang hollow, like the whole rest of him.

Still, he had gone down to town today and bought fencing supplies, and he had run into his former coach at Big R.

Normally, he would have kept his head down and kept on walking. Assume that the man wouldn't remember him. And anyway, sometimes Ryder didn't much have the desire to get into nostalgic conversation with people. Because nothing about that time was nostalgic for him.

Dreams he had to leave behind, and fresh grief and loss.

But he remembered what Logan had said, so he had started talking to him. And he had found out the old man was retiring. He hadn't been head coach for some time, but he'd been assistant, and the school was looking to hire someone else. And of course he remembered Ryder, and still thought he was the best player to have ever come through Gold Valley High School.

Assistant coaching football wasn't something Ryder had ever given much thought to. And he supposed it wasn't necessarily a vocation in a town this size, but he didn't really need it to be, considering that he had a ranch to work.

But now he was thinking about that. Getting back into football. Doing more than just watching it on TV on a Sunday.

He had taken his number, and had put in a phone call. Just his name, and the word the coach had already put in had netted him an interview.

And when he sat down to dinner that night, he knew the whole family was thinking they were going to have to avoid his foul mood, but he decided to surprise them instead.

"I'm applying for a job."

Iris and Rose looked up. Logan, to his credit, didn't really react.

"What kind of job?" Rose asked.

"Assistant football coach at Gold Valley High School. Junior varsity."

"Wow," Rose said. "I didn't know you could still... Well, I didn't know you still remembered the rules to football."

"Of course I do, squirt," he said. "I'm not likely to forget something that I used to live and breathe. But yeah, I figured it was high time I did something with those skills. There has to be some good to come out of it. Otherwise, it's just sitting there and I'm not using it."

He would have said that it was impossible for him to feel excited about anything at this point in time, but he felt mildly excited about this.

No, it wasn't his life being put back together in the way that he wanted it. But it was taking some of the pieces that he was left with and shaping them into something different.

Finding something new.

He supposed there was something to be said for that.

"I'm happy for you," Logan said. "It's a good thing."

"Well, I don't have the job yet. My old coach is the one leaving the position, and he's recommending me for it. So I mean, I'm going to have a bit of a personalized recommendation, which never hurts. But you never know. There might be somebody all lined up ready to take the slot."

"Nobody who would be as good as you," Rose said, and her blind loyalty to him made up for her brattiness of a few moments earlier.

"Would you have been a football player, do you think?" Iris asked. "If it hadn't been for us?"

"I would have been the wrong kind of man if I had turned away from my responsibilities. Not a man that I could've been proud of. It doesn't really have anything to do with you so much as the shape of the life that we ended up with. I'm not unhappy."

"You're not?" Rose asked.

"I mean," he said. "At this current moment I could be happier. But I'm… I'm doing something. All right? You know, Sammy said that I was retired. And now I think there's something to that. And you all think that you're obligated to me. Because I took care of you, or whatever bullshit. But I think if I would have done more than just sit around here all these years you might not feel that way. I mean, I chose to. I need you all to know that. I don't feel stuck here. But I did think that maybe picking up a hobby wasn't the worst idea in the world."

"That's good," Iris said. "Because I think sometimes I do worry about that. I know you've dug in and chosen to be here, Ryder. You're the most responsible man I know, and I do wonder sometimes what you left behind."

"I'm in the most important life that I could be in. We all sacrificed. We all came together. And no, our lives aren't the same as if our parents hadn't died. But we have life. I was thinking… You know, I am not significantly younger than Dad was when he died. And I'm about to become a father myself, whatever happens with Sammy. It would have been impossible to not be affected by their deaths. But we can't go on living for those deaths forever. Still, I think they would've been real proud of what we made here. And there's not a whole lot more I could ask for than that. That we made something, that we became something that they could've been proud of."

"Dad would have been proud of you," Rose said. "Because you are the reason we're still here. You're the reason the ranch is still here."

And he was proud of that. But still, it was difficult to feel triumphant when he had all those things but he didn't have the woman that he loved.

He went in for his interview the next day, and it went well. By that evening, he'd gotten the phone call that he had the job, starting at the end of August. Colt and Jake would be around when the cold settled in. Between them and Logan any work that might get missed by him would be well handled.

It had all happened so quickly, and it wasn't something that he was particularly able to fully process.

It was all so strange. Had all come out of nowhere. And here he was, living an entirely different life, yet again, than the one that he'd been planning on living.

He was used to grim grit and determination. Used to putting his head down and taking what life had dealt him.

He agreed with Logan on that score. That he needed to get out there and make something of himself, so that he could for sure know that he was in a life he chose.

But he didn't agree with leaving Sammy alone.

No, he needed to go talk to her. Not because he didn't trust her. He trusted Sammy. He really did. And he'd had a lot of thinking time over the past few days.

What he wanted to do was make sure that she knew exactly where he was coming from. That she understood what love was to him. And what it truly meant.

Because there had been a lot of talk about love, and he had wondered if she understood what it meant to be loved by him. But he realized he hadn't explained. He had said that he loved her, and before that he had shown it in a thousand different ways. But in all fairness, she had shown him the same. She had shown him love.

And things had only changed and gotten complicated now.

So he wanted to make sure that it wasn't just the words, but what those words meant.

They had made vows, but they were generic marriage vows.

Vows that everyone made as they stood up there at that altar.

But he had gotten a ring that was just for Sammy. And he needed to make sure that the vows matched. That the sentiment behind the word *love* matched.

He knew from Iris that Sammy was still in town, because he knew that his sister had run into her out on the street. But he didn't think that she was staying in town. No. He was pretty sure he knew right where he would find his wayward bride. And he was bound and determined to go and find her. And make sure that if she turned him down again she knew exactly what it was she was turning down.

SAMMY HAD GONE out looking for answers in just about every place but the one that had first raised the questions.

She had been avoiding the conversation because she didn't want to have it. She had been avoiding the conversation because she was afraid of what it might result in. But she couldn't avoid it anymore. She wasn't sleeping. She didn't want to eat, but she needed to because she was gestating a life so she was forcing things down that tasted like sawdust and sat in her stomach like a rock.

She needed answers. She had needed them for a long time. But more than that, now she was ready for them.

She had destroyed what she and Ryder had. She had destroyed their friendship. Their romance. Because she was afraid.

It was all bound up in seeing herself as a burden. In seeing herself as not enough.

It was all bound up in this toxic relationship with her mother, and it needed to be finished.

Ryder was right. He couldn't do everything for her.

He couldn't protect her from whatever was happening between them; it was impossible. Because now, finally, he was pushing her, rather than shielding her, and it was time for her to do something with that.

He'd said after the midwife that he couldn't have the baby for her. And he trusted her to be strong.

Well, this was all wound up in that. He couldn't do this for her, either. He couldn't make her not afraid. He couldn't make her okay.

She had to try and find a way to do it for herself.

She took a deep breath and walked up to the front door of the house that she hadn't been to in years.

She had come over when her father had died.

But it was the first time she'd been back inside since that night they'd gotten in the fight. Since he had followed her back to her little caravan and unleashed his full temper on her. She had gone back because she had thought that her father was the barrier in keeping her and her mother from having a relationship.

But she had begun to realize then that he wasn't.

That she had anger for her mother that was all kinds of separate. Over the way she hadn't protected her.

And that her mother had anger that went right back at Sammy.

For doing what her mother couldn't. For leaving.

Except now...

She had left Ryder. She had run, just like her mother had said.

She had to sort this out. She had to fix it.

She knocked on the door.

And her mother opened it.

"What are you doing here?"

"I came because… I wanted to tell you that you're going to be a grandmother."

Her mother looked down at her stomach. "Really? Did you go out and do that to spite me?"

The fact that Sammy was quite so predictable galled a little bit. "It was a reason, yes. I wanted to prove that I could, in fact, be a good mother. That I do understand. But while I'm sure that I can be a good mother to this child, I don't actually know how to be a well-rounded person. And I blame you. I blame you, and the fact that you didn't protect me. That you made me feel like I was worth less than your husband, who quite frankly, Mom, was a piece of shit. He was. He was awful to you, he was awful to me, and he wasn't worth a damn."

"That's your father you're talking about," her mother said.

"Yes. It is. And I know that I'll protect my child in a way you didn't protect me. I had to leave, Mom. I had to leave to protect myself because you wouldn't. Ryder had to step in to protect me because you wouldn't. And now he wants… He wants to love me. And I'm scared. Because I'm afraid that somehow I'm not worth it, and that comes from you. And I swear to God, Mom, I will never let my child feel that way. Ever."

"You always were above yourself, Sammy. Some people have to live hard. It's not their fault one way or the other."

She looked at her mother, and she saw that she really believed that. That her mom believed that this was some kind of hand of fate, and that they couldn't have escaped it even if they'd wanted to.

And Sammy realized that by surrendering to the pain in her life she was living that way, too.

That because she had been born into something hard, she was letting herself have half. Have less.

And it was easy, she realized. Easier than asking for more.

Her mother wasn't under her father's thumb, not anymore. But it was still fear that ran her life. And suddenly, it all became clear.

"At some point, it is your fault," Sammy said. "It wasn't your fault he abused you. But what about your life now? At some point, if you don't make the choice to demand more, to demand better, if you don't stop hiding, it is your fault. This is my fault. It's my fault, this thing with Ryder. He loves me. And I've been too afraid to open myself up and let him, because Dad made me so terrified to ask for it. To think that I could want it. And you… You've never done a damn thing to make me feel like I deserved it."

"Why should you deserve it?" her mom asked. "Why should you deserve it when I didn't?"

Sammy's heart twisted. She felt a certain amount of sympathy for the woman standing in front of her. The woman who looked so much like her. With curly blond hair and bright blue eyes. But she was defeated. And this was what happened when you didn't let love into your life. This was the future she had to look forward to. A baby wouldn't save her from it.

A positive attitude and the best of intentions wouldn't save her from it.

If she let her issues become bigger than hope, then this was what waited for her.

She had seen a glimpse of it a couple months ago when she had decided that she wanted to change rather than stay in the past. But she had decided to do physical things to make that change. And she had ignored the very real spiritual healing that needed to happen inside her.

Because that was the hardest part.

Not changing your circumstances. Changing yourself.

Putting away the things that you had always believed. Digging deep into your wounds, rubbing antiseptic into them so they could be cleansed, even though it was going to hurt.

"We can't have a relationship," Sammy said. "Not like this. Not while you're intent on dragging me back into all that. Blaming me. Accusing me of things. And I'm tired of hoping for one. I'm going to be a better mother."

"Is that what you came here for?" her mom said. "To insult me?"

She shook her head. "No. I came here because I knew there would be answers. I sort of hoped it might be answers that would fix us. But I can't fix you. I can only fix me."

She turned around and started to walk away. "There you go," her mom said. "Running away again."

Sammy stopped. "I am," Sammy said. "I'm running away from all this useless wreckage. And I'm running to where I always should have been."

When Sammy got back up to her camper, the sun was just sinking behind the mountains, casting a rosy glow on everything around her. She needed to think for a while, needed to sit with the changes that had reshaped the landscape of her soul after that conversation with her mother.

And she let herself feel it, all of it. Without that protective layer she'd built up to cover her pain over the years.

That protection she'd been so desperate to protect.

That protection that would do nothing but turn her into a hard, bitter soul who could never be more than an abused and neglected daughter.

Who would never be able to be the best mother she could be.

The best wife.

The best person.

No, that protection didn't really keep her safe. It kept her separate.

It kept her from being whole.

And she let it go now. All of it.

She missed Ryder. She missed having bacon with him. She missed her bowl of fruit.

She missed every single thing about him. Leaving him had been like chopping off an arm.

She hadn't realized quite how much she relied on him to function in all ways until she didn't have him around. So here she was, functioning without him.

She had told herself she maybe needed to do that.

For him.

But that was a lie.

She was forced to examine herself, now that she was spending so much time alone. So much time in the quiet. There was nothing shocking she could say to distract herself from what was going on. She simply had to sit in it. And that was uncomfortable.

Deeply so.

She had been thinking a lot about how their relationship had begun. How she had come to him. Baited him until he had become her friend. Offered him sugar in exchange for sanctuary.

And he had given it.

She had offered up pieces of herself. But never the whole thing. Because there was a reason that she had slipped into bed with him all those nights. Because she had wanted his comfort, had wanted the warmth of his body. Had wanted to be near him.

But she had been afraid of real intimacy with him.

She had gotten sexual attention from other men. *Any* man but him.

Because the cost of intimacy with Ryder was always going to be high. And it was always going to be one that she would find it difficult to pay. In the rosy evening light, she stood up. Then she took her shirt off. Her skirt. Her underwear. And she stood there, completely naked, letting the sun warm her skin. She closed her eyes, a tear tracking down her cheek.

She loved him.

With all that she was.

But she was afraid that she wasn't enough. That if he knew that she was just a trembling girl in her heart, not an outrageous, brave free spirit, he wouldn't really want her.

That he would resent her.

And it wasn't even so much that she was generous and wanting him to be happy, so much that she just… She never wanted to be the reason he was unhappy with his life. And she had been that. For both of her parents.

She felt small and selfish and miserable, but she spread

her arms wide and tilted her head up toward the sky, open and vulnerable and trying to will herself to simply be in it.

To love him. To love him and to know that there would be no guarantee it would never end. To love him and know that she couldn't guarantee his happiness forever.

To know that she couldn't guarantee her own bravery, that she might run scared sometimes and need to be held in his strong arms.

That sometimes she might need him, and other times he might need her.

That they were both going to have to learn what love looks like together, if he would still have her. After all this.

Her heart was bruised, and she didn't know quite where to begin.

But she supposed it would have to start with bravery. And no sugar cubes this time. Just her. But then she heard footsteps off to the side, and she looked over and saw him. For a moment she thought she might be hallucinating. Because it was Ryder just like she always fantasized about him.

Black T-shirt, black cowboy hat and snug-fitting jeans. He looked disreputable with his dark whiskers covering his jaw, and it was sort of wonderful because there was nothing disreputable about Ryder Daniels. Except…he could be, with her. Could be rough and tender all at once. Shocking and sexy and steady and faithful.

He was everything that she wanted, everything that she needed, all contained in one man, and the realization was scary as hell.

"It would figure, Samantha, that I would come searching for you and find you standing naked in the middle of the woods."

"How exactly did you find me?" She fought the urge to cover up. To hide. Not because she was naked, but because she was vulnerable.

Honest.

Because she was staring her fears down instead of pretending she had none and it made her raw.

But he was the one for those fears.

He was the one.

"Because it's your place. Where you used to come and watch us when you were afraid of joining us, even though you wanted to. I figured that was where you had gone off to. And I also figured that if I was right... That if I was right I might have a chance."

"You came for me," she said.

"I know you wanted your space."

Tears began to flow freely down her cheeks. "I need you to know that I was coming back to you."

"And I need you to know that I wasn't just going to let this happen. There are things in my life that have happened that were bad. And I didn't have any control over them. Not one bit. But this... This I do. And I just felt like while there was some breath left in my body I needed to come and tell you again that I'd be here. And that I needed you to know it was a choice I made. This life is a choice I made. No, I didn't choose to lose my parents. But I did choose to stay. I chose to stay at Hope Springs because there was always something there for me. My family. And you. Maybe I did stay because of you. But it wasn't because I'm a martyr. Yeah, I have been one. It's true. But not in the having of you. In the wanting you and not taking you, yeah. But this is not me being a martyr, Samantha Marshall. This is me being a man. I love you. I love you the way a man should love a woman. I want to lay my hands on you only to cause you pleasure and never to cause you pain. I want to protect you and never cause you harm. I want to be your husband and the father of your children. That's what I'm here for."

Every defense inside her crumbled, and the ones that didn't go on their own she knocked all the way down. Because she was ready. Ready for this. Ready for him. Ready for whatever might come next.

"I... I'm a coward. I wanted to pretend that it was about you, but it was all about me." She took a shuddering breath. "I just came back from seeing my mom."

His body went stiff, and she could see he was ready to fight. To protect. "And?"

"I don't want to be her. I didn't think I could be, because I saw us as being so different. She stayed. I left. She is still in that house, still outwardly clinging to all that same pain, and I'm here. I have my jewelry. I thought... I'll have a baby and I'll change my life. But I'm still living there, too. In my heart, I still was."

"It's hard to move on from hurt like that," Ryder said, his voice rough. "I know how it is."

"I am so afraid of loving bigger than myself. In a way that I can't control. But I do. With you. It's so all-consuming and huge. And it has been all this time. And I could never let you be my everything, Ryder, because I was sure that that would destroy me. But it won't because of you. That was what I was missing. That I needed to trust you. Trust us. I asked for love once and it was like looking into a black abyss. But you offered it to me without me ever having to ask. And more important, you've shown me what love looks like all these years. I was just afraid to call it what it was."

She took a sharp, jagged breath that cut her open, and she bled her heart out before him. Let it flow like a river. "I was afraid of giving myself over to something. But freedom…real freedom is this. Not letting the past decide how loud we get to live and how big we get to love. Real freedom is living, and not just hiding. And that's what I want. Not just life, but this life."

"Did I catch you communing with nature?" he asked, his grin lopsided.

"I was being vulnerable," she said, taking a step toward him.

"I got you." He wrapped his arms around her and pulled her against his chest, and she felt enveloped by his strength. Free to be as soft as she needed to be because of him. Because he was the kind of man whose hands were there to hold her. To cradle their baby. Whose muscles would only ever be used to protect. And never to harm.

"I'm sorry," she whispered.

"I wanted you to know," he said. "I got a coaching job."

She tilted her head up and looked at him. "You did?"

"Yes. And it's because of you. All the things we went through to get to this moment. Painful or not. So I don't need you to apologize to me. We both had some work to do. Because you were right. There were things I needed to address. I am happy. I want you to know that. I've spent years being happy because of the family we've had here. And you are part of that. Not shoved in here stitched in sloppy, not an afterthought, but a key thread that holds us together. That held me together. I told you. You've been my light. My warmth. Don't ever underestimate the power of that. Cold kills you. Darkness makes you insane. The sun is the source of life. You protected me all this time. Don't think you didn't. Don't make the mistake of believing that I somehow was the one protecting you."

"I guess we were just what each other needed," she said softly. "I needed to hide in your shadow, and you needed some light."

"I like that," he said.

"I love you," she whispered. "I have loved you all this time."

"Me, too. It was just part of breathing. And you know you never think about breathing, until you do. And then you become unbearably conscious of it. And that was what happened with me. I realized suddenly how much I love you. It was hard for me, because I was looking for it all to be like my parents' marriage. Which from the outside seemed like something that… I don't even know if it was that. Because you can't know. You can't know what goes on between two people in love, not really. But I had this idea in my head, and I didn't think that the crazy, dark feelings I had for you could possibly be that."

"Crazy?" She lifted her brows. "Dark?"

"Yes," he said, his expression turning feral, and she loved it. "The exact kind of feelings that you avoided. The exact kind of man you avoided."

"Tell me more."

"Possessive. Obsessive. I had this feeling… This… You're mine, you know? I felt that way from the time we were kids. That you belonged to me."

She leaned forward and bit him on the chin. "Then you belong to me. And you know, I only dated men who were nothing like you because I couldn't have you. I wouldn't let myself. And dating an approximation of you would have only been sadder, and more obvious in what I was attempting."

"Really?" He looked smug and satisfied at that.

"Really."

They just held each other in silence for a moment, before she spoke again.

"I'm scared," she said. "A lot. Just in general. And I've been running. I've been running from that fact. From me, for so long. Looking at my mother scared me, because it was like looking into a future version of myself, but I didn't see that. So I decided to have a baby to make a change, all without changing myself. Making big changes on the outside is so much easier than changing your heart."

"Sure." His voice had gotten scratchy. Husky.

"But this was the journey that I needed to go on. This one. Right here. Where I had to get right down to my own heart and quit standing in my own way. And admit that what I was looking for was right in front of me all along. But I was going to have to be vulnerable, be real to have it. So this is me. I'm scared sometimes, and I act the way that I do to keep people at a distance. But you know me better than anyone else. And I want you to keep knowing me. Keep being with me, even when I'm a mess. Please. Please love me through all of that, Ryder."

"I promise," he said. "And I am a stubborn, taciturn old man in partial retirement. I'm set in my ways. And I'm going to be a pain in the ass about water birth. Do you think you can accept me, knowing that's it? That this is me?"

"Yes." She rose up on her toes to kiss him. "It's not that I didn't know how to love you," she whispered against his mouth, "it's that I didn't know how to accept you loving me."

"And you can now?"

She nodded. "Yes. Because not accepting love when you have it is the real tragedy in this life. I've felt it for myself, sitting up here, weeping. I won't do that. I won't waste love. Not love like this, not our love. Not after all the love we've missed."

The breeze whipped up, skimmed over her bare skin, and she shivered.

"Time for us to go inside," he said.

"That sounds like a very good idea."

He carried her inside, and this time when he made love to her, she kept her eyes open. Kept them on him. So that he could see how much she trusted him. What was in her heart.

All the love that she had for him burning bright and brilliant in her soul.

Ryder Daniels had always been her rock. Her safe space. Her protector.

He had always been the love of her life.

All she'd had to do was become brave enough to recognize it. Because of his strength, she was. And she knew that it would be like this for the rest of their lives. That he would be the rock and she would be the sunshine for their child and for each other. And that they would be a family.

Forever.

* * * * *

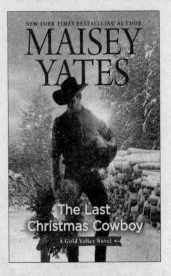

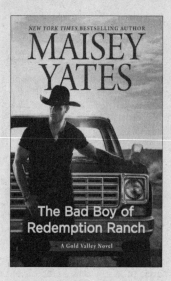

Get 4 FREE REWARDS!

We'll send you 2 FREE Books plus 2 FREE Mystery Gifts.

FREE
Value Over
$20

Both the **Romance** and **Suspense** collections feature compelling novels written by many of today's bestselling authors.